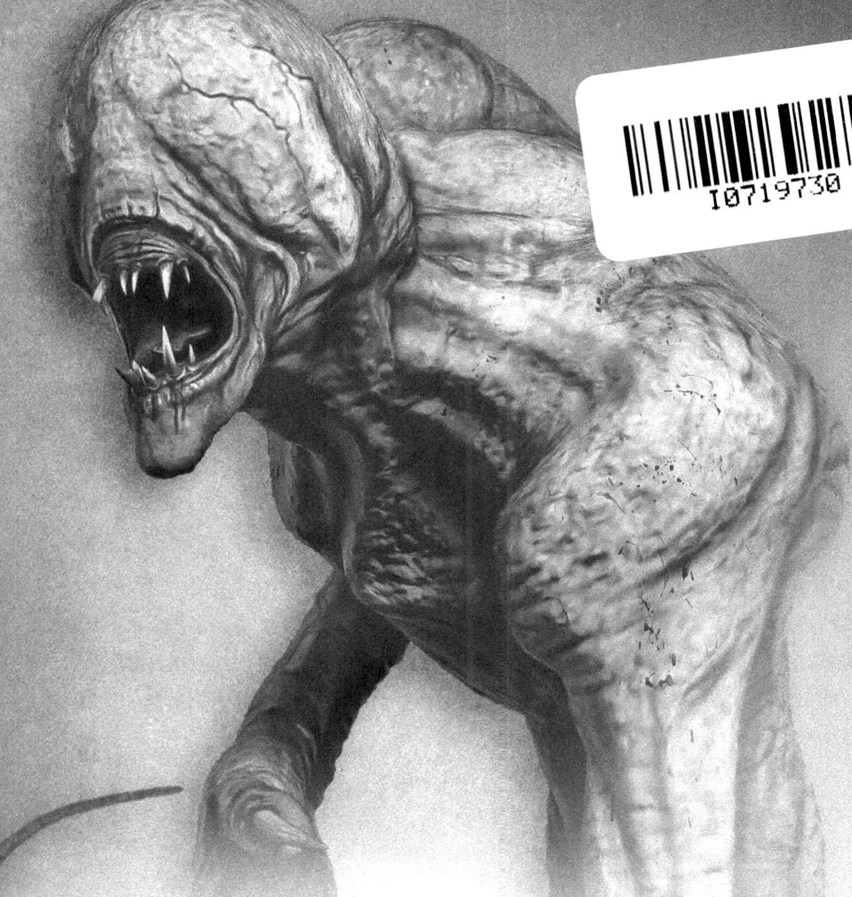

DESTRUCTION OF JUSTICE

THE MONSTERS AND MEN TRILOGY

BOOK TWO

LAWRENCE DAVIS

DESTRUCTION OF JUSTICE published by:
WILDBLUE PRESS
P.O. Box 102440
Denver, Colorado 80250

ISBN 978-1-957288-65-9 Hardcover
ISBN 978-1-948239-05-9 Trade Paperback
ISBN 978-1-948239-04-2 eBook

Cover Design and Interior Formatting by Elijah Toten
www.totencreative.com

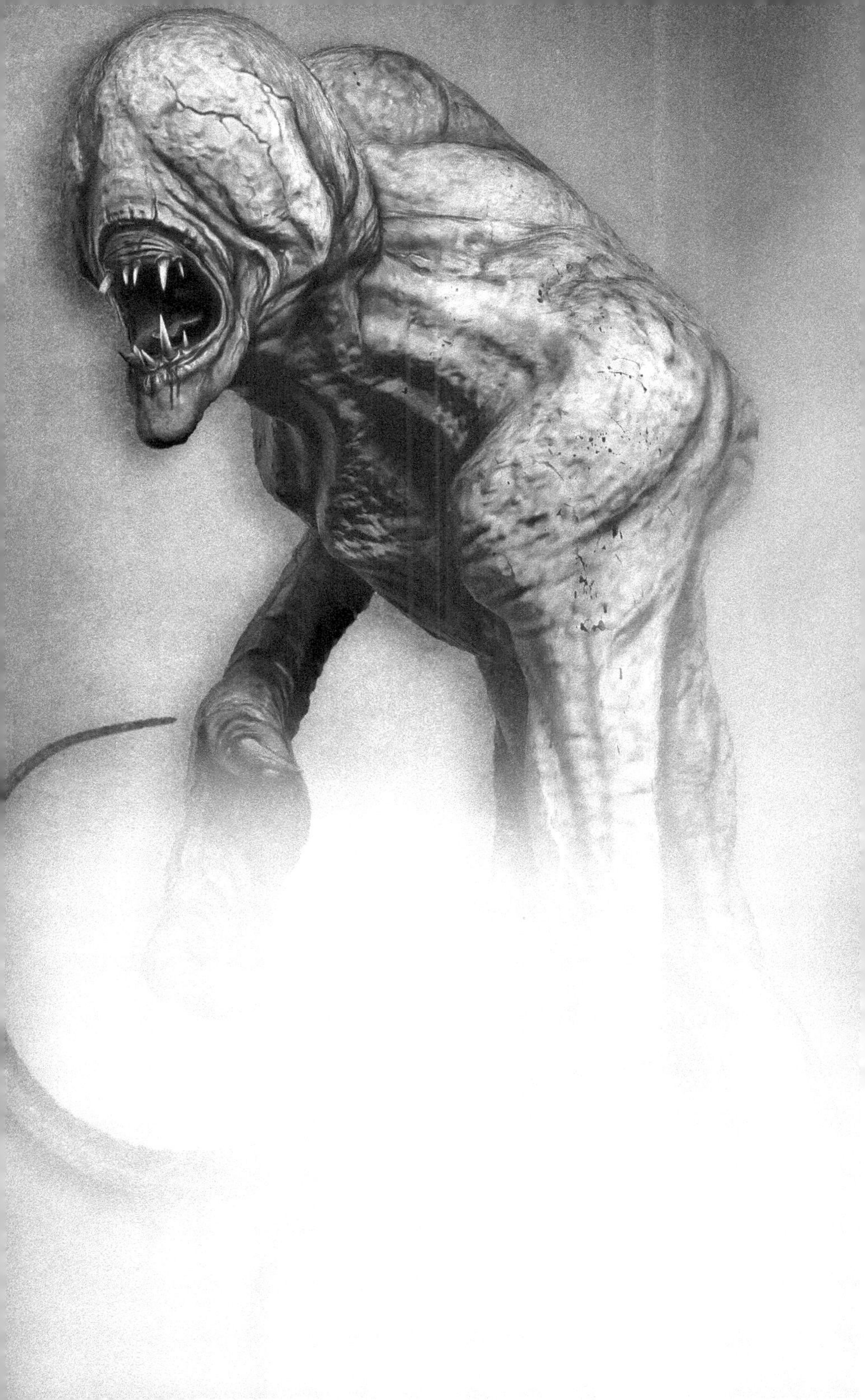

*This book is dedicated to my father, Jim Davis.
If there's one thing he taught me, it's everything.*

PROLOGUE

The abomination tearing down the rain-slicked street sending shards of grit in every direction was an unstoppable force. Bulbous ape-like arms ending in cruel curved claws found easy purchase on the street, twisting the asphalt into submission and launching the creature forward. Its reptilian head was thick with bone at the crest of its skull, and it had a broad snout full of jagged teeth that tore through everything that had been thrown at it so far. And if that wasn't enough, there was a spiked, three-pronged tail slashing behind it—each barb armed with a different venom. Gruesome stitching infused its hide with magical runework, showing the Frankensteinian beast for what it was—a collage of the most fearsome creatures in all the realms, patched together to create a singular killing machine.

An idling truck lay ahead of it in the street, its frame battered from the fight. In the passenger seat, Johnny B gripped the neck of his guitar and stared down the beast. "Any ideas, Muscles?"

The soldier sitting in the driver's seat wouldn't have answered even if he'd heard the question.

The elf seemed like a slight thing next to Grove, but he was tougher than he looked. The leather-clad goth rock'n'roller was just about to ask again when the engine roared as Grove floored it.

"Right," quipped the elven karaoke king. "We ram it. Brilliant."

Grove smashed the horn, clueing in the two others trying to stall the monster of his impending kamikaze attack.

Only Xander—Shapeshifter, Regulator, Rogarou or Doorman, depending on the need of the moment—could stand toe-to-toe with it for more than a minute. Then another thundering backhand from the monster sent the burly shapeshifter tumbling into a lamppost. Its flickering light extinguished like the last remnants of his power. The Regulator stood nearly eight feet tall in that form when upright, and still this hodgepodge creature towered over him. Even with Xander's supernatural speed, it was able to track and intercept his every approach with a swat. Fixated on its fallen prey, the scent of a near-kill proved irresistible to the creature, so when the truck barreling down the proverbial pipeline came within striking distance it couldn't react quickly enough.

That was what they were betting on.

Grove snatched Johnny by his studded collar and dragged them both out the open door—or rather, the opening that remained after the door had been torn away in an earlier skirmish. The SUV smashed headlong into the beast's colossal body, crashing to a cold stop from sixty miles an hour. Thick arms clutched the flanks of the battered vehicle, crunching the side paneling and collapsing the frame, reducing the once-mighty vehicle to an oversized accordion.

Xander, his canine head bloodied, turned to watch the savagery as the beast shredded the truck. The Concrete Monk lay motionless on the other side of the road beside a bloodied brick wall, face-down and unconscious in the grime. The man had managed to stave off the abomination on his own for longer than any of the rest could.

Johnny B, the last one still largely unscathed, mounted the half unconscious Grove, who had taken the brunt of the beating from their unceremonious exodus from the truck. "Come on," he said, frantically trying to rouse the hard-bodied warrior. Both of them lay soaking wet in the middle of the road, the flamboyantly dressed elf straddling him; it might be hard to live that down on another night—but this night was different.

Tonight was the night they'd tried to put themselves between a friend and a Blind Judge—an enforcer of the In-Between's laws—a juggernaut sent to deliver the council's judgment to those who dared disturb the precious Balance.

Beaten but not defeated, the soldier spat a mouthful of blood while pawing weakly at one of the magazine holsters on his hip. Luckily, Johnny B seemed to take the cue for what it was and scrambled to flip it open just as the gigantic surgical nightmare of a thing shifted its possessed narrow-slitted eyes back to them.

Johnny B started crooning a slowed-down rendition of Bon Jovi's *Blaze of Glory*. There was nothing commercial about his solemn reimagining of the song. A shaky hand retrieved the gadget stowed away in the magazine holster, a small black device with a big red switch on its side.

With an awareness no mere beast should have possessed, the monster's eyes widened just as the punk rock elf flipped the switch, a devil-may-care smile plastered across his face.

***

Just down the road, Janzen was fighting against the hammering of his heart, the boil of his blood, and the burn of each struggling gasp of air while sprinting to try to help his friends.

His people.

His family.

Close enough for a front row view but too far away to offer any kind of help, he felt a wave of heat from the explosion as it washed over his rain-streaked face illuminating an expression of pure horror. The Blind Judge, huddling around the mangled truck, surrounded by his closest confidants, his dearest friends, stood at the heart of a gigantic fireball some four stories high. The aftermath left smoldering asphalt, flipped cars, sheared and broken telephone poles, and shattered windows as far as the eye could see.

Behind him was a bone-rattling *boom*, then another.

The fire hissing in the distance had nothing on the one in Janzen's merciless eyes.

"You," Janzen heard himself say, in a voice that couldn't have belonged to him. The wet in his eyes wasn't from the heavy rain, and the rage that flowed through his veins was too much to keep bottled up.

Behind him stood a towering machine, a dire contrast to the beast at the center of the eruption. Where the former was a network of limbs and parts scavenged from enslaved beasts, this golem was forged from mythical metal and shaped carefully into an indestructible tank. Its expressionless countenance illuminated by the rich sigilwork etched across its behemoth metal mass.

The second Blind Judge squared off with the artificer.

CHAPTER 1

Two Days Earlier

"You could use this for like, so much stuff...I mean, *anything* really: Corporate espionage, surveilling cheating spouses, evidence gathering....I would have been okay with any of that," I said. Grove had the bastard I was berating in a hurtlock, making him a captive audience to my monologue. The scumbag in question was Nicholas Greene: late twenties, greasy black hair, unflattering clothes. He had that whole I-live-in-my-parents basement' vibe. He was gangly and malnourished, and his room looked like an altar to off-brand energy drinks and discount pizza. If I was going to give the word "disappointing" a face, it would be his.

"But spying on babysitters and moms? Come on, man." I looked at my hands. In one was a mason jar full of some kind of gunk. He'd called it an *elixir*. In the other I held a soldier figurine which I waved at Grove. "Kinda looks like you."

Grove glowered at me and tightened his grip, squeezing an unflattering yelp from Nick. Being pinned between my buff business partner and a computer desk wasn't an enviable position.

"So, with this stuff—"

I lifted the jar.

"—you can form a psychic connection?"

Next, the toy soldier.

"And with some Focus you can actually see what it is he's seeing? That's a nifty trick, man. Real nifty. How'd you even figure this out?"

"I—ow, uhm, well, argh!"

With a theatrical sigh, I gave him a look of doubt before nodding for Grove to relent. Not without his own qualms about it, he more shoved than released Nicholas. We were both a little peeved; this case was earning us pennies on the dollar because we'd taken it from a scared sixteen-year-old girl.

She swore to us that a toy kept creeping around the house of the kid that she'd been babysitting, and it got so bad that she was starting to have nervous breakdowns. The once valedictorian-bound teenager was now being drug tested by her exhausted parents and counseled by an overpriced shrink who kept reinforcing the suspicion that she was in fact, crazy.

At first, we had no idea how to approach the case—how do you catch a phantom stalker? Turned out it wasn't hard after all, and it didn't involve any magic, just some rudimentary detective work. Nick here was quite a fan of hers on Instagram, and he'd left a trail of electronic hearts a mile wide leading us right to his door.

"Talk. This whole pathetic social outcast thing doesn't earn you much sympathy with us. You were stalking a sixteen-year-old girl Nicholas. That's fucked up, you should probably get some help before you hurt somebody worse than you already have, or somebody hurts you worse than we already have."

After a beat to let the threat sink in, I held the jar up.

"How'd you get this?"

"I bought it," he said in a sullen tone. My silent partner complimented my sour look with a slap to the back of Nick's head. We made a good team in this respect, other things, not so much. Still, when it came to the presentation of a unified front, we couldn't be outdone.

"Ow! What? I did."

"If he's gotta hit you for every snide remark you make, this is going to be a long day, and as of an hour ago, we switched from the young lady's dollar to yours."

"That's not fair!"

Grove slapped him again. Couldn't tell you how he knew to do that one. Just a sense, I suppose.

"I bought it," he whined, rubbing the back of his head, shifting a sneer to the bruiser behind him. "At that carnival thing that just came through. Some guy way in the back, he made a big thing about being able to *see through the eyes of any and all.*' I don't know, seemed kinda hokey until he grabbed me with some of that stuff on his hand, and I could see me through his eyes. It was creepy kinda, but cool."

Interesting. Something like this wasn't a cheap parlor trick.

"How much?"

"Five grand."

"Five grand! How the hell did *you* manage five freakin' grand?"

"I design games," he said, gesturing to a poster hung up on the far wall. It was Kingdom Killer, a wicked game about a wronged barbarian gaining hellish power in order to take down the establishment that wiped out his archaic tribe. I was in the middle of playing it through for my third time.

"No way! I love that game. Holy crap, how do I slay th—"

Grove cleared his throat.

"Right. Okay. So, you bought this stuff, and I assume he gave you instructions for using it?"

"Yeah. Yeah, he told me the whole, like, way to use it, what to do, everything."

Cradling the mason jar of pungent-smelling goo, I screwed the lid on and turned all of my attention on the kid.

"Tell me everything."

***

Daydreaming was one of my least favorite habits, but one I'd caught myself doing frequently. I found my stupor interrupted when Grove took his hand off the steering wheel and pointed to the jar I'd been staring at. Grove was young, but only in body; his eyes had a clear-sightedness that spoke volumes about him. We'd spent the last few months as partners, working and living together; building a rapport that was quickly becoming seamless.

"Small stuff is easier to control, but apparently the drawback to it is that this stuff's exhausting to use even a little bit," I said. I'd gotten a kind of cursory breakdown of how the goo worked from the twerp we'd snatched it from. "Not sure how it works exactly, and it's gotta be some incredible stuff if it's able to give a passageway to power for someone who isn't naturally gifted. The more you use, the more you can control, and the more it drains out of you. I suspect it's habit-forming." We'd installed a tablet on the center console which picked up on what I said and relayed it to Grove with closed captions. Probably not ideal for driving, but it was far more reliable than lip-reading. I caught a glimpse of his face. His expression was quizzical, not skeptical. We had too much trust for that at this point, though it was good to see him starting to question everything with a newly educated mind.

Grove didn't have any magical talent, for him this was all a scholarly pursuit. It was easier to fight something you knew, and though we hadn't come across anything heavy since the Stalker, it was good to see the Boy Scout sticking true to the old motto to 'be prepared.'

"Did you see him? Clothing loose and dirty, like he's been ignoring food and basic hygiene for a while? He's not taking care of himself. For him to be able to write code and design on that level takes solid know-how. I know a lot of those guys tend to be reclusive, but they do go out within their own tight-knit community—contrary to popular belief. He's been fixated on this stuff. Even when you had him twisted like a pretzel, he was seriously considering making a grab for it. He was acting like an addict. My guess is that this guy gave him just enough to get him hooked, and knew he'd have a customer for life. Next time that carnival comes to town, we're gonna be there."

My hope was that the kid would be back to himself in a bit. I might not have the most intimate knowledge of magical mechanics, but I did know the most fundamental principle: give something to get something. The ins and outs of a hustle I completely understood, and in this case, a lot of the trade-off was dangerously close to being one-sided. This stuff was the equivalent of a gateway drug, one where the price it extracted was far higher and more insidious than the user was aware of. The longer a person used it, the more they wanted. And when they got desperate enough for more, they would reach into darker and darker places to re-experience the power that they had come to love.

On the way back to the office, I called the client and told her she was off the hook for the bill and that what she'd been seeing was some wonky gizmo created by a local pervert: basically a toy-drone, and that now it was destroyed; an explanation more within her realm of understanding than the real story. I stuck the perp with a hefty bill—after all, I wasn't running a charity and I figured if he could pay five grand for the goo, he could certainly afford to pay my fee. This solution was better for him than a beatdown—although I hadn't entirely ruled that out if he failed to pay.

⁎

Cleveland had a way of imprinting itself on those of us who came up here. We're a sturdy people, usually a bit too blunt or abrasive, and we skew pretty blue collar. It was a tough town, but I don't know if I would want to live anywhere else, crazy as I'm told that is.

Our shop was right outside downtown proper, a little north toward the industrial side of the city. Circle Protection Agency was a play on the fact that my work as an artificer all begins with a circle. The shape was the oldest ward known to mankind, predating written language.

Ours wasn't a big spot, just two window panels with our logo and the company name above it. The door was framed in old brick, with a dedication plaque mounted beside it. It was our touchstone—literally. Grove and I each placed our hands on it every time we entered the building. When we first came together as a team, we'd done so with a third person—the person who'd brought us together. At the end of one very rough week we ended up losing her, but not before she quite literally saved the city.

Maybe more.

It was heavy stuff, especially since we specialized in the proverbial lower end of the totem pole. We dealt mostly with minor wayward beasties, novice practitioners making trouble, and every now and then something like what was laid at our feet today. Something a little more.

Inside was a fifteen-by-fifteen room with desks in the middle facing each other. In the back we had three blackboards. One where we collected our scattered writings, theories, and sightings. One where we pinned articles about local goings-on and settled cases. And in the middle, cases that still seemed to be pending or problematic, the ones that we'd yet to resolve. There was a narrow hallway off that wall that led to a second room, an annex where we worked out and trained. Since taking on Grove I'd stepped up my physical fitness routine, and by stepped up, I mean I went from twelve-ounce curls at the bar to actual weightlifting and running. When it came to sparring, both of us found out that we had a few things we could teach each other.

For my part, I'd been tutoring Grove on what I knew of the world beneath the world we lived in. We talked of the lore, separating fact from fiction. I'd attempted to give him a rudimentary breakdown of artificing; a thing that took a specific kind of talent that was impossible to teach. It was a gift. Without over-complicating it, sigils had base templates to draw from, but a person had to *feel* the way the magic infused an item and inscribe runes using a kind of sixth sense. I took to it criminally fast, especially since I never really became the prodigal son that some expected me to be. For most, it took a long time. It wasn't in the cards for Grove though, and that didn't seem to bother him in the least.

"What're you thinking, food-wise?"

Grove un-holstered a pistol and cleared it, taking the round out of the chamber and setting it down on his desk. While he thumbed through menus, I pressed play on the answering machine. The contraption was old school, especially in the age of cellphones, but we were both equally paranoid and preferred to keep it low-tech in the office. Grove's paranoia was born from a fear of Big Brother, mine from the boogeyman, same phobia, different mask.

"Maybe even try our luck at the Last Lo—"

The door banged sharply, smacking the wall hard enough that it almost ricocheted back into the faces of the two figures bursting through. Luckily, the woman had enough of her wits about her to catch the door before it could crack her right on her full head of scarlet hair on its way back. The intercepting hand left a print of blood, which smeared as her weak arm slid down from the exertion of even having to lift it. She was beautiful in an ageless way, with piercing eyes that stabbed straight to your fast-beating heart and seized it still.

Gale was a big fish in a small pond here in Cleveland. She was without rival in terms of raw power as well as knowledge as far as I could tell. The last time I'd seen her magic at work, she was able to fight a godling to a stalemate before finally relinquishing some ground, yet never giving it over. It was a feat so impressive I hadn't the right kind of eloquence (or time) to really impart just how awe-inspiring an accomplishment it was.

When she stood upright, she was just shy of six feet tall, but right now she was painfully hunched over, her body propped up by a much smaller man. Donovan was my new mentor, a master Tinkerer and gnome with whom I met every week to refine my skills. Our lessons were usually tight-lipped and combative, but I was learning at too quick a pace to allow my pride to fuck it all up for me—no matter how badly I wanted to shove his head through the workbench.

Both of them had the look of someone who'd come out the losing end of a bad fight, a look I'd worn all too often. Their abrupt entrance earned them the barrel of a gun from Grove, who despite being aware of who they were, hadn't lowered it yet. Like I said, he's as good a partner as there could possibly be. I had to admit that I was alarmed—and not just because of the way they looked. Donovan had swapped his usual stoic aspect for sincere panic, and he was straining to keep Gale off the floor. He had a pretty ugly wound on his left leg, and another on his right flank which was gushing blood in syncopated rhythm with his elevated heart rate.

My place was their last resort, which meant that either whatever was after them came from official channels, or it was just so big and bad that they were acting on pure survival instinct. Our silent stare-down said everything without any of us having to actually utter a word out loud. Gale was trying her best to keep some semblance of dignity about her. Her jaw clenched with effort as she fought to keep the pain off of her face, as if looking impassive would help anything. Pride is a funny funny thing, isn't it?

Donovan, on the other hand, was easier to read than a pop-up book, which caught me by surprise. He usually had the kind of poker face that players at professional tournaments trained a lifetime to master.

I looked at Grove and, when he finally acknowledged me, mouthed for him to get the med kit. One of the many benefits that came from having a partner with a military background was that we trained constantly and prepared ourselves for every imaginable eventuality, with emergency medical care being near the top of the list.

"Lockdown," I said. Another contingency laid out by my hyper-vigilant partner was a protocol to button us up. The last shred of bravado broke in Gale and relief flooded over her bloodied body as I jogged past both of them to close and lock the door. I hit the switch next to it, which lifted a panel with a number pad on it. With an ease that came from muscle memory, since my stringent associate insisted on countless repetition, I punched in the code to put us on lockdown. Hurricane shutters slammed over both of the windows and the door. Inside, the electricity went off the grid and a series of emergency lights popped on.

I shoved Donovan aside and ahead of me, a little more roughly than I intended to, and took his place under Gale's arm. She was taller than me, but even with her athletic build she was feather light. I suspected she had some kind of hollow bones like most elvish types—but now was not the time to ponder that. "Of all the doors in all the city, you had to walk into mine…" I said.

Despite the violence she had experienced, Gale smiled at my Bogart reference as I hustled us to the back. "I thought that would appeal to your inner gunslinger, and even more to your love of Casablanca," I said with a smile. I always worried whenever I said something even whimsically flirtatious to Gale, mostly because she reminded me too much of a hot Praying Mantis.

For a moment I thought she was shrugging, but I realized that she'd actually passed out cold. The back room was much bigger than the front, and every corner was filled with all kinds of training equipment: boxing gear, replicated melee weapons, barbells, weights—even a pair of cots for overnight duty. Donovan shot me a concerned look. I got the sense that he didn't think this was the best place for us to stash Gale.

I wrapped my other arm beneath her now-limp legs and scooped her up. Grove started dragging away the old high school wrestling mats we'd bought from a shady second-hand store to reveal a large cellar door that led down to our basement.

"Take her," I said, handing Gale over to Grove, who was much more confident in his balance than I was in mine. I waited at the top of the stairs and offered Donovan my shoulder, which he took with a pale hand. He thanked me with an appreciative look before we started down. Managing to get the best of a Tinkerer was a big deal, especially on his home turf. There's no way Donovan didn't have his place warded to the proverbial nines to deal with any and all manner of potential issues, which made this big deal even more impressive. Before they showed up at my door in this condition, the idea of something handling the Tinkerer and putting

Gale on her ass simultaneously would have been unthinkable, yet here they were.

The sub-basement was shaped like a big cylinder. It was an old bomb shelter built back before the city began regulating that sort of thing. Grove settled Gale on the bed we'd prepared and set to lighting torches.

Donovan's dubious looks were starting to subside, and when the room lit up, they disappeared completely. I'd taken the time to carve, trace and imprint every kind of protective sigil and rune that I could find, from the most fastidious and archaic to the ever-evolving stuff being done at the few modern institutions of magic. The trick was in keeping to what I knew, which was based on subtle manipulation and sheer craftiness. None of it was meant to thwart scrying eyes or repel an attack, all of it was simply for misdirection and guile. It was designed to bounce a seeking spell back on itself, spinning any inquisitive energy signals so that they continuously circled the very quarters they were probing. Determining where either of them was would be a nuisance and a major league pain in the ass for even the most accomplished practitioner. One sigil would redirect a spell into another sigil, which would in turn do the same to another, each of them imbued with a small sapping quality which wouldn't challenge the actual power of the casting but instead weaken it with every deflection until it just evaporated. A house of mirrors would be envious of the confusion it inspired.

If you can't be strong, be smart…And If you can't be smart? Cheat.

Normally the impression of just how stunned my mentor was would be kind of a Hallmark moment for me but given that this recent encounter had nearly killed Gale and had grievously wounded him, I didn't have time to gloat.

"Sit down," I told Donovan. Before he could object, I shoved him down onto the other bed.

Grove had laid Gale out carefully to examine her. Just before getting to work, he paused and gave me a wary eye. Luckily, as I said, we'd come to understand one another well enough to be in sync. While I had his eye I said, "She's still got a physical vessel, same rules, amigo. If it's bleeding, it's bad. She's probably going to need an IV and some bandages."

Donovan, a guardian of not only Gale's business but the woman herself, was about to voice a complaint when I tightened the tourniquet, I'd slid up his diminutive leg while he was watching Grove work on her. It sank into sensitive flesh, cutting off the circulation and eliciting a yelp. Donovan was a gnome, but when they passed to our world a kind of glamour concealed any of the tell-tale traits of his natural heritage that would make him stand out to us—save his height of course.

"You could have warned me," he said through gritted teeth.

"Right back at you. Stay here." I climbed back up to seal the cellar door. The locking mechanism turned, setting into motion a steady soundtrack of bolts engaging before I came back down. I wasn't too keen on locking myself inside but given that this was a situation I knew quite literally nothing about, *and* that it was serious enough to bring these two clamoring to my doorstep half-dead, I figured it was time to exercise a bit more caution.

"So," I said, plastering the most sarcastic grin I could muster across my face. "What's new with you?"

"We were attacked," he answered, his voice flat.

Gasping and wide-eyed, I covered my mouth in feigned shock before falling into a deadpan expression. "You two what, pissed off the Stalker that got through the portal last winter and needed me to play clean up? Some old flame of Gale's doesn't want to pay alimony for their little hellspawns anymore? Mrs. Never-Blink thinks you and Gale got more than a working relationship?"

The last quip was for him. I probably shouldn't have been so cavalier, but annoying humor was a go-to for me; a kind of defense mechanism—some might even argue that it's my default setting—so even if I wanted to curb my behavior, any attempt at that would just flat-out fail. Everybody has their way of dealing with things, and this was mine.

"No." Donovan's voice dropped an octave, his sunken shoulders fell even further, and a desperate expression washed over a face I was used to seeing as unflappable. He turned to watch Grove as he cut Gale out of her bloodied clothes and gently covered her with the blanket we'd laid at the end of the bed.

It was really hard not to respect the guy.

I decided to soften my approach and set aside my proclivity to remind the world what an asshole I am with every utterance and try to usher Donovan back to the present with a reassuring hand on his small shoulder. "Whatever it is, together we can—"

"She's being hunted by a Blind Judge."

For the first time in memory, I was rendered completely speechless as I felt the clutch of despair drag me down into hopelessness.

CHAPTER 2

Blind Judgment

"That's impossible." I might have been gaping at Donovan for one minute or ten, it was impossible to tell. "That's like, an act of…I mean… a Blind Judge?"

"It's true." Downtrodden and dead eyed, Donovan looked physically and spiritually exhausted. "I would know the Dreadnought anywhere, that is what came for us."

"Dreadnought?"

"How much do you know of the Blind Judges?" He asked, his assessing eyes returning to their clinical mien. Given the circumstances, I saw that as a *good* sign.

"Like… Nada. Zachariah told me it's 'an inescapable death sentence,' that's about it. Something about a house of gnomes and a tribe of goblins or something, having a ritual trial when the 'Balance' is broken, and they send their champion after the offender. Wasn't really in my wheelhouse. I feel like I've got the bones of it but not much else. If I had to guess, judging from the style of my ... *Curriculum*, that kind of stuff was going to come later."

"That's the gist of it, yes. The In-Between is the dividing space between our world, the Veil, the Abyss and the Beyond. The Masarou tribe and the House of Unet are keepers of the Balance. These two, the oldest goblin tribe and the royal line of Gnomes, are in control of the Judges. If there's an accusation, they investigate, take it under advisement, make a determination, and if justified, decide which of the Judges to send out to deal with the offender."

"There's more than one?"

Donovan nodded. "The one that came after us was from the House of Unet. Their champion is the Dreadnought: a golem of Earthcore steel."

"Earthcore, so that's like, strong…like uh," I paused, looking for the word; my forays into proper studies had been stunted, to put it mildly. "Mithril?"

"Mithril?" he asked, his tone unreadable.

"Never mind. It's from The Lord of the Rings."

"I'm aware," he said, having recovered some of the characteristic condescending superiority that I'd come to know and hate so much. "Yes, somewhat; it's particularly good steel. It's immune to the hottest of flames and tempered in such a way that the density is just astounding. Each limb weighs countless tons. They work anti-magic into every inch of it too. It's resistant to almost every element, and all but impervious to traditional magic."

"Oh, good. I thought this would be...you know, tough."

"It's impossible you idiot! And don't be so flippant." he replied.

"Well, if it's impossible, it does tend to take a lot of the pressure to succeed off," I said.

Donovan usually despised my cavalier wit, but this time his disapproving stare shrank away, and the beaten down Tinkerer actually chuckled—if only at the absurdity of it all.

"So they send this thing after big-time magic wielding types, right?"

Donovan nodded.

"It's a single-minded wrecking ball?"

Another nod.

"All right. No strength comes without sacrifice, and that will mean a weakness. What do you know about it?"

"Nothing, to be truthful. What I do know sits just on the fringe of my consciousness," he said.

That didn't make any sense. "What do you mean?"

"I mean I don't know anything about it, even though I built it." Donovan displayed an unflinching stare on his face, his tone neutral.

For the second time in the same hour I had been struck speechless, and even found myself leaning back to better absorb this startling news.

"You *built* it….The Blind Judge. That was *you*?"

My animated zeal drew Grove's attention. I waved off his furrowed brow and confused expression, gesturing at Gale so that he kept his focus on her.

"Well, not just me. I am an heir of Unet—albeit disgraced and disavowed—still one of the Royals, nonetheless. When my House exiled me, they took my knowledge of the golem from me before casting me out of the In-Between, which was my home, and sent me into this place. I was the architect though, yes." Donovan looked past Grove to Gale. Despite being bloodied and bandaged, she seemed peaceful. Gale was an uncompromising pillar of strength and integrity, but the one theme I'd been taking note of lately was her affinity for those who had been cast out. Everyone in her circle was a stray. Take Xander for instance, Gale's life mate. In the simplest of terms, he was a werewolf whose pack had run him out. He'd become persona non grata to them before falling into the bar matron's lap and Gale took him in. It was not her style to dominate through fear, instead, her people swore an oath of fealty to her out of appreciation and adulation. And while there was profound reverence for the woman, the obedience of her castaways was a product of love.

"Why?" I asked. When I saw the confusion on Donovan's face, I clarified: "Why did they throw you out?"

"It's a long story. In short, I did something unbecoming of royalty. I fell in love with someone beneath my station and my heritage. Her name was Ja'Sune. She was a goblin."

Ah, a 'West Side" love story….It fit but I was surprised that Donovan, usually so reserved, shared all of this so openly. Love had a way of dispensing with one's usual reservations, I suppose.

Sure, I had a momentary reservation about the *Goblin* bit—but this was a wacky world, and we already had enough judgment.

" Ja'Sune? Beautiful name." I wasn't so absent of empathy that I couldn't extend a tiny bit of kindness. After all, Donovan had really furthered my education in our craft with no real payoff for himself as far as I could see. "So," I continued carefully. I was already familiar with Donovan's pensive mask, so I strove to remain both patient and soft spoken as I tried to walk him out of his thoughts. "We have to figure out the procedure for this whole judge, jury, executioner thing and see if there isn't a way to slow it down, or, I don't know, get a retrial."

I rubbed my recently shaved head. Focusing on the prickly-soft sensation was a nice way to get my mind working. "This place will do for a spell," I said, wincing as I caught my own accidental pun. "But with Gale's power signature it's going to be hard to keep her concealed."

Donovan raised a finger, then untucked one of his necklaces from beneath his tattered shirt. The circular pendant contained an old emblem, one I wasn't able to recall from any of my studies. Before I could open my mouth, he answered the question written on my face: "It's a masking vessel, her power is in it. Although its signature is mostly hidden, if they're close enough, they will still be able to pick up on it. It's a dampener, not a solution."

"Gonna have to do a little better than that D." The mention was enough to goad him into a bit more of an explanation, while I examined the symbol on the pendant. It was an iron cross kind of build, symmetrical, with a design encircling the cross-hilt point, where a glowing amethyst stone was embedded. One with an admittedly alluring resplendence that transformed the gem into something even more enchanting. It seemed almost alive—like a living current of color.

"The…*aspect* of Gale that came from the Veil, the Power in her that originated there, is now in this vessel, and it will dampen any ability to track her, though it will make her weaker while she is separated from it."

Knowing I'd regret it, I held my hand out expectantly. Donovan looked down at my opened palm and then up to my face and said "what?" With more patience than I actually had, I shared my logic with him. "Donovan, *this* is one of the places they'll eventually come looking for her, so it would be best to keep them off the scent and get it out of here. Give it to me so that I can get it out of here and keep it safe—especially since it's got as much the feel of a hand grenade as it does any kind of solution."

"No!" he cried, betraying a shocking amount of passion for a man who always kept his cool. "This is my responsibility."

We locked eyes in a confrontation that felt almost physical. That was the very line I used when dragging Maria's lifeless body out of Lake Erie, barely managing with my one good arm but determined to be the one who completed the task.

I gave him a terse but unenthusiastic nod and stood up. Donovan moved again, slipping the pendant back under his shirt next to his heart. If it was anyone else, I'd have ripped it out of their hands, but I realized that Gale must have trusted him completely, or she would not have put her magical essence inside the thing. Grudgingly, I backed off, thinking it was probably her best chance to stay hidden, which is why she must have done it in the first place.

"If you help us—" he began to say.

"I'm helping you." I stood, and that got Grove's attention. I signed that we were heading out. In our ever-evolving process to find amicable middle ground, I had taken the time to learn some American Sign Language, and Grove had made it a point to be more expressive so that I could pick up on his cues. For all the headache this kind of silent communication could create, it had its benefits, and as more time passed, we started to fall more and more into step with one another.

"Anything else you need to tell me about this?" I asked.

"It has something to do with the lake," he answered.

Where we lost Maria. She was the person who prompted us to start this crackpot company in the first place. We did it with the hope that we could help someone else someday should they find themselves in something way over their heads like she did. Of course to this point, we hadn't handled anything quite that hot—our focus had been aimed at maybe keeping some girl off the menu of a vampire or something, or a guy from being cursed by a really angry ex-lover or wife. Stepping into a dispute set against a borderline demigod like Gale was far above my pay grade; a fact that was now occurring to me for the second time, establishing a potentially troublesome pattern.

"There's plenty of food and water here. Everything is completely off grid, and you should keep it that way."

The gnome, apparently surprised by my willingness to help more than I already had, struggled to his feet, but every time the opportunity to thank me came up I made sure to interrupt him.

"Don't talk to anyone," I said as Grove headed upstairs. "Make sure she rests. If you need to get hold of me you can't, but I'll check in on you with that—" I pointed to the wall, where there was a metal box next to the medical kit.

"What is it—a portal? Some kind of security camera?"

"Not exactly." My sheepish response stoked his suspicion. Donovan went to the box, unclasped the metal latch and pried it open. Inside was a Styrofoam cup with a string that went through the bottom and ended in a knot. The look I got was perfectly contemptuous, which just made me smile.

"Really?" he demanded.

"Yep. No magic residue, no electronic signal, nothing to hack; that's what you never get, sensei." That was a title he hated, and one I employed as often as appropriate comedic timing allowed. "The higher up a problem is," I said, illustrating my point with one hand stretching skyward, "the easier it is to crawl under it. You beat a big power with better technology by lowballing it. Scoff all you want, nobody's gonna detect that thing or find it except us."

It was a rare win; he seemed less stupefied and more begrudgingly impressed. I took the victory in stride however, saving my shit-eating smile for when I turned to follow Grove out. It was important to appreciate something like that, since it seemed I was about to join the losing team in a one-sided beatdown against an undefeated adversary, you know…just another day at the office.

CHAPTER 3

The Last Love

Since my own version of the story was abbreviated, I parroted all of it back to Grove as best I could. When he asked me to explain the difference between something like a Stalker and a Blind Judge, I explained it as the difference between a big jungle cat and a Tyrannosaurus Rex. Neither was ideal—both could kill us with ease—but one afforded a relatively more reasonable chance of survival than the other.

We cleared off our joint desk and dropped an assortment of gear onto the surface. Grove had emptied out his savings to buy some really incredible body armor, thin as a sweater and scaled. The rifle Kaycee had given him was still a favorite; its silver blade gleamed as he handled it. A spiked hammer coated in the same rich silver hung at his hip. I waited as Grove stashed a few other pistols and knives on his person.

My setup was much the same. I secured the broken bat to my lower back across the line of my waist, then donned my leather bracer and put a satchel of marbles in my pocket. The skeleton key necklace I put around my neck was refashioned, and I'd recently added two bracelets to my right arm where my broken watch used to sit. Once we had piled into our truck, I settled an aluminum bat between my legs.

"Are we going to go talk to Kaycee?" Grove asked.

Kaycee was like a surrogate older sister, she owned the magic shop across the street where she sold parlor trick accessories, the kind of stuff a low-rent Houdini or some backyard illusionist might want. Ironically, beneath the gimmick magic floor she had a second store that catered to a completely different clientele; real practitioners, legitimate magic occultists. It was ingenious really, not to mention an endless source of entertainment for me. Watching some two-bit sleight-of-hand hack sneering at a seemingly decrepit old man speaking Creole, not knowing the guy in front of him was a bona fide warlock was hysterical—at least to me it was.

"This is different than last time. Some very big powers are involved in this one, and we're going to have to toe the line even more than before...well, not us obviously, but anyone we might bring in. A Blind Judge is the end-all, be-all, and it's a foregone conclusion when you send one of them after someone or something. They're the alpha dog of everywhere except for maybe the deep, deep parts of the Abyss and the Veil, and even then, I doubt anything would be eager to cross the thing. The Dreadnought itself is like magically bulletproof, and it's the size of a monster truck, so I think it would be best for us to take this thing one a step at a time."

We'd worked out a system of talking at the red light and, since he wasn't one to interrupt (a proclivity of mine despite my claims to the contrary), I could usually get my whole point across before it was time to go again. Since my signing was still pretty shoddy, we relied mostly on lip reading and the tablet.

We pulled up to the Last Love, the bar that Gale owned, and her misfit band of outcasts operated. It was still outside, almost unnaturally so. This wasn't normally a bustling street—but it wasn't usually this dead either. It seemed almost bleak out here, but it wasn't surprising, not to me at least. One of the biggest things about us regular folk who are both historically and perpetually underestimated, is that we're good at tuning-in to our instincts. There was something just under the surface, leaking out from under the door, and we could feel it as we approached the entrance; a dreadful feeling that was suffocating, and very unlike the usual cozy ambiance you'd find inside. The bar was notorious for never being empty, no matter the day or time—never quite packed, but never completely thinned out either; just a steady flow of people coming and going.

We stopped at the door. I checked the sidewalk in each direction before bending over to break the glass with my elbow. My jacket was imbued with a tougher texture than just the leather it was made of, and it caved easily without ringing my bones. I turned to find Grove looking at me with disapproval.

"What?"

He poked the dangling cluster of warped wiring that hung off my necklace, asking, in a rather abrupt fashion, why I didn't use it. The incantation infused into the metal made it into a skeleton key, but it was a one-off trick, and it took me a few hours to break the key back down.

"What if we need it later?" I asked.

The skeptical look he shot me revealed his strained tolerance.

"Just stow the righteous do-gooder shit, alright? We're already way out on a limb for this chick, and if we get her out of this mess, she can buy another window." I shouldered the heavy door open and invited him to take the lead.

"Gale is our friend," Grove added. "You owe her a new window, *and* the respect of using her name."

This was a losing battle, and while I'd like to pretend it was an impasse, the truth was I'd end up paying for the window because it was the right thing to do. It was such a small thing really, especially in the grand scheme of all that was happening and was about to fall on our shoulders, but that's what made Grove what he was: stalwart. To him, no matter the circumstance or situation, you did the right thing, period. Breaking the window to avoid an hour of work didn't pass muster with him.

"Fine." Once we were in the stairwell, we readied ourselves. I rolled up my left sleeve and unlatched the broken bat from the small of my back. Grove opened his jacket for better access to his guns and unlooped the big, western rifle that Kaycee had given him. Despite my aversion to guns, I'd fired that weapon and had a blast doing it. We'd gone to the range a few times a month to develop a better knowledge base for me to build on, in case I ever had to use a firearm. I'd thought I'd gotten pretty good until I learned that standing still at a range and firing at your own pace in a controlled environment wasn't a realistic way to gauge your abilities. Ever since we'd moved to stress shooting—firing while moving and under duress—I'd come to again realize that I was still absolute shit with a gun.

Constricting tension set the stage for a very anxious trek down the stairs. It was dark and quiet, and every whisper-soft creak of the stairwell made me think my heart might explode. Normally adrenaline had a way of inspiring a kind of reckless fearlessness in me, but unlike cases where we'd be contending with some low-end scumbag, this time we were dealing with the kind of menace they sent to put down the worst damn things in all the known worlds. To put it into perspective, Gale was always the last bastion of hope for us when we got in over our heads. If not for her intervention at Lake Erie last winter, we'd all just be memories. As powerful and damn-near omnipotent as she was, this thing was a level above; it was what they sent to rip a god from their impervious perch and remind them what it meant to be mortal. Taking on a demigod, godling, or legend is a massive task; taking on what they sent to retire them with extreme prejudice and a flawless track record, is whatever beyond impossible would be….Infinitely impossible maybe?

Downstairs was a giant room divided into two sections. If you hooked around at the stairwell the bar was immediately to your right. It stretched out on the far wall and displayed a vast array of booze. Not that the choices really mattered; Gale would take the measure of anyone who cozied up on a stool and fix them whatever she decided was appropriate for them. You took it or you left it, but either way you damn well paid for it. The back of the room contained a few oval tables, more comfortable chairs, and a pool table which I had never actually seen anyone use.

In the opposite direction was a stage. Any local singer or band who thought they were worth a damn wanted to come through here. Gale found the best talent in town and gave them a taste of the limelight. What was best about it, was that everything was acoustic, so a rowdy crowd had to dial back the rambunctiousness if they wanted to get a good listen to whoever graced the stage. The place inherently created an atmosphere that encouraged listening, so when the designated entertainer was ready, everyone settled down. This was really for the best because Gale loved her music and hated to have it interrupted, and should it be interrupted, she had a bear of a man doubling as a bouncer on hand to deal with things. The only thing Xander liked more than violence was keeping Gale happy, so it went without saying that if he could accomplish both of those things at once it was a banner moment for him. Beyond the stage was a series of tables loosely situated in rows, with enough room between them for staff to navigate.

Overall, it was a comfortable place with a warm ambiance. The more I came, the more I realized it was kind of an unofficial place for the outcasts of our world to congregate. Gale wasn't a saint, the woman didn't have it in her to be so selflessly benign, but beneath those scary slanted looks and prickly quips was a woman who prided herself on her ability to look after her own.

The reprimand Grove gave me earlier, which had felt so dramatic, hit home. I was one of those lost boys who'd hung my hat beneath the roof she'd provided for all of us. I turned to him, once we were on the bar level, and signed him to keep his eyes out while I looked behind the bar. That same unnerving quiet that had blanketed the place outside was even more pronounced in here… as if the air itself was too tense to circulate. The atmosphere was charged with a dread which had settled itself in, making it almost impossible to appreciate what the place was like before. Trying to figure out why the surrounding space was soundlessly screaming at me to focus on it was also becoming a bit bothersome, and I couldn't shake the feeling that I should be paying more attention to it.

Once behind the bar I started more meddling, going through some seemingly mundane papers: bills, some offers, more bills. It was funny to think of Gale trying to do something like balancing a checkbook, handling payroll, or paying taxes. It just tickled me.

Suddenly there was a ruckus upstairs, an abrupt one that had me bracing as if for some big impact. Grove was standing at the foot of the stairs facing me and couldn't hear the commotion, so even though I had come to regret breaking the window at the entrance, I grabbed one of the glasses from the bar and hurled it past him to get his attention. Obviously, the noise of the glass shattering didn't do anything, but the blur of movement in his peripheral vision registered and was enough to do the trick. The muzzle of his gun swung my way as he whirled into action. I pointed up the stairwell we'd just come down, and Grove shifted the dangerous end in that direction. I was about to leap over the ledge and throw myself into what I assumed was going to be an ugly one-sided fight, when I saw him relax. The relief unwound every damn inch of me. If the Blind Judge had a protocol to try to end anyone aiding and abetting Gale and found us here in these tight quarters—assuming it could somehow fit—we'd be dead before we got a chance to even have at it properly.

Grove's posture went from relaxed to concerned in an instant, and before my line of sight would allow me to see whatever was coming down, he took off up the stairs. I heard some kind of talk and a throaty laugh before they began to work their way down. I saw the person Grove had gone to retrieve, but he was tough to identify at first. I saw tousled, shoulder-length hair matted with blood and some kind of smeared mud, and clothing torn to absolute shit with a left leg dragging listlessly. It wasn't until I got a glimpse at some tribal tattooing—and not that "tribal" crap you see taped on the walls of tattoo parlors, but the real stuff—that I realized who it was. Granted, I wasn't going to make fun of anyone with the other kind of tattoo either since I had no room to talk…. I was wearing a leather bracer on my left arm as if it were a socially acceptable fashion accessory.

Xander was one of the toughest beings I had ever come across. Not only was the Rougarou—affectionately known as The Regulator—big and menacing, he had a deceptive cleverness about him that made him more than just mere muscle. Rougarou were a kind of werewolf, although from my understanding they were bigger, and instead of falling victim to some kind of feral mindset, they seemed to keep a lot of their higher functioning. Xander, at the Lake Erie fight, had gone toe-to-toe with a massive Stalker and managed to walk away from the skirmish alive and in reasonably good shape. If something had caused him this much damage, then whatever we were dealing with was every bit the nightmare I feared it to be. As impressive as the burly doorman was, the fact that Grove was managing to not only steady him but literally shoulder the bulk of his considerable frame spoke volumes about Groves physical abilities.

I stopped myself from leaping over the bartop to help, mesmerized by what I was seeing through the not quite average two-way material that formed the wall under the bartop. From the customer side it looked like an ordinary wall, but from behind the bar, you could look through it and see what was really there. I watched Grove helping Xander down the stairs, with one distinct difference. I saw what Xander really was beneath his human shell: the revealing spell that Gale had evidently placed on the wall was proving quite useful tonight.

I didn't wait long. Xander was in rough shape, and being a ruffian himself, it was tough to imagine anything that got the best of him so thoroughly relenting for very long. Time wasn't on our side. Still, I lingered long enough to appreciate Gale's craftiness. She used to lecture me on the importance of keeping what you can and cannot do to yourself, insisting that mystery and reputation were as real and as useful as the other tools of the trade. She'd cultivated a deceptive environment where her most obvious, most frequently used power was a gift she didn't even have. We had always assumed Gale herself could see through every glamour, disguise, or mask, but it was the power infused in the wall…just another trick. I really could learn a lot from her.

"We need to get him out of here," I said.

Hustling around the bar, I grabbed a bottle of bourbon on my way over. Grove had wisely deposited Xander on a chair before mourning his blood-stained shirt. I dropped the uncorked bottle on the table and Xander snatched it up, lifting it in my direction for a makeshift salute. He downed half the contents in one pull.

"What'd you do, kick the door down?" I asked.

"What?" he asked. "Oh, you mean the broken glass? I don't know what asshole did that."

"It was open."

"Huh?"

Xander's head canted back slightly as the warm liquor started working its way through him. "Yeah, it's just stiff, you gotta muscle it a bit; I mean it's easier from the inside, but yeah, it wasn't locked. Probably just some punk kid."

"Probably." Grove's stare began burning a hole in the side of my head, a sensation I could only adequately answer with a raised middle finger. "How'd you make it out?"

"The thing isn't interested in me," he said. From what I could tell, the amount of blood he'd lost should have killed him, and the severity of some of his visible injuries lead me to believe that if he were anyone or anything else, it would have. "Once I couldn't move it just went on by, leaving me for dead. It's unstoppable, man. I threw everything I had at it, I threw everything around me at it, didn't do shit but pause it long enough to give me a swat before just moving on." I'd never seen the man defeated before, which was disturbing. Xander wasn't just beaten up; he could deal with that. Something about this incident had taken the spirit out of him. I knew what it felt like to receive a beatdown but put up a good fight; to show some grit and go down swinging hard enough to leave the other guy with the knowledge that despite winning, he'd been in a brawl. Being systematically taken apart was different. That wasn't just losing, it was having the fight ripped right out of you. I didn't think Xander had ever dealt with that feeling before, and it was showing all over him.

"How long is it going to take you to recover from this?"

Xander did an admirable job of lifting his head up enough to drink, while looking down at the same time for a cursory self-assessment. He belched before answering, filling the air between us with a distinct, boozy sting. "Three days, at least. Maybe longer. Hard to say. What's the lunar cycle right now?"

"That makes a difference?" I asked.

"I dunno. Maybe? It's weird, there's a lot of us. I mean, a lot of types." The fact he wasn't sure was another callback to the broken-home-history he'd come from, so I didn't press. But how little he knew was actually startling.

I was inclined to agree with him about the weirdness. The whole mythos of vampires and werewolves had been mutated, bastardized, dramatized, misrepresented and misinterpreted. My feelings on vampires notwithstanding—apparently there were more than just the fear-inducing variety I was used to contending with—it was the same with shapeshifters. I did know that I wanted to learn more someday, but the thing that I was most curious about at the moment was why Xander didn't know about his own lineage…but now wasn't the time for education. Kneading my brow, it occurred to me that while Xander was very cunning in many ways, there was a lot he tended to be dense about.

"Does it matter?" I asked.

He shrugged, chugging. I was about to push it, irritation written over every inch of my face, but then I remembered he'd been an outcast; there was a chance that he actually didn't know.

"Alright, three days," I said, looking around. The bar was desolate, and it wouldn't do us any good to operate like it was business as usual. "You've got to come with us then. We've got to stash you somewhere for you to lick your wounds." I couldn't help it; the shoe fit, and I snickered.

Xander, already not my biggest fan, told me with one sharp look in no uncertain terms that his hatred for me had just grown exponentially. I didn't care, it was a good pun, and I couldn't resist an opportunity to be punny.

Grove and I got to either side of the mastodon of a man we were now going to try to carry out of here, and managed to pull him up with little fanfare, save damn near throwing my back out in the process. I was grunting and straining, but Grove was staying as stone-faced and unreadable as ever.

"You boys need to either play nicer…" a singsong voice called down to us. It was masculine, but just barely. It was one of those things that defied explanation, no matter how articulate, but even a simple utterance seemed melodic, "…or figure out some kind of safe word."

All three of us turned to the stairwell we'd just been preparing to climb, only to see someone standing in it. His outfit looked like it belonged on the cover of a thirty-year-old fashion magazine. Ripped skintight jeans sitting so low on his bone-thin hips that they exposed smooth alabaster skin. Every finger had a ring on it—some more than one, and he had a guitar strapped to his back. His mohawked hair was rigidly spiked, to the point of defying my very elementary understanding of hair product—and gravity for that matter. Nose ring, lip ring, enough earrings for ten people. He was wearing eyeliner, which to his credit did accentuate a startling set of sterling gray eyes. His shirt was proudly boasting a band I'd never heard of, and I do know obscure pretty well. He was tall and had the posture of someone decidedly feminine, and the voracious look in his eyes when he glanced between Xander and Grove told me that this was not a mistake in his styling. Untied boots bloused out, yet never slipped from his feet as he sauntered over to us.

"And you are…?" I asked, as I released my hold on Xander and saddled Grove with all the weight. (I'd like to say I felt a bit of remorse about it, but if the kid wanted to act as if it wasn't a burden, I wasn't above letting him.)

"Johnny B," the stranger said, never once affording me a look, though he offered up a dainty wave to my partner.

"Johnny B?" I asked.

"Johnny B whatever you want him to be," he answered smoothly off of my unwitting set-up.

I laughed, despite myself.

CHAPTER 4

New Allies

Grove and Johnny B. managed to get Xander up the stairs with surprising ease. It helped that Grove was in peak physical condition and refused to be outdone by anyone, especially a waif-thin bony punk rocker who looked like he'd stepped out of the 80's NYC music scene.

"You're an elf." Stating rather than asking. After navigating around them, I shouldered the busted front door open so they could half-drag, half-carry Xander out to our truck. The drunk shapeshifter managed the trip with minimal grunting and growling. Pulling the back door open, I let Grove deposit him inside so I could check the dodgy bandaging we'd applied, knowing he would heal exponentially quicker than anyone else involved in this budding shitstorm.

"Aye." Johnny had storm clouds for eyes, constantly shifting in color and shade, like silver mist curling off the lake on a gray day. They were breathtaking really, and the only thing that kept me from outright gawking was the provocative grin he gave me.

"What're you doing here?" I asked.

"Tonight is my night," he answered, sighing theatrically. "What did Gale do now?"

"She's in trouble," I answered matter-of-factly, taking some of the glibness out of my own tone. It worked, because the look I got from the rock star now was a lot more serious. I sensed that some of his shtick was a gimmick, but I wasn't sure how deep the charade went.

Johnny B sighed. "Bad?"

"Very."

Deliberating on the broken door for a bit, Johnny took a minute to consider. Grove was by my side, but I signed for him to keep quiet. Elves perceive time differently than our kind, even if they don't mean to. It could come off as rude, and when they went into a pensive state like this it could take some time. By contrast, they tended to view us as juvenile because of how hurried we seemed by comparison.

"I'm coming with you," he said, breaking out of his thoughtful reflection as if no time had passed. "Hey muscles, open your lid."

Grove's poor eyes went so wide I couldn't keep myself from cracking up as he shifted an unsure look from me to the androgynous elf who seemed determined to make him as uncomfortable as possible. After a good laugh, I took the keys out of his hand and opened the tonneau cover so that the smiling miscreant could drop his strange-looking guitar into it. I had never seen an instrument quite like this one; it had the traditional shaft for the stringing, but where they all started from was where the whole classic guitar thing ended. It curved down and then sharply up like a very wide-drawn U, and the back tip was sharpened to a deadly-looking point. It was orange, too, impossible to miss.

Grove regained his flat affect by the time I threw him the keys. I contemplated getting in the back, for the sheer comedy of it, but ultimately decided to take shotgun.

"Take us home Chewie," I said.

"How are you Han when he's the roguishly handsome one?" Johnny B asked as the truck started moving. Grove wasn't looking at him and couldn't hear his quips so when his verbal dagger missed the mark, the man actually pouted, which got another laugh out of me. I liked Johnny B.

"He can't hear you," I said, turning to explain. "He's deaf."

"Oh God, so he's got like a wounded warrior thing going for him too. I can work with that."

I slapped Grove's shoulder. "This is why you should wear looser shirts." He answered with a perfectly perplexed expression before turning back to the road. I was pretty sure I saw him give the barest shake of his head, before I turned my attention back to Johnny B.

"Why do you want to help Gale? Honestly, I should be reading you the riot act or giving you the fifth degree but we're way out of our depth here and backed into a wall before it's even begun. That," I said, pointing out at Xander's prone form, unconscious and bleeding black ichor, "is our big gun, and he's already been thoroughly handled."

"Gale and I have history," Johnny said, examining his meticulously manicured nails. It seemed a foppish gesture, yet there was something decidedly predatory about the man. I suspected that the behavior was designed to throw people off and distract them from his brutally violent side. A broken titan was in the back of the vehicle with him, having been systematically fractured, and Johnny was still unfazed. That kind of unflappability took practice, and the kind of self-control that can only come from one place: experience. "I might not like the bitch, but she ain't my enemy."

"That's reassuring," I said, salting an open wound with my flat, expectant look, waiting for more elaboration.

"That should be enough for you."

"It isn't."

"Well, too ba—" With just a gesture of my thumbed-out fist Grove violently jerked the car to parallel the cold concrete sidewalk we'd been driving by, and Johnny's head ricocheted off of the passenger window. The elf had a curse on his mouth that never found breath because I had the tip of my aluminum bat pressed just beneath his elegantly pointed chin. The elf looked from me to the weapon, noticing the glowing sigil work that had been carved into it.

"That's pretty shoddy work, Artificer."

"Ugly yet effective," I volleyed back with a smile that begged him to try me. It wasn't a patented look, but damned if I don't know how to sell it. "Like me."

"Is this about me and Muscles?"

He was funny and I liked him, which was why I pressed the bat closer instead of driving it into his throat.

"Playing it fast and loose kid?" Now the pseudo-sagacity of the elder elf came out; all of them could shift to the veneer of a kind of elder statesman and condescend to you, as if that would somehow convince you to change your act.

"Last time shit started going wrong in my town I had to kill a Stalker, a pack of vampires and face down some kind of dark goddess from the Abyss, so tell me again how you think you're out of my weight class."

Something akin to a proverbial *'a-ha!'* kind of light bulb switched on inside of him. He lifted his arms to signal defeat. "Gale was my mother before she became what she is. It's complicated but suffice it to say I am still harboring some affection for the old bat. And looking at me like that isn't going to make it any different. Take me to Kaycee, she'll back my story—that is where we're headed, right Janzen?"

Great, the guy knew my name, and he had delivered it with a sharp, sly smile. It was like the severity of this all was just washing right over him. This time it was me who paused to consider all the implications of what he'd said, but eventually I just signaled Grove to start driving again.

It was quiet, and just as I was about to try and think all of this through, Johnny piped up from the backseat.

"Didn't expect that…" It was a conspicuous comment, hanging in the air like bait.

"What's that, little sister?" My own snarky comment was only just contained by a tempered sneer.

"You got some darkness in you, is all. I heard you come from a house of good guys, so it was just unexpected to see that much menace—especially in a man as young as you. Dad not hug you enough?"

"Me? No. My family was great, but we played Monopoly so much it taught me not to trust anyone. Shut up," I cut the rocker off as he sucked in air for another comment-to-question combination. "I have to think."

About ten minutes later we were outside the magic shop.

***

"*Don't look at our place at all if you can help it,*" I mouthed to Grove, not wanting to draw any attention to it. He was a little thrown by that, but I could see his mind wheeling around to what I meant by it. I wasn't sure who was watching us, or if we were being watched at all, but I wasn't taking any chances. You know what they say, it's only paranoia until you're right: then you're a genius.

Not a minute after we pulled up, another truck pulled up behind us. It was an old, run-down, thirty-year-old pickup. More dents and rust than any consistent color, except for a yellow hood, some green paneling, and lots of exposed primer. Before Grove could overreact, I stilled the hand going into his jacket and gave a furtive shake of my head.

I jumped out of the SUV and went around to open the back, trying to work out how we were going to get the now-unconscious Xander out of our vehicle and inside the shop. A bell chimed, a kind of serene symphonic sound, and Kaycee stepped out to greet us. Still sitting in the backseat, Johnny B hadn't moved or uttered a sound, and I had the distinct feeling that he was halfway to jumping up front, throwing the thing into reverse, and beating it out of there before she saw him.

"Well lookie here, it's Johnny B. Come'ere honey." And just like everyone else who hung around here for more than a minute, his fear evaporated, and the bone-thin elf couldn't help but excitedly tiptoe over to Kaycee and accept a big, bosom-trapping hug. She pulled him back to look him over. "Sex Pistols called; they want their outfit back."

"Thanks," The rocker said through a laugh. "You borrow the Gingerbread Hag's costume?"

"Play nice young man." Kaycee returned his laugh with one of her own, idly roping an arm into his skinnier one before turning toward us.

I stepped aside so that Kaycee could get a clear view of Xander's condition.

"Well, that's perfectly terrifying," she said. "What did he get into this time?"

"It's a lot more than just him," I said, trying not to sound too intense. To help me fight something decidedly bad was one thing, to get involved in something as convoluted as this was would be asking too much…way too much. "I need to keep him here for a few nights."

Kaycee, a maverick in her own right, did a remarkable job of looking at me, then past me to our shop across the way, and back at me without making the slightest move of her head. It was hard to tell—unless you knew what to look for—that our quaint little security shop was in lockdown mode. She was the one who had helped me build and ward the facility, so she understood the implications without needing to hear it.

"Sure. Who should I charge, you or him?"

"Definitely him."

"Does he even have a salary?"

"If not, you'll get some killer peanut butter-filled bones out of it."

I could tell the joke didn't land well when everybody gave me quizzical looks all at once.

"He's….You know...a….Because dogs like bones, and peanut butt….Never mind."

Grudgingly turning to Xander's prone form, I tried to get a good grip and pull him out. To my surprise I managed to sit him up, even dropped my shoulder under him, but when I went to hoist him up, we went down hard. Luckily, the sidewalk broke my fall.

"He has denser muscle and bone than you, that's why he can grow to be so big; he's probably a few hundred pounds heavier than you think." Although informative, Johnny B's statement wasn't very helpful with regard to getting me out from underneath Xander's exceptionally heavy body.

"We only got him up the stairs because he was still managing to bear most of his own weight," Johnny elaborated. "Now you tell me?" I said, annoyance written across every inch of my face while I looked up from under this mountain of Rougarou flesh, as if I should be grateful to learn this *after* I'd fallen with Xander on top of me.

After Grove extricated me and I got to my feet, we stared down at our latest charge, still sprawled on the pavement and out cold. Kaycee and Johnny B were locked arm-in-arm whispering to each other. The driver's side door of that strange pickup finally opened with a wince-inducing wail of warped metal pieces fighting against each other. Jay, Kaycee's enigmatic husband, was a very big guy, and while he didn't look like he was in peak physical condition, he was thick and very strong, and had a scarred face that was locked in an eternal scowl. Jay was tall but not towering, imposing without coming across as intimidating. I think I'd heard him speak three or four times in all the years I'd known him. My biggest challenge was to not rudely stare at him. Jay only had one arm—his right, the left had been severed from the elbow down. Most assumed he was a veteran, but the truth was far more magical—literally—than that.

"Jay," Kaycee cooed sweetly, and even though *soft* wasn't the right word for the gruff-faced guy, it did seem that some of his scowling faded when she said his name. "We're going to be watching Xander for a few days, can you give them a hand?"

I *almost* made a joke, but Kaycee's glare and the certainty that Jay could rip my own arm clean off and beat me to death with it was enough to hold me in check. Plus, what I saw next confirmed my suspicion. Jay looked from Johnny B to me, then to Grove, and finally to the face down Rougarou. He didn't answer Kaycee's request so much as just emit a kind of guttural, grunted acknowledgement. Jay knelt down, turned Xander over, grabbed him under the arm and lifted until he stood straight, and then effortlessly threw him over his shoulder. That simple… this mountain of a man that I couldn't have moved if my life depended on it… and this guy, with one arm, did it with ease, and never once showed any sign of strain. Just picked him up and threw him over his shoulder like a sack of potatoes.

"Holy shit," I said. Grove and I were visibly stunned, and even Johnny B seemed to bite back some of the smugness from his face. Kaycee untangled herself from the rocker elf to open the door, whereupon the bell chimed twice; the first, a low ominous bass and the second, a more piercing echoing sound.

"You know," I said, "now I'm even more worried about the fact that I don't think he likes me."

"He doesn't," Kaycee answered as she stepped back outside to where we had gathered around the entrance.

"Oh. Good to see my sense of people isn't broken."

"No, no, no, not liking you is kind of… Well, that's actually kind of good for him, he hates Johnny."

The elf feigned a wounded expression, one that left as quickly as it came. His factory setting seemed to be this kind of half-cocked smirk and he fell back into it as his default. I could see where that would rub someone raw, especially someone as reserved and soft spoken as Kaycee's husband.

"He likes Grove though," she added.

Grove was unmoved by the revelation, which was probably why the one-armed barbarian had such an affinity for him. That, or they were cut from similar stuff. My guess would be the latter.

"What is Jay?" I asked, not sounding nearly as nonchalant as I'd hoped.

"Strong."

I hadn't been expecting a straight answer, but I'd be lying if I said I wasn't surprised by the scowl on Kaycee's face; it told me not to ask a second time. Blurting it out was stupid, but in lieu of what I'd seen and how little I knew after all this time, it was just kind of a knee-jerk thing. Curiosity killing the cat and all.

"So, why don't you take me to the store to get some milk, hm?" She wiped her cherubic fingers off on her apron, airily drifting to the front truck and waiting for one of us to open the passenger side door. Grove complied, upstaging me in the process, so Johnny and I just shuffled on into the back. Once inside, we did as instructed, and drove to the store so that she could get milk. On the way, we took the time to review all that we'd been through recently.

***

"A Blind Judge," Kaycee echoed thoughtfully. Johnny B noticeably drew within; his vibrant disposition seemed to sink when the reality of what we were dealing with came to light. The severity of his expression was shared by the shop owner who, milk in hand, was staring out the window on our way back. "I can't remember the last time one of them has been sent over to take someone. Even for someone like Gale, it seems excessive."

"She's not one of us anymore," Johnny said. "Maybe it's overkill, but she's strong, so I guess they're thinking better safe than sorry."

Kaycee was not charitable with her tenderness, so I was a bit surprised to see her offer it so openly to the singer. "She's strong, but she's not that strong. She's still her, even if you think that's changed." Whatever Kaycee meant to imply, it wasn't meant for me, and since I didn't have the energy to analyze every little exchange between them, I let it pass. Johnny B. seemed to get it loud and clear, but whatever she meant, I didn't get the sense that he agreed with her.

My suspicion was that with this information, we'd lose Kaycee's further assistance. With her restrictions, she already had to be exceptionally careful about what situations she stepped into, but this was something she couldn't tread on at all, and I wouldn't expect her to. Maybe she would do it for me (as egotistical as that may sound) but not for Gale; their relationship was ice cold. Judging by the look painted across the face of the androgynous karaoke king rocker it seemed like I was at risk of losing his help too.

Kaycee and I had a very surrogate family-type relationship, and like most families, we had to respect the fact that there were certain limits to how much we would intervene in each other's lives. The paradigm between Grove and I was less surrogate and more symbiotic. He had just shown up six months earlier when I was in the middle of the shit with the first stalker like a avenging angel, and we've been together ever since. Johnny B was still an unknown, which was part of the reason I got a bit dodgy when he started asking questions.

"Is Gale—" he asked.

"She's safe."

"Where?"

"She's safe," I insisted.

"What's the matter, don't trust me?" he asked, cornering me with an impish smile that accentuated the awkwardness between us.

"No." Candor was my oxygen, so if he thought I'd get uncomfortable getting blunt with him, he was sorely mistaken. Despite my tone, the edge never quite left his smile; I wasn't sure whether I respected or hated him for that.

"I don't even know where to start on this one Janz," Kaycee said, stealing my attention. "I mean, if you find out who is levying the allegation against her you can call them on it in court, they do have a check-and-balance thing they do, but it's not like anything you've experienced: they play judge, jury, and as you've already seen, executioner. To my knowledge, a Blind Judge has never failed; they're unstoppable, single-minded juggernauts." She spoke with a sadness in her eyes, one that told me she'd borne witness to the devastating destruction these things could visit on someone. I knew without asking that she felt for me, because I had never seen her look so downright hopeless before.

It all traced back to the lake, there was no doubt in my mind about it. Before that, Gale was notorious for her ability to stay uninvolved with local happenings, both ordinary and extraordinary, and she never once stepped out of line. Neither had her people, except maybe when Donovan had taken me on as his apprentice, but his tutelage was private, and since I wasn't any kind of player it seemed unlikely to cause a stir this big. An infraction like that conjuring up a Judge would be like giving a death penalty to someone for jaywalking. If that had been the case, they could have sent the Judge after me instead of Gale and I wouldn't have even lasted long enough to bring this irritating mystery to the surface. Worse, I hadn't even known that a set of accords or guidelines actually existed; I always assumed that most of the talk about direct intervention in "the Balance" was a series of suggestions… more a matter of tradition than practice.

"Do we know which Judge is after her?" I asked, despite already knowing. Sadly, it was all about misinformation and duplicity in this life, so playing stupid was a sure-fire way to get people to show a hand they were trying to keep close to the chest. It helped me discern how much people knew about the current situation and the politics that were driving it.

Johnny B seemed confused by the question, but Kaycee adopted an intrigued yet knowing expression. She was well aware of what I meant by what I asked, but curious as to how I'd come to learn about it. I had a knack for reading people and it was especially difficult to veil an emotional reaction from me if we'd spent any kind of real time together. It came from my back-alley education—street and sidewalk schooling weren't ideal, but it made me into one hell of a hustler—and the age-old adage ain't wrong…it's hard to hustle a hustler.

Kaycee and I volleyed a few silent speculations back and forth with pointed looks, until she let out an exasperated sigh.

"It's going to be the golem, from the House of Unet. The Dreadnought. You can slow it down with brute strength, but it's got an impenetrable defense mechanism; a ward that reverses almost any kind of magic that gets thrown at it. And for someone like Gale… I don't think they'd entrust that to the tribe."

"Alrighty then," I said. "I got it from here. I'll be in touch tonight." Kaycee flashed a face of concern, but expertly masked it for the benefit of our mixed company. She gave Grove an affectionate squeeze on the arm before he shouldered open the door and exited. I got out and gave her a hug, then seamlessly slid back into shotgun position, leaving Johnny B still sitting in the backseat.

"Supply run," I announced, and sent a long text to Grove so that my actual partner could have some insight into what I was planning next. Whereas Johnny was absently amused and aloof, as if that was his default setting, a grimmer and more determined look washed over my partner's face as he read over what it was that I was planning on doing next. We met the fact that the elf didn't take the cue to get out of the truck with a shrug before heading off.

Our first stop was only a solid baseball throw away from the shop; it was a storage spot in our little warehouse district. We backed in, rolling out like we had rehearsed it—which we had, and got started. Johnny slunk out behind us, watching as Grove made short work of dialing a code into the security panel on the outside of the garage.

I could tell the beginning of a question was forming in the back of the singer's mohawked head as his eyes surgically picked at the contents of the unit. Admittedly, it was quite a sight. The boxes inside were all labeled, stacked and organized so that we could easily navigate the crude pathways that they created. Grove grabbed one up to load into the back of the truck, and while Johnny hadn't actually asked, an inquiry brewing inside those curious eyes was quite evident.

"There's power in being underestimated," I began, bobbing my head from left to right as if I was trying to formulate a coherent thought out of the concuss-riddled helmet I lovingly referred to as my head. "If you survive it, that is. You try harder and you learn to be adaptable. It's what Darwin actually meant when he described the *fittest*. We survive by not assuming anything and knowing just where we are in the food chain of this thing." I motioned toward the contents inside the room as Grove stowed away the box he'd plucked free a moment before. "We've got a grab bag for every kind of baddie you can think of—as well as a few we've only heard rumors about—and each one of them has multiple contributions from our little band of merry men and women. Say what you will about the Boy Scouts, that motto is an exceptionally useful tidbit." *Be Prepared* was a mantra for us at Circle Protection Agency, and we stood firm in the belief that it was the only chance we had at enjoying any kind of longevity as we trudged the road of our ill-advised career path.

The musician kept a steady bead on us as we loaded up, begging the question as to what the elf was actually *doing* here. "So where we goin'?" he asked. His silky voice grated on me as it queried from the back seat in some kind of accent that he had adopted as if that would elevate the question and cajole an answer out of me. Uncharacteristically, I kept my mouth shut rather than give a knee-jerk answer that I would regret later.

My eyebrow lifted as I swiveled in my seat to stare at him, giving him an opportunity to extricate himself before going any further.

"Ignoring what is obviously a complicated and probably screwed up past between you and Gale," I began, " if you start riding with us, the moment you get on the radar of whoever it is that is after her, you'll be stuck on our side of this fight." The warning either didn't register, or he was every bit as cocksure as the flippant expression of smugness he was aiming at me. "Us… a guy with a bunch of guns, and a shitty Artificer… against a Blind Judge that just handed your mum her ass, as well as her pet wolf and a bona fide Tinkerer."

Johnny feigned contemptuous indifference, examining his manicure and humoring me with an occasional nod.

"So you're going all suicidal for a mom who kicked you to the curb?"

His expression split into a fierce smile, as he crossed his legs and folded his well-kept hands in his lap. "I'll show you mine if you show me yours..."

"Touché." I replied. After all I thought, I wasn't exactly a banner example of mental and emotional health myself, and it wasn't as if I'd come from a functional household either.

I retrieved the GPS between Grove and me and input the address to the restaurant beside Lake Erie, the closest landmark to the brutal battle that went down that fateful night.

CHAPTER 5

Retracing Steps

Gale being beaten was believable, even though I wasn't going to be insolent enough to say as much out loud. Her being caught unawares is what perplexed me. I didn't suspect an inside job because both Donovan and Xander had nowhere else to go when she took them in, and each coveted loyalty, albeit in their own way. Johnny B was a reasonable suspect, but the guy actually seemed concerned for her well-being. So he was either wasting time leading us to a trap or throwing himself smack in the middle of all the mayhem. Between the arguable clairvoyance of the bar proprietor and the eerie intelligence of Donovan, one of them would have gotten a whiff of suspicion if it was someone in their inner circle. I didn't trust the Elf, but I did trust that Kaycee wouldn't have sent him with me if she thought it was a problem. That was the deciding factor for me because I trusted Kaycee's instinct more than I trusted the North Star.

At the lake we'd thwarted some pretty heavy hitters; a fight like that was bound to be connected to this, and it was the only thing we could really think of. You don't even attempt to execute a plot as bold as the one we encountered without having some kind of major pull. With the kind of clearance it would take to try something like that, I wouldn't be surprised if they had the know-how and juice to try to blackmail Gale too.

If the conspiracy ran that deep it wasn't too far of a stretch to think that they had gotten to whatever board, assembly or council was in control of these Blind Judges. Truthfully, this terrified me. Whatever the governing body was—and however it had come to power—it believed in the righteousness of the hammer when handing out punishment. To think that this group—formidable enough to force both the Veil and the Abyss to operate secretively—had been infiltrated and manipulated was horrifying.

"So… music?" Johnny B. was asking.

My contemplation had blanketed me so much that while whatever started that question was lost on me, the tail end was enough to rouse me and get the message.

"Yeah," I clicked the radio on, and some garbage top-twenty started churning out. "Sorry, with Grove I just kind of fell into the habit of silence."

"The deaf thing?" The guy was a bit abrupt, and I wondered if this was what it was like talking to me since I was a star student in the school of candor and boorishness.

"Yeah," I answered, laughing. "The deaf thing. It kind of became a thing, and before long it was kind of peaceful. I talk a lot, so silence can definitely be golden." Sorry, I couldn't help myself.

"You appreciate what is said more when you do not speak. I get it." Even now the melody—one that was cantankerously catchy—was being perfectly matched with a corresponding rhythmic kind of drum-rolling against his denim-clad thigh.

"What do you hope to find out here?" he asked.

"A lead."

"So you're some kind of detective?"

Percolating how best to answer, my shrug was noncommittal, and my silence didn't validate any position.

"Private eye, with dangerous dames coming in at all hours, selling you a sob story and sending you on an adventure that's ripe with danger?"

"Read a lot of dime store novels kid?" I said, finding myself smiling, though quietly I thought of the *Casablanca* quip I fired off for Gale when she first fell into my lap.

"This certainly has the feel of one."

"I'd shop this story for a few bucks, but I can't imagine who would want to read it."

Practiced silence from the talkative man cued me to continue with the original point I had deviated from.

"I do security mostly. Tracking stuff down isn't really in my wheelhouse. Still, I'm capable enough and notoriously persistent. Evidence is a shred of truth. Pick up enough truth and you'll find your way to the whole thing. Truth acts like pieces of broken glass; as long as you know to put the whole thing together before trying to make any sense of it you should be alright."

"Hm." His pursed mouth seemed to indicate that he was impressed. I asked a question without giving voice to it with the look I cut over the sharp slope of my shoulder.

"Just didn't expect anything quite that profound from someone like you," he said casually.

"Human?"

"Simple."

"Fuck you."

"Throw Muscles in and we can talk," he said, flashing his teeth in a lusty smile.

I laughed and he joined me, our amusement muted by the impending darkness of what we suspected we'd find—but for the moment, the banter felt good.

"What's your niche?" I asked. I figured if we were going to be running shoulder-to-shoulder in what would inevitably become a throw-down, it would be wise to know what we could come to expect from him.

"Niche? You make it sound like a parlor trick, or some kind of sleazy sales tactic. Are you asking me if I have any talent? If I am a practitioner, a wizard, an artificer, or all of the above? Then no. I'm none of those things."

"Then this is double crazy for you to come along with us, isn't it?"

"I can take care of myself. You don't live with such extravagant flamboyance the way I do without learning how to handle yourself. Plus, I tried to tell you before. I sing."

"Sing." My skepticism was delivered in my tone. "And there is some kind of power in that?"

"There is when I'm the one doing it."

My confusion was written all over my face, which hadn't a clue how to keep anything off of it.

"Singing is the closest that an everyday nobody comes to using magic; it can influence mood, and it can inspire and motivate. Music is magic without magic, and music with magic is just…so much more."

It didn't even register on the list of the weirdest things I'd heard today—let alone ever— and there was a part of me that could identify that line of logic pretty quickly. Magic is an infusion of emotion, mathematics and thought. We can quantify it as energy all we like, but we didn't really have a finite definition for any of this anyway, so singing…why the hell not.

We managed to get to the restaurant without incident. By now it was dark out; the sunken sun no longer spreading its warming radiance, having given way to a cool cutting breeze. The blanket of night seemed a lot more stifling than was reasonable to expect so early in the evening. I wouldn't ever voice it, but my suspicion was that this uneasy feeling was born of that awful night half a year ago. It had done irreparable damage not only to everyone that was involved, but the landscape itself had been scarred. We parked far enough away to remain discreet and walked into the thicket of forest instead of toward the light of the nearby dock bar and eatery. I waited until I was confident that we were well out of sight and earshot. It was a good trek from where we parked to the designated location. None of us spoke, which wasn't entirely unexpected considering Grove hardly ever did, but the chatty Elfling's silence was a little surprising. It wasn't a bad thing because it gave me time to reflect; the quiet after the chaos allowing me to sift through all that had been dropped on me. Sorting things out uninterrupted was a luxury that I didn't usually get, especially while shit was still happening.

I opened my mouth to speak, but the singer interjected before I could get anything out.

"So what happened here?"

I knew it was a question I should have expected. Hell, if my suspicion that this connected back to what had happened was correct, it was actually a fair question. What I was unprepared for, was the reality of being back here again. It was completely different than just thinking about this place, that night, and what had happened. And I was being asked to give voice to those memories, and it hurt like a mother fucker.

"From what I have been able to gather, Some crazy amateur-hour cult actually managed to touch base with a big bad something on the Abyss side. She only gave them the time of day because somehow these assholes had within their ranks, a bonafide Wanderer. Of course, she—the Wanderer, Maria— didn't know the extent of her own power, or what they —the cult—were actually about. Nor did she know about the big bad something and what it was up to. End of the day, they tried to use the lake as a kind of conduit infused with her Wanderer energy to open a portal between our world and that one."

The singer gave a low whistle, appreciating the gravity of the revelation. Coming across a Wanderer—not just happening upon them—but finding one at a point where they hadn't yet figured out what they were and what they're capable of, was extraordinary. A Wanderer is a being that has a mysterious piece of the In-Between inside of them. The In-Between is a living sentient power whose job it is to keep this world separate from the Abyss and the Veil. Maybe even more…I don't know for sure. One time I thought I heard Donovan mention something else in addition to those realms when he was talking about the magical worlds, but I might have had one too many to be sure. I do know this: a Wanderer is extremely valuable because that piece of the In-Between inside of them can be used to form a bridge between worlds; to open portals from one to the next, and the fact that they were an untapped well of magical power only increased their value to some, and their threat to others.

"I think Maria—the Wanderer—started to get a little suspicious of what they had been up to, but by then it was too late.

The cult had brought a Stalker to our world and sent it after her. We intervened, and it ended up being one of those insane plots that would usher in an end of the world kind of headache. We thwarted it of course, being the badasses that we are," I said, as I struggled to keep a straight face and deflect the pain. I was trying to be cheeky and inject a little levity into the telling to help me swallow the big lump of regret that was trying to choke me, but it wasn't really working.

"Yeah, that bit got out. You two jackals taking on a Stalker, eh?" said Johnny B.

"It was mostly him." I hitched a thumb at Grove, who was kneeling beside the box from the trunk and taking inventory of its contents.

"I can believe it."

"Anyway, it all came to a head when those bastards got Maria and managed to gut her enough to try to open a portal. It didn't work. We stopped them—all of us: me, Gale, Xander, Donovan, even Kaycee." I tried to stuff my heartbroken soul behind some failing stoicism.

"And the Wanderer?"

I shook my head and was relieved Johnny let it go so easily.

"Anyway, it's the only time Gale has ever gotten involved as long as I have known her. I even checked with some people who keep a better ear to the ground than I do, and they agreed that she's never before stepped over any of the invisible balance lines."

Johnny sneered, though he fought through it well enough. "She took her station and neutrality seriously, so I believe it. She wouldn't put herself out there and go against the status quo. Trust me, bitch orphaned me for a raise. Anyway…" he broke off, taking a breath. I understood the need to share some contempt out loud, so I let him vent. "My point is, I'm leaning toward agreeing; if this is all centered around meddling, there's a good bet that this is the only time she's ever done it. Must have been some heavy shit."

"It certainly had the look of it," I said, turning my eye to the shoreline where I nodded for them to follow. "The portal was crawling to an open, and it looked as if she had an entire gaggle of Stalkers to send over, whoever this evil bitch from the Abyss was. One did get over actually, beside the one we killed." It was massive, it dwarfed the one I fought—the one I literally had to drop a building on to kill. Xander managed to go toe-to-toe with the thing, which was a testament to his abilities and showed me just how far up a creek we were. This new threat, this powerhouse Blind Judge, The Dreadnought, had been able to cast the doorman aside with frightening ease when they crossed paths earlier today.

"What did get me—" I began, turning to Grove so that he could read my lips, "—was how organized it all seemed." I had a working theory that had troubled me for a while, and since we had ended up back where it all started, I figured now was as good a time as any to give it the long overdue time of day. I didn't do it often, since I power-talked so much (my mom used to say I would talk to a dog if it barked), so I usually spared Grove from my incessant ramblings. "I would bet a good portion of my debt that the Stalker that got through was some kind of established leader. But from all I've read, they don't really have an organizational structure. The ones we saw were lined up and waiting—they were expecting a portal. If anyone was toeing the line and venturing over it, it was the chick from the Abyss. She wasn't just planning to cross over; she was planning an attack."

I tried to defend my perpetual zoning out as less an attention issue and more a kind of spontaneous meditation talent, but even I had a hard time buying that particular line of bullshit. Recalling everything from that night was difficult for a multitude of reasons. The loss of Maria still plagued me; it was a haunting, consuming reminder of just how out of my depth I was and would continue to be. Knowing that this catastrophe—though averted—might have landed one of my very few friends in extremely hot water, was a consequence that was very disturbing to me given the price we'd already paid. My recollection was spotty at best since I'd actually been knocked unconscious a time or two that night. Even when I did have the fortitude of character to look back on it all there were still a lot of missing pieces. I guess two concussions in the same week is not exactly optimal for memory excellence…who knew.

"Hey!" Most people gave me a kind of barely tolerant glare when I seemed to detach myself from the present conversation, but Johnny B wasn't one of them; he opted to give me a hard shove. "Did they?"

"Did they what?"

Grove answered on my behalf, shaking his head *no* which was poorly received by the elf.

"What?" I asked, still confused.

"They never got the other Stalker? I mean you—you never got the other Stalker?"

"Oh," I said. That was a fact I tended to gloss over when speaking in mixed company if ever it came up. "Yeah, well, it and Xander fought, and we had some dark elves come over and that split our fo—"

"Stalker! Get to that."

"Yeah, no. After everything that happened, we just never got a bead on it. No macabre incidents or bloodbaths or anything, our attempts to scour the city came up with nothing. And before you get all loud about it, it's harder than you think when you've barely slept for a week, been fighting off a crazed cult and a darkling Goddess, are distracted by ninja elves and you're just trying to get off a doomed boat. Just give us a break, ok."

"What if it's still around here?" he demanded.

"We fight it off while you sing it a lullaby." The sweetness of my smile was a mocking gesture, one reflected back in his own pierced face.

"Come on," I said. I tried to find myself a nice clearing, and a smooth spot where I could unroll the parchment I was carrying. I brushed aside what little debris impeded its placement on the ground, and once it was situated, the grimoire orientated itself the proper way so that true north on it was aligned with true north on our world. Weighting each corner of the map with rocks, I looked up and continued to adjust it until I was satisfied that it was centered under the correct constellation. Bones aging faster than my years cracked as I stood upright, carefully stepping onto the delicate tool. The aviator sunglasses I kept in my pocket came out; who doesn't wear sunglasses at night, right? As perfectly ridiculous as it looked, the glasses had a carefully calligraphed runework up the frames all the way to the lenses.

"Nice look, Maverick," Johnny B jabbed at me.

"Sun never sets on a badass dude."

I requested silence with a finger, cutting Johnny off from issuing another irritating retort. The gravity of the situation demanded that he obey, which was a small *win* for team sarcasm. Grove had laid out the inventory from our box of tricks and tools, and then proceeded to go work with an e-tool (a hybrid shovel-like instrument from his time with the military) creating a circle around us in the dirt. The parchment was then torn into precise, individual pieces, each with a single symbol on it which were then buried inside the gutter of the circle track with extreme care. Each image aligned with a particular star, drawing power and light, which made the entire circumference glow with a faint green hue.

There is an essential synergy between the Artificer and his tools that has no counterfeit; the sigils do the bulk of the work, but you have to ignite their function using your own power and focus. Luckily, it didn't take a lot of power, even less if you knew what you were doing. I'd gotten better at using my natural ability, most of that thanks to the tutelage of Donovan. Steadying a held breath, I drew from my own energy and focused to create the catalyst.

Through the lenses I could see perfectly; there's a kind of greenish hue on them to match the glow that washed over our own shared space, but the color didn't distort what I actually saw, it only affected the appearance. It wasn't quite like the night vision we see in video games and movies—it was a little more illuminated, and the shade of green vacillated between sea foam and dark forest.

"Give me your hand and close your eyes," I told Johnny B. He seemed a lot more reluctant than I would have expected, but after his period of deliberation I felt the delicate pianist-thin fingers fill my own. I slipped him a glyph'd marble. Once it was in his hand, he gasped and then let out a short chuckle. Johnny now saw the world as I did through my lenses. I dare say he might even have been impressed, as I noticed him bringing the small sphere up in front of his eyes and really examining it; elves already had incredible vision, and this magical marble would only bolster it.

"I'm looking for any kind of energy signal and this place has got to be ripe with it. We just have to separate out what's us and what isn't."

"Okay, and what exactly are we trying to pinpoint?" he asked.

Color started coming to life, some of it yawning in the sky and stretching far and wide, while elsewhere it seemed to just barely present itself. In the placid lake I saw blue for the water, but not like an average blue water—it was electric, volatile and crackling. The hue blossoming in the sky was an acrid black, almost anti-color. It felt like a vortex, and I imagined that anything near the mouth of the portal that ripped apart our sky was bound to have had some of the good in it forever siphoned out.

"The Stalker," I answered.

"*What!*" Beside himself, Johnny ripped his hand from mine, forcing me to turn and acknowledge him.

"The Stalker. We need answers and to be honest, it's the only one on the bad side of what went down that's here…and…well, not dead."

"You brought me out here to *stalk* a Stalker?!"

"Well, when you put it like that it sounds kinda silly," I said, pulling a faux thoughtful expression.

"You're insane."

My smile reinforced the accusation, a smile that was quickly enervated by what I saw coming up behind him. It was soundless; the northern wind favored the predator that was crawling toward us; it had specifically picked that avenue of approach so that the passing breeze was not contaminated with its very signature smell. They had one—Stalkers—they stank, but it was a different kind of foul. It wasn't like rotten eggs or spoiled milk; it was a scent that had the promise of pain in it. Death smelled like that: acrid and despairing. Normally the sight of the thing could stun someone to a standstill, but not me. Not today. Not now.

Not ever fucking again.

It saw me looking at it; its twitchy stillness a paradox only a peak predator could pull off, and while it was taking the time to measure me, I was doing the same. I didn't have to fight to keep the wretched cologne of fear off me because I wasn't scared. Johnny was. It was written on every inch of him—I didn't need any preternatural or predatory sixth sense to feel that—but I wasn't. Neither was Grove for that matter, his stare steady and strong.

This monstrosity unwound to every inch of its menacing eight feet. Before seeing this one, I had assumed that Stalkers were a lean breed, with dense, compact muscle that allowed for both strength and speed without sacrificing too much of either. This one showed me otherwise. Though I wasn't sure if Stalkers had a pack mentality, my impression of this one was that it was an Alpha. It was at least a foot taller than the one I'd killed 6 months ago, a few hundred pounds heavier, and the bulk of each appendage was considerably greater. Veins ran like steel cords under its skin and made me think that the sinew beneath was so strong that it was capable of ripping me in half while accomplishing the motion so swiftly that I would literally be unable to see it coming. Instead of a needle-thin snout, its maw seemed almost oversized: there was no jigsaw puzzle of patchwork hair, either. The Stalker we'd put down was a mangy runt compared to this one, which had a full diffused mane of night-black hair that helped it blend better.

Johnny had taken up a tactical position behind us. The stare-off felt like it lasted an eternity, though I couldn't imagine it having been more than a minute.

"If you don't come out and find a way to talk to us, you're well on your way to being dead," I warned the thing.

For the first time, it made some kind of sound. I had plenty of trouble picking up on anything in the human social contract—nuance of expression was impossible for me to decipher with any kind of success (and that was with my *own* breed)—which should have made me hopeless in trying to gauge what it was the Stalker was doing…but I could swear it was some kind of chuckle I heard, though to what end, I couldn't say.

"Don't believe me?" I continued. I was courting death here, and as dangerous as it was, I couldn't help but be tickled by the fact that though I was at risk of being set upon by one of the few things in all the worlds that could rip me limb-from-limb without much effort I still had my sense of humor. "Take a sniff." I wouldn't stink of fear, and this was a creature that lived off of it.

"The air has changed. You're marked. You're the last living witness to what went down here six months ago, and you know stuff you shouldn't, stuff above your pay grade."

I could see it thinking; the stall from outright violence was clue enough of that, and its internal debate was downright palpable, a welcome change of scent since my olfactory sense was a little tired of being so badly abused by all the offending odors. It swayed, slithering down to all four limbs and taking a testing stride toward us. The advance wasn't friendly, which was not wholly unexpected. It was a gamble, but I was confident of the gambit.

"Fine," I spread my arms out, daring it to commit. "See if you can take us with our new elemental sorcerer…. Try us," I said, my challenging sneer ripe with a barely caged delight at the prospect of the beast making such a mistake. That's how a bluff worked; you didn't just try to squeeze an inch out of the lie—if you were going to lie, you had to go big or stay home. "Once you limp away from us, it ain't like you're gonna survive the Blind Judge they set after your ass."

I wasn't going to scare the thing; it was probably well aware that I had done everything except throw an actual kitchen sink at its now-dead underling in order to make it out of our contest alive….Actually, the condemned building did have a working bathroom—so I did in fact throw a sink at it….I thought with a smirk.

Not only was this stalker a more physically impressive specimen, it was a second—or at the very least a high-ranking servant to that dark Goddess—so it was very likely that it was well aware of how high up on the food chain it belonged. Truth was, when something was a pariah from the land it came from—a land governed solely by might, where the Stalker had not only survived, but thrived—there was precious little that would outright scare it.

Except a Blind Judge.

These weapons of choice from the House of Unet and the Tribe of Masarou had flawless track records, having taken down everything they had ever been unleashed upon, and had done so without incident. With the help of my glasses I felt the thing arrest its prowling momentum. Grove seemed to feel it as well, and Johnny B perked up a bit, seeming to better understand my play.

"You either talk to us and give yourself a shot," I said with a nonchalant shrug that actually had some sincerity to it…"or stay tucked away out here—the first place the Judge is gonna to think to look for you." I couldn't care less if the thing wanted to be stubborn and end up dead or not, what I did care about was getting the information I needed.

A second nerve was struck; Its teeth were bared in a kind of knee-jerk reaction, and I knew that even if this thing wasn't a big orator like I was, the wheels began to turn in its ancient mind—and just like any of us, this Stalker not-so-secretly coveted survival above all else.

"Hold." Its voice sounded so primal that one might mistake it for a growl if you didn't have an ear that could sort through the baritone and bass. It rasped cruelly, all while a sickening soundtrack of cracking bones and painful grunts started up, its body warped and drew in on itself, and developed into a human form. The process was gruesome, and it was difficult to watch the body painfully break and rupture itself, folding in on itself, twisting at impossible angles and bending back severely. When it was all done, the body laid there, bare naked as a jaybird. It breathed laboriously trying to keep itself present and centered after such a gruesome transformation. Credit was due—it managed to get to bare feet and collect itself quicker than I might have imagined. Still, it was hard to look away, and the three of us standing on the shore were shocked, our mouths dumbly open in the aftermath.

The Stalker king, biggest and baddest of them all wasn't a king at all, it was a queen. It was a woman.

And it was *hot*.

CHAPTER 6

Unlikely Allies

"Do you want a shirt or something?" I offered.

The Stalker gave me a level, mildly annoyed look. She was just under six feet tall and fit. Lean muscle dense enough to give her an alluring shape: Rounded hips, strong thighs, an ample bosom and a stomach fractured by deep divots of muscle. It was hard to ignore since she was naked and cavalier about it. Maybe not cavalier exactly, but indifferent maybe? Unperturbed by her own nudity, she was waiting expectantly for us to abide by our promise to fill in some of the blanks.

I liked to believe myself a man of at least some integrity, but it was hard to stay in good character when she crossed her arms. I felt like a prepubescent boy on the cusp of my first acne outbreak. She had nightingale black hair, and what had previously been a menacing mane was now simply lovely. Half her head was shaved, and her scalp was marked with some kind of scarred design. It was archaic symbolism turned aesthetic, deeper than just some clever scribbles. There was also ink around her left eye, circling it in a fashion that if she were an actual human would have me think she never wished to be gainfully employed again. A crooked X intersected the circle; I had my suspicions of it being some kind of a brand but thought better than to ask about it right now.

"Somebody is trying to clean up the mess that happened here a few months back," I started.

Creature of the Abyss or not, everyone had a tell, and she flashed hers. I couldn't consciously pinpoint it, but my sixth sense told me that even if she hadn't literally *blinked*, she blinked.

"Which isn't wholly unexpected to you," I added.

Her look soured, but that didn't deter me. Not a lot did. You didn't act the way I did, at my age, without having had your ass kicked a bunch of times. One more wasn't going to make a bit of a difference to me.

"Look, I'm talking, but you're giving nothing. Right now we have a Blind Judge roving the city, probably making its way out here right now. Hell, for all I know it's on our tail looking for you."

Instead of pushing the point I tried to let it simmer, hoping—as I had suspected earlier—that the whole self-preservation doctrine that we lived by was prominent in her species too. It took longer than I would have expected, but finally it seemed like the wind went out of her sails. She was too sharp and proud to be deflated, but I could tell she was as close to afraid as something like her could be.

"I am not sure what I can do to be of any assistance," she said. Her eyes were hard to hold. They had an alien quality, slit down the middle with a living darkness within. "We can't expect to win against a Blind Judge."

I articulated my first thought while chewing on my second. "There's some kind of tribunal, a court, right? The people in charge of the Blind Judge, who control it, have been beseeched by another party for a restoration of order. If we can get to them and argue that it wasn't us that put this whole thing out of balance, we might be able to stop the whole thing before it goes any further. It's the only reason I can think of that one of them would be here. So long as we can testify that none of us directly did it, there's a chance this thing can blow over us without further consequence."

"Are you suggesting that I betray my master?" she said. It wasn't the threat of her voice that had a way of sapping some of the strength out of me, it was the deadly calm of the utterance while showing hints of elongated teeth. She was not only smarter than the first one I encountered, there was a lucidity and cunning in her eyes that made me wonder if she was smarter than the rest of us. Every one of us dropped hand to weapon, but I knew that diplomacy was our only real hope here. Forget trying to defeat a Blind Judge—a Stalker was challenging enough, given how much trouble we'd had with a pint-sized one of her ilk. There was no way any of us could afford this fight.

"I want you to realize that your master has betrayed you. In order to prove her point, she can't have any evidence as to what was done, and you know what you are? A living, breathing piece of evidence. Yes, you're both our alibi and her fatal witness. And while I don't envy your position, you have two choices: come with us, or linger here until whatever she's sent to retire you shows up."

I could see an unspoken thought being processed, so I forged ahead.

"Now if she had gotten it right the first time with the Blind Judge you might have had an out, but she didn't. So she's fully aware of the fact that since she didn't stamp us out in the first place, we're going to fight back. We all know that the best route for that is to go and find proof for our side of the story…which the respective courts probably will do even if we don't succeed."

Their name more than mine carried the effective amount of weight to be threatening.

The next pause was wrought with a dreadful tension as we tried to sway the Stalker from the only allegiance it's ever known. As with most that were countless centuries old, it didn't take just a small amount of time to consider something; no, it had to make the whole world wait on it until we were all awkwardly shifting around within our circle. The musician started fumbling through his phone, checking social media updates, and even nudging Grove to show him something they both laughed at. I tried scolding them with a stern, what-the-fuck look, but neither seemed all that bothered by it, though Johnny did put the cellular device away.

"They make smaller tablets than that," I couldn't resist saying.

"Bite m—"

"Okay." We'd been quiet for the whole of her contemplative tenure, and then she gives us her answer the minute we broke our silence—go figure. Despite myself, I could barely contain the relief washing through me. Releasing air I didn't realize was trapped, I looked skyward as if some godling had intervened and exonerated us from this venture going catastrophically wrong. Grove also audibly breathed, that white-knuckled grip coming off the hilt of a sawed-off shotgun he kept at the low of his back.

"Good," I said, rubbing my brow. "Alright, we have to get back to town and get a plan together. Johnny, give her your jacket."

"Why?" The singer and Stalker said simultaneously. One out of confusion, the other out of licentiousness. Scowling, I turned a flat, tempered glare at Johnny until he did as I asked. "Driving around downtown Cleveland with a naked woman in the backseat is going to attract a lot of attention we can't afford right now."

Unfazed by her nudity, the fiend shrugged into the jacket and had the wherewithal and understanding to close it up and cinch each buckle. Her lower half was still kind of problematic, but you know what they say, one thing at a time.

"Alright, one down and one to go."

"Another…?" Johnny B asked vaguely, trying to clear up his confusion.

"Person," I said, giving an up-nod of my chin at the Stalker. "More muscle. Hey punk rock Barbie—" Johnny B was nice enough to signal to the Stalker that I was speaking to her. "—What's your name?"

She strained after the question, before answering in a guttural growl that I guess could have passed for some kind of identifying moniker. I doubt I had the vocal capability to replicate the sound even if I had a desire to do so.

"Sam good for you?" I said.

She didn't blink, but Johnny nodded and Grove, who reads lips, looked so woefully confused that I just enjoyed the stumped stupor written all over his face.

"We'll call her Sam. Grove, can you bring the truck to the clearing right before the tree line? I don't want anyone at the restaurant seeing us come out of the woods with a half-naked lady."

Ever the soldier, my silent partner pivoted away and took to a light jog while we started walking in his wake.

"Who's this other person?" Johnny B asked.

Thumbing through my own phone, I found the number I was looking for and grimaced at the realization of how much it was going to cost me.

"He's… Well, not a friend exactly, but the best-kept secret in town. A hired gun, though not for anyone doing something shitty. Problem is, it's expensive just to talk to him, and just talking to him is no guarantee of assistance." I staved off whatever questions Johnny was about to ask with a raised finger.

"Half Moon Pizza? Yeah, I need to order 50 pies for delivery."

CHAPTER 7

The Concrete Monk

It was my aim to arrive with the pizza, or just as it was being dispersed to the starved masses. There was a part of me that wanted to be announced by way of my philanthropic deed, but the truth was that this wasn't done out of the goodness of my halfway-decent heart. My hope was that this would warrant enough consideration from my soon-to-be host who would see my credit-killing sacrifice as noble enough to grant me an audience. I'd like to believe there was some altruism in there, but I knew better than to try to lead with that; it would be an insult to the man I was here to see. Honesty was key to this man who could see through every lie. Impure motive or not, so long as it got me an audience, it was worth the price. I knew 'The Cause' was his kind of righteousness.

The homeless shelter was a lot busier than I think anyone would like, even worse was seeing a new face or two arrive every day. Times were hard and sometimes all it took was a bad break at the wrong time to put you into a tailspin that could cost everything. I never looked down on people like this, I remembered more than one occasion that I had walked the streets of Cleveland on cold nights with nowhere to lay my head and knew that I was just a single tough stretch away from being one of them. The staff were busy with the rowdy crowd enjoying the food while a movie was played through an old school projector. Staying small, I took up residence in a back corner. It didn't take long to find who I was looking for.

Guy J. Smith on the nametag, an obvious alias if ever I saw one, was hard to miss. He was a man at the end of his youth but not yet old, a stocky-fit hybrid, with a generally amicable affect and a warm disposition. His strawberry blonde hair was unkempt in a way that wasn't fashionable, just wild. His eyes were oceanic and kind of spellbinding. That booming laugh was infectious and undeniable. We exchanged a look, but I knew not to come across as expectant. The guy fraternized with each pocket of people, checking on them in turn. Although he was dressed in ragtag clothing—torn layers of hand-me-downs—he had an air of quiet authority about him that made him seem downright regal. The staff conferred with and deferred to him while doling out more slices of pizza. Graciously refusing a warm slice with a smile, he reached into the baggy blazer and produced a crumpled bag of sunflower seeds. Taking the time to look over his domain once more, he filled a fingerless gloved hand with a loose fistful of the seeds and tossed them back.

When he finally got the time to navigate his way over to me, we were quick to embrace. The bear paws he was passing as hands grabbed me to pull me into a solid hug, then held me by the shoulders and pried us apart while he examined me with those kind eyes.

"Janzen Robinson. Good lord, it's been a long time. You look well," he said with a head tilt. "And you don't look fat at all. I'd heard you'd gotten fat. I would say *less* fat, more ... *Seasoned*."

"That's code for *shabby*."

"It is."

"Hey!" I made the mistake of playfully slugging him in the shoulder for the pseudo-slight. I say mistakenly because it was like punching a slab of stone. "You look good man, really good."

"So, what can I do for you?" he asked, cutting right to the chase.

Leaning back, hands over my heart, I feigned being wounded, and before I could start a diatribe about how hurt I was he interrupted me.

"Save the bullshit, you wouldn't come here unless something was up. Plus," he said, hitching a thumb out to the populace he kept company with, "I got my sources. I know what you're doing with yourself these days." The homeless were a hell of a resource if they trusted you. There was no rival in information gathering and networking; they saw everything while almost never being seen. Invisible when in plain sight. Masked in tolerance, I could tell he was contemplating how he felt about everything I'd done of late and was still doing. "It's good, good for you, good for the city."

Guy wasn't a big talker, and neither was he big on the sharing-is-caring part of friendship. He valued time and hated when it was wasted. I took the compliment in stride and kept moving.

"I need muscle," I said, glancing up at him. He was above average in height, but only barely. Thick bodied and strongly built, he had a similar build to my own, though with that Irish blood of his, he couldn't endure any direct sunlight on his skin for more than an hour unlike me.

"Eat more protein after lifting heavy stuff."

While he was supremely kind to the downtrodden, he was kind of abrasive to almost everyone else; very dry and direct. I'd known him more than half my life, so I was a bit desensitized to it.

"I'm in deep water and about to drown. You know I wouldn't come here unless I didn't have anywhere else to go. I know you hear about everything in this town, and that you know the last time I was in the thick of it and in a bad way I didn't come to you—did I?" I asked.

That one hit, even if I was a bit gruff about it. Sarcasm was normally the bread and butter of my life, but right now I wasn't in the mood to deal with cutesy curtness. There was a part of me that hated that we had to get down to a nitty-gritty, brass tacks kind of conversation so quickly after not having seen one another for so long. *Guy J. Smith* was the outsider and only other survivor of the old group my now-dead mentor once led. He didn't involve himself in all the happenings of the city; in truth he really only cared about playing shepherd to the homeless who were ripe targets for the supernatural communities that needed people to prey on. It was easier to pick them off with sickening regularity and not have to deal with the unwanted attention which would normally follow a missing person's report. Sadly, most of these people had no one left in their lives to look for them.

That never sat well with Guy, and so in a roundabout way the prickly fighter became a kind of champion for them. Guy J. Smith wasn't just a scrappy fighter who shied away from fisticuffs all honorably until there was no other option either. No, The *Concrete Monk* was the undisputed bare-knuckles champion of the world. I thought the moniker was spot on actually; I'd seen him accomplish unspeakable physical feats without so much as a strain, bending steel in the same hands that cracked asphalt. We both took the loss of the group hard; I think both of us blamed ourselves for not being there for the final fight that did them all in. Before losing them all, he and I weren't very close, and not for any particular reason. It wasn't as if there was some kind of discord, we just didn't gel. We didn't keep in touch either, though whenever we saw one another, we enjoyed it; sharing exaggerated stories warmly and asking after the other sincerely and not just out of some tired-ass, dutiful obligation of the social contract.

Neither of us did niceties very well anyway.

"I'm in a corner here and I have very few people who can get my back—and most of them are green. They haven't been in the thick of it like you and I have. If I'm going to focus on the problem and try to find a way to un-fuck it, I need somebody who can keep the ship upright while I'm doing that. I'm in trouble *Guy*, and I'm asking for your help."

The silence is disconcerting, because I am in every bit as much trouble as I am telling him I'm in, and saying it makes it even more real to me. Peril was actually a better word for it, since trouble usually could be solved or at least piggybacked onto a less severe predicament. Guy shifted from his posture of stoic consideration to a flash of congeniality as one of the local denizens stopped by to exchange a greeting and celebrate the slice of pizza they carried. In the simplicity of the moment, as the gruff-faced fighter softened with a pious sincerity, it dawned on me that while Guy and I may have never seen eye-to-eye and never been outright friends, there was a kindred spirit in us. We both fought against the scourge of oppression and the inevitability of bad being brought down on good, and that created a kind of kinship. We did good work—great work—separately and together, even if we weren't the greatest of friends.

"I'll grab my coat," he said.

"That's it?" I was surprised, though not as much as I would have been had it not been for the epiphany I'd had a moment before.

"You asking for my help?"

"Yes."

"Then that's it," he said with a shrug.

***

We moved in a silence that was serene, not suffocating. I'd forgotten what it was like to walk beside a controlled and calm person. It was reminiscent of my mentor, and the proximity alone was a soothing balm to my addled mind and grated nerves. I thought of trying to strain out some small talk, but it never came, as if there was nothing to be said between the two of us.

The Concrete Monk wasn't much older than me, but in comparing us you'd rightly guess him to be both my senior and the better put-together person. That was particularly damning when you took into account the fact that he didn't just dress up as a homeless man but was in fact without a home. He was a giant among men without that gargantuan size to overstate the fact. My musing on the way he was moving—with the confidence of a proficient fighter and the balance to match—was abruptly interrupted when those ham hocks he called hands snatched me and ripped me clear off my feet. I'm not taking liberty with the description either. The man snatched me up as if I weighed a fraction of my two-hundred-*ish* (I'm still working on it) pounds. Muscle memory and training kicked in and I was just about to try to extricate myself or retaliate, but that thought was interrupted more than my stride when a harrowing BOOM followed by the foul shriek of metal twisting and the impact of it compacting itself into the brick wall right beside me. Unfortunately, it was an all too familiar soundtrack; the screech of steel mixed with the hiss of a destroyed engine was like fingernails on a chalkboard to me.

I was trying to get a grasp on what was happening, but before I could lift my head, there was a tug on the back of it as Guy spun me again. I barely caught a glimpse of his blurring body exploding into action to throw a kick. There was a grotesque impact that was seconded by a forced expelling of air, a small window of background noise after the chaos of the first, with crunching metal added to it all like an afterthought. I followed instead of fighting the momentum and found myself righted on my feet beside the Concrete Monk, wide-eyed as I surveyed the situation.

Before me was a badly wrecked economy car, its front end still smoldering against a brick wall that was spider-webbed with fissures and cracks from the crash. Sprawled out against—or embedded into—the car was a guy who was tattooed head to toe, groaning from being kicked into the vehicle. He was muscular and bald, with what I would suspect was a habitually hard look on his face, which at the moment was twisted into an almost irritated grimace.

My newest ally, the aptly named Concrete Monk, had swung my body out of the way of the impact and kept guiding me to the point where the follow-up attack by this unidentified male was evaded by him whipping me around this cement dance floor. He was about to close the distance on the attacker when it was my turn to intervene.

I gracelessly tackled him and sent us both careening down into the paved sidewalk just as a spell that I had detected sailed directly overhead. Shards of magically condensed and sharpened ice stuck into the wall. Our eyes watched the spectacle and then we turned our attention to the other side of the street and the source of the attack.

Turning our heads at the same time to look across the street for the source of the attack, we saw a bald woman covered in tattoos from head-to-toe standing there, glaring at us. Those tattoos weren't just any kind of ink; they were sigils etched into her skin, imbued with power that allowed a person to draw ambient energy and use their body as a conduit to cast quick spellwork. It was a little crude, which was kind of my niche, but a lot more effective than the stuff that I tended to put together. It was more effective because the work—the ink—wasn't done by some low-brow caster or middling artificer; it was the product of the most elite Tinkerers in the known worlds…the House of Unet. As some of the thrumming madness subsided, I realized that she had somehow launched the car at us, and that her partner had come roaring in behind it.

These were members of the Marked: the private police force of the Unet. The unofficial peacekeepers and enforcers of the law, the law set by the Unet without any input from the rest of us. A lot of those old Zachariah lectures were coming back to me now— though never quite quick enough.

I had landed on top of the monk after my tackle, and he was on his back with his arms around me. Looking down into his face I asked "friends…?" my terse quip ripe with sarcasm. I used his shove of my arms to get myself upright while keeping an arm down and out to return the favor. The monk wordlessly took my arm and pulled himself up, and together we turned to look across the ocean of asphalt at the female Marked One. Her accomplice pried himself out of the car he'd been kicked into—the same car he'd seen fit to aim at us like a battering ram. We each eyed our respective attacker.

"You think my friends go around trying to run me over?" he answered softly with a skeptical look, one I scowled at before grudgingly allowing the expression to melt away into a resigned nod and shrug combination.

"Fair enough."

"Our fight isn't with you, Patrick of the Last Gate," the male agent said. It seemed that he was attempting to sort through something, and I suspected that he was trying to understand why the Concrete Monk was standing by my side at all. Of course his befuddlement could have been compounded by the fact that he'd been drop kicked into a sedan a moment ago. It seemed that the combination of those two things really shook him up, though he still had enough presence of mind to start berating us in an extremely authoritative tone.

"Patrick? Like Sponge Bo—"

"Another word and I leave you here."

I zipped my mouth, which was now spread into a shit-eating grin. Of course leave it to me to focus on making an adolescent joke about a totally reasonable name and pretend that I didn't hear that tidbit about the *Last Gate*.

"Leave now and we will consider this a simple misunderstanding," the woman added, her voice lacking any kind of femininity. If the word gnarled had a voice, this was what I'd imagine it to be.

Part of me wanted to tell Patrick, the Concrete Monk—champion of the downtrodden, defender of the defenseless—to just leave and stay out of this mess. It was quickly becoming a disaster that was most likely going to evolve into a full-blown catastrophe. It was written plain as day across his cherubic face that he was considering his next move, but before I could open my mouth and let him know that it was okay to tuck tail and run, he shifted again, sending another snapping front kick into the chest of the unsuspecting male Marked One who had been slowly moving toward us. This time, since he did it without twirling me around, I got a front row seat for the spectacle. Even if he'd been confident that the ragtag freelancer wasn't going to side with me, I thought it had been a bit brazen that he'd so carelessly approached us. I couldn't tell if it was surprise or pain that contoured his face into such an ugly showing of disbelief, but he was off, sailing into the rear end of the car this time, so that when his lower half clipped it, he was sent tumbling head over body across the trunk and deposited on the other end. The female Marked One was quick to react. I managed to intercept her, stepping in front of Patrick and sending a pulse of will to my wrist; the bracer came to life, lifting and fanning out in a circle. The leather plating completed the evolution, creating a makeshift buckler shield a little smaller than a beach ball. This time she'd picked fire, and it smarted, and I stumbled as the sheer force of it actually pushed me back, the melting leather and heat giving the air a terribly unique signature. No mistaking that smell. Still, I was able to absorb the blast of fire with the buckler.

The surprise across my face probably didn't convey confidence to my new partner, though I had little time to think about it and even less to react. She opened her other hand, rigid fingers harnessing an unseen force as the tattoos up the length of her forearm thrummed with an awakening power.

"This part of your small favor, kid?" the now-annoyed redhead grumbled while grimacing.

"You're getting soft in your old age… *Patrick.*" Sentiment wasn't really my thing, and the fact that a man I respected more than any other was paying me a compliment forced me to fall back on my default setting: jackass.

"Growin' old is earned," Patrick answered, ever the more mature one.

Despite the dread of another overwhelming case, the promise of violence, and risk to my own person, I couldn't help but smile. Caustic as it was, this had the same kind of liberating carefree feeling I'd experienced a few months prior, standing back-to-back with a friend as if we were in some old black-and-white gunslinger film. Even though I couldn't see it, I felt our shared grin creating the calm before the storm in a unified battle as we charged our enemies.

***

I hit the wall nearly as hard as the damned car that had just barely missed pancaking me at the beginning of this skirmish and tried to keep my mind present so that the waxing blackness eating at the fringes of my consciousness wouldn't swallow me whole. Rushing a spell-caster? That was a special kind of stupid.

Spellcaster.

The realization slingshotted me back to the present. I barely managed to shove off the very wall I'd just slid down to avoid another wave of crackling green power. It took a sizable chunk out of the brick, which provided me with a pair of important insights: first, while these Marked weren't terribly powerful, their ability to conjure and hurl spells came with an unrivaled swiftness so that the volley of it seemed endless and relentless. Second was that in order for her to be able to channel that kind of raw power, she had to do so using herself as a conduit and project it out, which meant that there had to be a tax on her person. Nothing in this world is free and that's especially true of magic. Suddenly the lean and chiseled body type was less a source of athletics and an arduous fitness regime and more a byproduct of the harshness of her chosen craft. Still, she was only human—no matter how enhanced, which meant that there was a limit to how much she could cast before the exertion sapped all of her strength.

There was nothing reassuring about the revelation, seeing as how I was having to sloppily tumble out of the way of yet another offensive. My mind was so rattled that I actually was mourning the fact that nothing I do is smooth and seamless. I caught myself wishing that just once I could do a choreographed tumble maneuver when evading something such as an invisible missile of raw energy and slide all slick to my feet into a readied fighting stance.

The third attack was crushing, my raised forearm and buckler-shield absorbed just enough of the impact to spare my ribs from a pretty thorough cracking. It did nothing for my bruised back though, as the sheer concussion catapulted me into the brick wall behind me. The aforementioned problem was now coming to light: while none of the offensive was particularly death-dealing, it came in such rapid succession that it was almost impossible to recover from one parry and get set for the next. I had been banking on her growing tired from funneling all that energy first, but the better bet was probably me growing tired of being brutalized.

I shoved off the wall, hoping it looked like I was less staggering and more determined, pulling the cleverly concealed bat I kept tucked on my back between my shirt and overcoat free. The female Marked One let sail the next attack and I took a good old-fashioned cut at it—except I wasn't looking to challenge the force or even send it sailing back, I activated the absorbing rune on the bat and allowed the energy to funnel in through the metal shaft into the weapon itself. Outside of our clash I'd probably look like a madman taking wild swings at the streaks of raw power, but none of that mattered as the first spell was siphoned away. The rubber grip around the hilt gyrated violently, the assimilated power climbing up every sigil like a ladder, but before I'd even had the time to wrestle with the implication and consider the ramifications, I was swinging away at a second attack, absorbing it as well even as it sent a jarring flash of pain racing up my grip and throughout the length of my now-taut arm.

As teeth-chatteringly brutal as the effort was on my side, the once inexhaustible woman across from me was starting to look a whole lot more human. She doubled over and went down on one knee staring daggers at me all the while. I'd been told that I had this kind of effect on women—mostly by women. There was a flash-in-the-pan stalemate that, luckily, wasn't long lived, seeing as I couldn't have held onto my weapon much longer. A dozen feet apart, she pushed an opening fist toward me.

And I, in a moment of well-thought-out strategy, threw my bat, end-over-end, for no other reason than it seemed like a good idea at the time. Now seeing as it was literally sizzling with energy—the metal humming from the excess of it and the absorbing sigils still active—it collided with her spell and there was a huge explosion.

The Marked member of the Unet may have been a better sorcerer, a savvier fighter, and far better conditioned than I was…but she had never been blown to hell and thrown completely across full streets like I had, so once again, experience trumped knowledge.

I vaguely recall the feel of an iron-like grip gathering the back of my outdated jacket and hauling me up and over a shoulder before carrying me off.

CHAPTER 8

"You're the worst hero I have ever met." It was easy for me to recognize the voice, especially given her inclination to mock me despite the fact that I was almost completely unconscious.

"That's why I go for that whole edgy anti-hero thing."

Kaycee smirked. "Anti-hero types are always so sexy."

"And elves are always so skinny."

My short-lived grin was wiped away by a swatting hand. I heard Kaycee inform the rest that I was as fine as was to be expected. We were all crammed into tight quarters, a gaggle of familiar faces mulling around my laid-out ass. The room was decorated with hand-me-down stuff, all of it sturdy and comfortable but none of it really expensive. The color scheme was decidedly earthy: greens, browns, all of it rustic instead of polished. It was cozy basically... homey. Toys were scattered all over; some were for her own children, some for her students; she'd quietly taken to schooling children who have talent in the mystical arts for the neighborhood. Her teaching flirted with rule-breaking, but Kaycee wasn't a top-tier, world-threatening practitioner, and she wasn't doing anything more than just instilling basic discipline and control. Really, she was just trying to keep what were historically ostracized kids from getting scared and inadvertently doing harm: letting them know they weren't alone.

What little money Grove and I did make usually ended up over here for that purpose. I often thought that if Maria had found a better community earlier on, she wouldn't have gotten into the thick of it with that bunch of dirtbag zealots.

I didn't enjoy the idea of dragging Kaycee and her kin any deeper into all of this, although strategically, this was probably the best place to rendezvous—what with my shop harboring known fugitives and all. I knew better than to voice those concerns, as she was a grown-ass woman, perfectly capable of her own decision making, a fact that she would pointedly remind me of in an extremely embarrassing fashion in front of anyone and everyone, should I go down that path.

Resisting the temptation to open my mouth, I swung my legs around the couch and sat upright, gathering what little sense I had left before taking inventory of everyone that was there. Grove looked as super heroic as ever; his deadpanned stoicism so impressive that I had to use a pair of words to describe it so as to really drive it home. Patrick, whose birth name I'd very recently learned, was looking like the inspiration of some Walt Whitman poem written about a sage vagabond. Reserved, though not as professionally detached as Grove—there was some parallel between them in body language and expression (or the cultivated lack of one). Sam the Stalker had adopted a style that seemed heavily influenced by Johnny B's own—I'd guess they wore similar sizes, and was I a gambling man, I would wager that those were in fact his clothes that she was in. So we had a pair of almost exaggeratedly good-looking people dressed like they belonged at a Dead Kennedys concert instead of out hunting some titan of the supernatural world.

"How long is Xander down for?" I asked. What was true of the mundane world usually ended up being so in the supernatural one, just with different variables. While I knew enough about what the doorman was, I didn't know enough about how long it would take him to heal or even what kind of injuries he was suffering from. All of that would play a hand in the timeline for this thing.

Luckily, Kaycee was a great resource with a wealth of knowledge that really couldn't be given a price tag. The Balance was important, and people handcuffed by those very vague accords were now more than ever bound to be cautious with what they did and didn't do; even with what they did and didn't divulge. This

Blind Judge tearing through the city and ripping asunder anyone or thing that dared to defy them was sure to have people who played the middle being more mindful of their actions.

"He's tough," she said through a thoughtfully chewed lip. "There's still no way he'll be back for a day or two though."

That should be great news. Normally, it would be. A day or two to lay low in order to get the man who was arguably our biggest gun back would be easy enough to do. But we didn't normally have an ultimate supernatural bounty hunter hot on our trail. "I'll assume that we're now on the radar of all those involved," I said, dabbing a bit of blood mixed with asphalt above my right eye. "And if I'm reading this right, first, we have to find the accuser and get more evidence" ticking off these points with my fingers as I spoke. "Second, we have to get the Unet to listen. And third, we have to get them to reverse the decision and recall the Blind Judge, since they are the ones who sent all this trouble in the first place. Effectively doing all their jobs and the dirty work for them. Sound about right to you guys?"

"The Unet and Masarou hear and handle any violation of the Balance pertaining to the In-Between," Kaycee interjected, saving me from stumbling through it. "They both will hear the case and then decide which of them will take on the duty of addressing the transgression." We were deep enough into the magic shop that we were inside her living quarters, so the very competent warding and spellwork she'd woven into the fabric of her home was shielding us. Again, I was torn; I was thankful for the protection and insulation from any spellwork, but also wrought with guilt over the fact that I'd gotten her knee-deep into another damned mess.

"Any chance the people scheming against Gale are in cahoots with either the council or the tribe hearing the case?"

"Cahoots, that's funny." The monk chortled, and while I almost regretted using such a cartoonish yet perfect word, I just chalked it up to a rattled brain and forged ahead.

Kaycee shook her head. "Doubtful. If it is the woman in black from the lake, she does have some incredible power for sure, but the Masarou and Unet serve the In-Between itself, which is… sacrosanct. I mean, it's beyond anything and everything, at least to them. It's the foundation of their entire society, the bedrock of their culture, hell, their very being. I could see one or two of each being swayed for personal gain maybe—and that's a weak maybe, with a healthy dose of skepticism on top, but the whole tribunal? No. Never."

"That's actually good then."

As if they were less individually minded and all sharing a connected consciousness, I felt them turn to me all together. I was about to talk but paused when I heard a loud bang. It startled us, but I just launched a short spell of silence while Grove navigated around to square up with me just beside the elven shop owner. If he didn't have a line of sight to my lips, then it was impossible for the man to read them. Ignoring the momentary confusion of everyone else, I waited for the almost imperceptible nod. Once Grove cued me, I continued.

"Well, I imagine they aren't going to be thrilled about being duped. We just have to figure out what the allegation is and then get some evidence to the contrary. Sam is a good start, but we're going to need more corroborating evidence." If this was anything like those awful procedural cop shows I'd spent the last year of my life religiously watching, the Stalkers testimony alone would just turn this into a he-said, she-said nightmare.

"One problem," Kaycee said, expectantly.

My expression invited her to take the floor and continue.

"Once a Blind Judge is set on someone, they keep going until they've got them—dead or alive."

"So we stay on the run until we get what we need: the identity of the accuser, the proof needed to clear these trumped-up charges, and a hearing to present our case and get the charges dismissed. Right?" Kaycee nodded at me to continue.

"With the appearance of both the Marked and the Dreadnought, it's safe to say that the council of Unet took this one, yeah?" I asked.

Another nod.

"Little guys, sour faced, no sense of humor?"

"Yup."

"Alright. So I've got to talk to Donovan and find out with more clarity how this is working so that we can unravel this before this big tin can comes along and undoes all of us."

I groaned to a standing position and shrugged into my outdated jacket, then looked at my partner. "Grove, take Sam across the street and wait to hear from us."

Johnny's lamenting sigh, theatrical and full bodied, let me know in no uncertain terms that he was hoping that the boy wonder was going to be coming along. That foppish demeanor sharpened to a suggestive grin, though it missed the mark on the girl he'd fired it at. Sam was just irked she wasn't going to be a part of the hunt.

"What am I supposed to do?" the Stalker asked. That her stunning body and angelic face belched a voice forged by unfiltered smokes seemed all the more hysterical.

"Try to figure out what I meant when I described soldier-boy as *ideal breeding material...*" quipped the rocker as he slithered over to my side, "and think about who has the biggest bullseye on them? Even if you got your fight and won, it would be a pointless battle that would cost us the war."

The Stalker seemed perfectly unfazed, mostly because she didn't understand any of that, even the innuendo about my business partner. Clearly, she wanted a different answer.

"We can move without notice if we're not bringing you along, and that'll give us our best shot at doing all of this minus any incident. You're going to have to trust me on this. Plus, it'll do me good knowing that another badass is with Gale and Grove, even if he is a life-sized action figure—I still worry."

"I'll attract notice? What about him?" she said, gesturing at Johnny B.

She had a point, but Johnny B seamlessly inserted himself. "I'd rather not be locked in a room with Gale and all her besties when she wakes up. I'll be good, I promise." He winked, which didn't bode well.

Kaycee handed me a backpack full of goodies, snacks for the road, various forms of magical ammo for work and some of the trinkets and gadgets I had been tinkering with over the last few months. "I don't like this. I'll be asking around while you kids go exploring."

I planted a kiss on Kaycee's cheek and flashed her a big smile. "Thanks, mamabear. Johnny, Patrick, let's go see if we can't find us a lead on who the accuser is."

CHAPTER 9

Conspiracy

Grove walked over to our shop beneath the glare of the fluorescent streetlights, the Monk beside him. Johnny followed a minute or two after them, doing his best to look nonchalant and failing spectacularly. Sam and I went the way of the sewer passage below, trying to stay unseen. I wasn't sure we'd had any eyes on us yet, but I didn't want to risk it. And while everyone else seemed confident that the preternatural court system we all were supposed to adhere to was beyond corruption, I was less than convinced.

We found Donovan in the sturdy cellar I had built, hovering at Gale's bedside while vigilantly watching over her still-sleeping form. She was on the mend, which would be another win for us if we could manage to get ahead of all this.

I broke our working theory down for him.

"With the Council of Unet, us having a witness is going to help," he said, shifting a look to our former enemy, Sam, who was tucked up in the back of the room while we spoke. I was sitting on an empty cot on the other side of Donovan, with Gale's prone and respectfully covered (and pretty thoroughly bandaged) body between us. We spoke in hushed tones. "They're very methodical. By the book, as you can imagine. The Masarou tribe is more likely to be swayed by pathos and charm."

"So this is good?" I asked.

"With the Masarou it would probably boil down to likability, and if you're at the front of this, well… Let's go with the pathos group."

"Hey," I said, a bit defensively. "I can be charming…. People like me."

It was unanimous. Nobody agreed. They all looked at me as if I was suffering from a delusional episode and they wouldn't even humor me by trying to make it something of a punchline. I guess I was the punchline.

"You aren't. You make a bad first impression. Bad second impression too. You just don't make good impressions."

"I grow on you."

"So does cancer," Donovan said.

That routine had run its course for me, and I shifted back to a flat affect. Donovan continued, "A decree is written on the chest of the judge, it's written in the All-Tongue." One cool trick of the trade was to make what I called palpable magic: magic that worked off the person, instead of the person working the magic. The All-Tongue was a trade secret that magically scribed a message that could be read by anyone who was literate.

"It said an accuser claiming Gale, a *not-quite* fugitive in the Veil, escaped here, to your world. It had something about what she supposedly did," I'd never seen him at a loss for words, and it was weird watching such a commanding presence in my life struggle for them. "They said that she was siphoning power from a ley line to weaken the crossover at the Lake, where the in-between is most vulnerable. Apparently, Gale is accused of trying to exploit the weakness and get into the Abyss. The woman in Black is claiming that if not for her, Gale would have compromised the entire Balance and thrown everything into chaos. I didn't get all of it, but that's the gist, and it's serious."

Donovan obviously thought it was the evil bitch from the Abyss too. Although the story of us trying to get into the Abyss seemed weak… after all, nobody wanted in there—not even the creatures haunting the deepest and darkest recess of that hellhole that lived there already. Of course, I wasn't privy to everything about the Abyss. From my very limited knowledge it was a dark, hell-scape with a structured tribal society and hierarchy. I didn't know everything about it, and even worse, the spare few who'd told me anything about the place may not have either.

"The lake. That's what we thought. Amazing how in her version of the story she flipped places and roles with Gale. The best lie is always a spun-up version of the truth, isn't it? Do you know any of the history between the woman in black and Gale? Anything we can go on…anything?"

Donovan's headshake was discouraging. I wasn't going to let the momentum sputter though, so I kept asking. Ley lines weren't unknown to me, almost every practitioner knew about them. They were universally discussed in almost every school of magic. Like a map of living power that was networked into the ground itself, they were channels of raw energy just beneath our feet.

"We need to see if we can dig up any record of the cult and their plan," I said. The thought had come to me abruptly, and with it a swarm of hope. "Those guys love to write in journals and record stuff. We get that, we can prove it was an orchestrated effort. We can prove that Gale—wait," I paused, shaking my head. "Fugitive?" I had used the term before because it fit and I liked making jokes about one-armed men, but he'd used it seriously.

Donovan closed up like the walls of Troy, becoming as unreadable as drunk cursive from the left hand of a righty.

"No," I demanded, hitting him with enough conviction that it was all I could do to keep some actual anger out of it. "We're about to take a deep dive, and I get that I owe her, but she's…you are asking me to go get into a boxing match with a damned terminator of monsters, so you back the fuck up. Is her being a fugitive going to have an effect on all of this? And before you even try to struggle with answering under one of those really long stretches of silence you thousand-year-living assholes don't realize is all damned day, let me remind you that time isn't on our side with this one."

Despite my soap opera anger, there was time spent having an inner monologue where I think he debated whether or not this was his to divulge.

"It'll put her on the map. Even if we can beat this, we'll have to leave." Donovan wasn't just talking about her. "All of us. The In-Between has a relationship with the Veil and once the powers that be on the other side of that curtain find out that she's here we'll have to move on. It's complicated."

That took the wind out of my sails—even if everyone else in my secreted chamber didn't quite put all the pieces together. Circle Protection having any weight to it was predicated on the fact that we'd somehow managed to get a handful of heavy hitters on our side. Basically, Gale was my big gun. She'd always been there for me, in the background. While we were out doing our song and dance, I was completely confident that if it ever came down to it, she'd have my back and help me fight the good fight. By weaving this version of the story, the woman in black had effectively divided the team. So even if she couldn't get a conviction and bullseye on our backs at the very least, we were forced to split our forces—not an optimal scenario for our side.

Worst-worst case, some of us died, so not only does our team get split up, but it would be significantly smaller. I hated her even more then, as well as myself—because while I was hating her, begrudgingly my respect for her amplified once over. It was an absolute pin, like in chess: no matter the direction we moved, she'd staged the battlefield so that we'd come out of this with a loss. The kind of power she could command was deathly frightening, and now to get a glimpse of her cunning mind wasn't any kind of comfort either.

"So," I broke our sound-sucking silence. "If we can get word to the council that Sam is willing to speak, that'll what, get them to at least stow the Judge?"

"It should. There's no way the woman in black can prove that Gale opened a gateway between the worlds, but the story will hold until we can prove otherwise. It has the advantage of being true from a factual standpoint: There was in fact a rift in the In-Between, so the sooner that they can lay that at someone's feet and hang them up for that offense, the better. The Unet and Masarou are actually more interested in hearing about the rift opening—

how they managed it—and making an example of them. The two tribes may be night and day, but they are single-minded when it comes to maintaining the integrity of the border."

"And what about the Marked Ones?"

"What about them?"

"I had a run in with a pair a while back."

Donovan's furrowed brow told me that it was unusual to have a run-in with them, but I wasn't going to push it.

"They usually work a case in doubt, or one that's directly affecting the In-Between. Think harbingers of the Blind Judge; the Judge is the indicator that their job is done. They probably got word late that the Judge was on it. Still, be careful. I know this is not the way you wish to conduct yourself, but if you run into one of them you need to put them down, period. They aren't on our side, and they aren't going to give you the benefit of the doubt."

I wanted to believe that this was one crisis averted, but I didn't really believe in coincidence, chance, or luck falling in my favor, and that was *before* I learned about all the wonky weirdness of the world. Now I was a solid skeptic.

"So our next move is to find some evidence from the cultists, and then track down who to present it to right?"

Donovan, who had turned back to caretaking and was diligently checking Gale's pulse and temperature, nodded deeply.

"Well, it sounds like getting you two off the hook is more feasible than we originally thought." I was terrible at hiding my disappointment, so I didn't bother. "At the very least we can get you all a head start on your escape."

The weight of another shared silence was a solemn reminder that our best hope was its own worst-case scenario for us anyway.

I waved at Donovan to follow me out of the chamber in which we'd secreted them and started my trek upstairs. It seemed longer than I remembered, and each step had a weight of finality to it that was so on the nose that I cursed my fondness of foreshadowing.

My footfalls announced my arrival, and on the main floor I found a pool of familiar faces looking expectantly at me. I nodded my chin at Grove and asked, "You have any contacts left with the police?"

Grove's shift was uneasy. Most wouldn't be able to see the discomfort beyond his reserved exterior, but it was easy for me to discern now that I knew what to look for. I motioned for the rest of the group to shuffle to the front of our office, which they did without complaint, though Sam cast a glance over her shoulder on her way out with Johnny and Patrick. Only Donovan remained with us in the annex. Circle Protection wasn't large, but it was large enough to allow for a modicum of privacy. Once at the allotted distance from the rest of our group, I let him carry on without asking what bothered him. That was important for our relationship, respecting boundaries; sometimes it was more than somebody just being embarrassed too.

"After the building thing with the Stalker, not really. My sister called in every favor she and I had to keep that from becoming an even bigger issue."

I should have known that that would be the case. If he'd any clout at all left, this part would go much easier, but we work with what we got.

"They'd collect evidence, right? Maybe notes, effects, whatever they found on the ship that didn't get ruined in the… you know, fighting, magic missiles, fire and, uh, sinking." Saying it aloud had a way of not only sobering me up but dampening my expectation of what we would find. Grove didn't seem discouraged, so I figured now should be one of those rare times where I actually shut up and listen.

"You'd be surprised, evidence does have a way of surviving. There might be something there that we could use."

"If only life came with one of those indestructible black boxes that are on planes…."

"That's a little dark, Janzen."

"I'm not sure the box is actually black."

Grove lazily signed *haha*, and that's how I learned that American Sign Language could convey sarcasm.

"So the evidence from the boat at Lake Erie is really our only chance?"

Donovan didn't look hopeful when I'd mentioned the remnants of the wreckage of that night, but Grove wasn't so sure. The gnome watched with more interest than I'd seen out of him well, ever.

"Let's sort this, yeah? It's worth a look."

Gnomes weren't the affectionate sort, so I should have expected him to stiffen at the companionable hand I attempted to set on his shoulder. Luckily, the awkwardness wasn't long lived, and the tired tinkerer just trudged back downstairs to attend to Gale.

I snapped my fingers, hoping it would light a fuse that would spread some illumination on a wobbled memory. My idiosyncrasies tended to be as taxing as I was. In my defense, during our last skirmish with the woman in black I'd spent half the adventure concussed, so full recall wasn't always spot-on for me.

"Who was that poor dude that we didn't get to in time—Frank I think?"

Grove nodded, not quite tracking, though given my excitement he could see that I was attempting to weave together a tapestry of some hope.

"If I was going to turn my back on my cult, knowing that they were about to do something insanely apocalyptic that I couldn't stop, I would probably go about collecting some evidence or something to bring up the ladder to somebody who could stop it, right?"

"It tracks." Military vernacular was so concise; if I didn't sound so damn ridiculous using it, I would do it more often. Unfortunately for everyone else, I was a talker, and changing that was no doubt utterly hopeless.

"Let's start there then, see if you can tap those depleted contacts one more time to find out where they're keeping anything left from the wreckage."

"It's thin, man," he warned.

"We know a sorceress elf who runs a fake magic shop to sell real magic products. Thin is a good day for us."

We had everyone except Donovan with us and given recent happenings I figured that this was a snowball-in-hell chance, so I wasn't about to get his already beaten hopes up just to suffer another crushing defeat.

We spent some time going back and forth over the details, how we'd split into team and what our priorities would be: Grove, Sam and Johnny could comb through the wreckage of Frank's apartment, while Patrick and I handled the much more delicate operation at the police station identifying whatever evidence remained from one of the worst nights of my life. Then maybe we could finally track down whoever was pulling the strings on this gigantic titan of destruction that was probably tearing around town looking for us even as we spoke.

***

In the end, none of the former colleagues could (or wanted to) lend a hand to Grove. That was a twofold disappointment. First it meant we had to break into a police station without any clue as to whether or not the stuff left over and cataloged as evidence was worth that monumental risk.

Second, I could see the hurt hidden behind Grove's practiced stoicism; the feeling of being rejected and ousted wasn't unfamiliar to me either, and I was intimately aware of just how hard that could hit when it was from people you considered your own. Late night bled into early morning, which was the best window of time to do this kind of thing. People suffering through the overnight shift were impervious to caffeine and complacent at this point, so this was our only shot.

I packed my bag, slipping the jar of transference gel I'd confiscated from the programmer along with an action figure I'd lifted from Kaycee's kids inside. I was not proud of the toy I'd stolen, but it was being sacrificed to a good cause.

***

So there we were, three a.m., a homeless guy and a high school dropout parked outside a police station. A police station we'd every intention of breaking into. The only reprieve from making this feel like absolute madness was the fact that this was an evidence depot tasked with crimes that hadn't the same heft or consequence of higher tier felonies. Stuff like traffic accidents, code violations, a strangely sunken boat on the lake…minor stuff. Still, it was a depot full of police who probably wouldn't care for our unsolicited intrusion.

"Plan?" he asked.

"Yeah, I mean, sort of."

"Brilliant." The sandpaper dry delivery let me know beyond a doubt that he was not happy.

"Look, maybe if we just ask about… or better yet, pretend to be some kind of credentialed columnist… we can get a look at…"

I was cut off as an alarm went off inside the police station.

It gave one harrowing, ear-splitting scream and then it cut off. The synthetic cry died out, but the human one that was in concert with it didn't, carrying on the glass-shattering tone for another two seconds before ending with a gurgle.

A moment of madness calmed by an unnatural quiet.

Patrick was on my heels as I shouldered through the door. We skidded to a stop at the smallest entrance landing just as all the lights went out.

CHAPTER 10

Possessions

It wasn't just dark as in the absence of light, it was an unnatural kind of blackness that was alive; a shadow accompanied by pulse-pounding dread.

"They cut the power; I can't see anything."

"Are you just going to narrate everything happening to us?"

Oh, if only he knew.

I shot him a murderous look, and while we couldn't help but volley some disparaging remarks back and forth, I could tell that he was as tuned in as I was to the fact that this blackout was no natural occurrence. We were within the belly of the station—a kind of transitional space where evidence from active cases went after they became cold ones. Even at this hour, with a skeleton staff, we expected to see someone—anyone. Instead it was just quiet. It was a foreign quiet, but one I was not unaccustomed to, it was the same kind of stillness that blanketed me whenever I shared space with a Stalker.

To our immediate left was some kind of kiosk for information; moving past it led us into a hall that split off in three directions: straight, left and right. The right dead-ended into a break room with a vending machine and some kind of coffee set-up.

It was also home to our first victim—or so I thought. All of a sudden, the face down deputy twitched, his face abruptly turning in a painfully sharp direction before uncoordinated arms clumsily got beneath the bulk of his body and started to push up. I was no expert on possession, but if I were a gambling man, I'd bet that this didn't bode well for us.

Once upright, the mid-forties, slightly overweight pencil pusher locked eyes with me and drooled black ichor through a toothy and sadistic smile.

"You…"

Nobody who addresses you with a punctuated and exaggerated "*You*" has good intentions or designs, trust me. The mouth opened to speak but the lips didn't comply with the sound that came out. It wasn't the first time I'd seen this; I was hoping it would be the last, but I wasn't gonna hold my breath.

The Concrete Monk was stuck somewhere between the urge to move and crippling indecision, the worst predicament for somebody who was a person of action. Of course, a grinning cop with black blood coming out the edge of his twisted grin and moving like a stilted marionette wasn't an everyday occurrence, even in our genre.

There was no fluidity in his limbs; it was as if the body was fighting through the last stages of rigor mortis. Lucky for us, that meant that when the creature reached for the pistol on the hip of the victim it was piggybacking, we had plenty of time to react; its stifled movements telegraphing his intent.

I shifted behind the monk, ready to reach into my makeshift utility belt of tricks when suddenly I was off my feet, slammed to the ground and gasping as the lungful of air I had comfortably settled on was evicted from me by way of a brutal take down, courtesy of the monk I had been standing behind a second earlier. I heard a shot fired, followed by a strange kind of shriek. Grove was a hell of a shooter.

I noticed the possessed cop was grimacing, its gun-wielding arm was down, and it was stumbling around seemingly at a loss.

"What are you doing!" Patrick screamed at me while I screamed back at the same time.

The start of a smile touched my mouth, but with a threatening fist raised overhead the monk let me know that if I was to call *jinx*, he would blacken one or both of my eyes.

"I was getting behind you to find a tool to use to try to handle this!"

"Behind me? What the fuck do you think I am…bulletproof?"

I blinked dumbly, the stupefied expression staying put even as Patrick pulled me to my feet, and we ducked into the waiting area designated in front of the information desk. The row of flimsy and uncomfortable chairs wasn't an ideal cover or concealment, but luckily, we got tucked behind the wall before the creature could collect itself. Snarling, searching eyes swept the room.

"I have an idea…" I whispered.

Patrick looked incredulous at the notion, and to be fair I had just kind of blindly assumed he was bulletproof and did in fact attempt to use him as a makeshift shield… without asking him if he was.

My bad.

"It's going to make this even more of a time crunch though." We both winced, not at the proverbial clock we were working with being abruptly shortened, but rather because my version of whispering was apparently loud enough for the possessed cop to draw a bead on us from behind the wall and take a potshot in our direction. It took a bite out of the wall, sending chunks of debris across our bodies.

The possessed cop matched the piercing noise of the gunfire with a toe-curling cry, his distorted face twisted into a grimace as he lowered the firearm.

My partner mumbled some kind of curse as I raced by him, ducking beneath a stiff swing from the cop and smacking into the far wall. Before I could take inventory of my surroundings, which was tough in all this darkness, I felt around the surface of the drywall until I found what I was looking for: locating the box, I hitched a finger over the lever and yanked down.

A piercing siren-sound, the wail of an angry alarm reverberated from above sending the harrowing, chilling call down every unseen corridor. Of course it seemed victory came with some kind of price, because there was a blinding flash of light every other second that took frightening snapshots of the whole place. I saw the cop turn to me, I saw two seconds later his face contour in horror and anguish and then he was buckled to his knees, bent distinctly at the waist with his face planted firmly into the tile floor, a pool of ebony ichor around his jaw.

"What. Was. That?" The Monk asked, carefully stepped over the prone body of the formerly possessed, and now sadly just dead deputy. He spoke in a strange cadence so he could slide a word in between each ear-splitting alarm.

"It's. A. Night. Geist."

The mouthful of air taken to speak was abandoned as Patrick pivoted and put his fist through the fire alarm, sending it shattering into a dozen pieces and sinking his actual hand a good foot into the drywall and clean through the rebar reinforcement.

That was impressive.

The alarm was still going though.

"That's. Not." I started. The sour look from my new partner suspended the rest of my thought, which I just waved off. He didn't care where the alarm actually was, not at that moment, and I found that watching a man shatter rebar with a gnarled fist was just enough to persuade me to drop the point.

The strange groaning and howling I heard between the sharp alarms reminded me that we were in the thick of a situation, so I hustled to the vending machine and coffee area.

"Find. Salt!" I yelled through the alarm as the strange ethereal crying became more prevalent. I was the first to find a small shaker, and I grabbed a handful more of the salt and pepper packets. I poured a line of salt from wall to wall at the beginning of each hallway before fishing out a handful of marbles that I scattered down their dark depths. Still kneeling with Patrick standing beside me, I whispered a word of power that traveled with some careful focus to each of the sigils carved into the marbles; they illuminated with a soft, blue glow.

Just beyond the blue glow, there were several living shadows shifting in the darkness. Any other day they would seem to be just a trick of the eye, but today we knew better. Standing upright, I started searching the rest of the entrance area, then waved for the monk to follow me while I rushed behind the information desk.

Crouched together, I leaned into the Concrete Monk's ear and explained loudly through the alarm, "They're Nightgeists—ghosts, spirits, whatever you want to call them that somehow fell into the Abyss."

I got a straight-faced look rife with confusion. I forgot that this stuff was all compartmentalized; there were vampire hunters who'd never heard of ghosts, werewolves that knew nothing about the Abyss. It was complicated, and everybody treated knowledge like some kind of card-hand that they had to play close to the chest. Information in our world was a kind of currency.

"Okay, Abyss, big dark world of scary monsters. We'll get to that, but Nightgeists are a creature from that world. They're cruel tricksters, usually they just push people off the sidewalk into traffic or scare people off a balcony. They influence through whispers and small illusions, but the strong ones have been known to possess people. They're rare and insidious."

By now the alarm has become something of a background soundtrack, at least it was until I thought of it, and it pushed its way into the forefront of my consciousness again.

"So they don't like sound?" Patrick asked.

"I guess not…"

"You guess? Aren't you an expert on this stuff?"

"Look, I don't go to your corner and tell you how to break skulls, do I? I guess he didn't like the gun after it fired, so I took a leap, okay? Do you really want to get into this right now?"

"Okay, fine," he conceded. "So, the salt?"

"Rumor has it that spectrals, phantoms, anything like that can't cross salt in their ghost-y form."

"Ghost-y?"

"It's a technical term. Look, if you're gonna make some kind of smart-ass remark every time I try to explain something, we'll be here all day."

I saw why everyone was so frustrated now with my incessant need to add a quip, comment or joke after every utterance. It was annoying as hell. Despite the life-or-death episode we were in, the Monk was matching my annoyance with mirth; he was messing with me. Now, of all times.

I like this guy.

"There're probably people here who aren't dead. We need to take a look around."

Stiffening upright, the Monk got suddenly a lot more serious. The prospect of still-living people hadn't dawned on him.

"And the evidence?"

As if on cue, I found a laminated map of the depot on the wall beside us and tracked where I needed to go before showing it to him.

"Break room—get there, drop them off, and then come back here and shut the alarm off."

Before he could ask how that was done, I pinpointed the electrical breaker just behind us. I had thought of making mention of it in the form of a sarcastic quip, getting my dig in as well as a little education, but the whole wall-punching, steel-snapping episode swayed me to momentary silence.

I turned my gaze down the hall leading straight into the heart of the building, the one corridor that was still thick with a living murkiness.

"I'll meet you there," he said, and I realized I'd only caught the tail-end of whatever it was he said before. There was a look of concern painted over his freckled face that I tried to placate with a cocksure smirk.

"You look like an idiot when you do that," he pointed out.

"You smell like urine."

We shared a shallow grin that was a poor mask for our mutual foreboding. He headed left toward the break room, and I started down the middle hall.

***

I wasn't even out of the hallway when I saw another face-down dead body, this one with black blood pooling out of a fractured jaw. It wasn't a law enforcement officer this time, but some kind of courier instead—I recognized the outfit. This struck me as odd, since it was flirting with dawn and was much too early for any delivery service to show up.

There was a scuffle a little beyond me, but this deep into the hallway the light from my marbles wasn't much help; I retrieved a few from the floor beneath me and carefully tossed them into the darkness ahead. I'd like to say it was because I was on a budget and that even in the thick of this life-threatening crisis, I could be economical—but it was just that I needed more light and didn't want to run out of marbles. This was a much larger room than the others we'd been through, extending a few dozen feet back. Inside, there was another desk that was completely caged in except for a small service window.

The evidence room.

I stepped carefully over the dead courier. The man had been possessed, and while I didn't have a lot to go on, I guessed that this thing had tried to gain access to this room, which was troubling for a host of other reasons. A courier could easily get into lots of places— a clever gambit that didn't work out for them.

Most troubling, was that it meant that this attack was designed and coordinated; a conscious effort to sabotage what we were doing here.

Startled by blurred motion in my peripheral, I ripped my wooden, broken bat free and summoned the buckler shield on my forearm into existence. The ruckus was hard to make out with the unnatural darkness trying to suffocate all semblance of light, but I soon saw what it was.

It was the female Marked One, her attire ripped to ribbons, black blood mingled with her own living red. She heard me, turning enraged eyes on me.

"*You.*"

See? Told you.

***

She was no novice to combat, and despite a myriad of grievous wounds she still managed to stand upright. Working her jaw, she spat out a blend of that black and red gore that was also coating almost every inch of her. The closed fist started to call on energy, gathering the ambient power from around her to transform into some kind of offensive spell.

"Wait, it's n—"

I got my buckler up in time to take a fireball head on, but the momentum that was carried through the blast staggered me back, tripping me over the body of the dead man in the process. Unfortunately, there wasn't enough force to throw my legs back up and over my head and try to tumble back to my feet, so I was greeted by the image of her standing above me with a stomping boot coming down right at my groin.

I didn't have my broken bat anymore: the dagger-like weapon had fallen out of my grip when I hit the ground, so I did the next best thing. I reached into my pocket and tossed the contents at her face.

It was leftover salt.

While it didn't need a word of power to activate, wouldn't explode, and wasn't lethal, it sure as hell was effective. Her stomp veered wide as she screeched and grabbed her face; perhaps she feared that it was something more insidious like acid instead of salt. Crudely kicking her stomping leg to buckle her over, I rolled to my feet and with a quick turn at the waist I sent my shield sailing right for her doubled over and exposed head.

It found purchase instead with a snapping front kick, one she threw with enough force that it knocked my shield-arm wide and exposed me to the haymaker thrown by her partner, the male Marked One. There was an explosion of pain and blood from my nose; blurred vision corrupted my equilibrium and criminally clumsy feet sent me right back to the tile floor.

"You will burn for this, Janzen Robinson, you and your whole crooked circle of saboteurs," she spat at me.

Fighting to process information was tough when trying to simultaneously stave off unconsciousness and quiet the cries of agony inside of my head, but I'm proud to say that I chortled at the word *saboteurs*.

"Thou hast underestimated me and mine, good knight…" I fired back in an admittedly slurred voice but still *nailing* the accent. I'm a regular at the Renaissance Faire.

On one knee, staring both of them down through the muddle of darkness, the waning blue glow and the wet of my own eyes it was clear as day that they didn't get my joke, and if they had, they didn't find it as amusing as I did. To be fair, not many people make a punchline on the heel of being punched, so I'll forgive myself if the comedic timing was a little off. I'd been told more than once I was like a bad 80s action film with my commentary.

"You can't just try to open the Abyss and not expect there to be some kind of consequence!"

That stopped me cold, after I managed to get my second leg beneath me. Did they think this was me? Even at a few feet apart we were shouting at one another because of that unrelenting alarm, and it wasn't like they were the type to try to listen to reason. The time for discourse was long past, and judging by their own mangled faces, they had both fallen victim to some thorough ass-kicking and horrifically unpleasant (so I'd heard) possession.

The Marked Ones used a kind of archaic tattooing, a type of artificery that was permanently infused in their flesh. It made them a living conduit for several types of magic, usually all offensive. Their ability to continuously hurl an almost unending array of attacks made them unbeatable at a distance, my best hope was to close the distance on them, where they could only employ their decades of brutal hand-to-hand combat training.

Hooray.

I couldn't backpedal—that might invite a moment of clarity for the two enraged enforcers and have them remember that a series of fireballs could quickly annihilate me. Instead, I charged shield-first into the guy. Normally no amount of training could compensate for a desperate, two-hundred-pound missile. To his credit he caught the shield edge in each hand, challenging and ultimately stopping my charge to a standstill, and while that could have been serviceable had it been just the pair of us, his quick-thinking and even faster-stepping partner had danced around our grapple and delivered a stomach-crushing side kick. If it wasn't for my jacket, ribs would have cracked; instead, it just buckled me over again.

The male still had a vice grip on my shield, and he used that to his advantage. With a fluid movement he turned at the hip, pulling his wide leg back behind him in the process, and then twisted to throw me over his hip into the wall. Well, more aptly he threw my shield, which I was attached to.

I hadn't even pulled myself off the ground before the female launched her next attack. I managed to find myself on my knees and intercepted her curb-stomp for a second time, absorbing some of it with my chest; pushing through the pain of the blow, I cinched my arms around her waist and hoisted her up with me while standing up. It wasn't nearly as graceful or technically sound as it sounds, but I tossed her—right at her partner.

I was banking that beneath all his tattooed, hardass facade there was still some chivalry at play and that that would give me an opening at best, and some time at the very least.

I was wrong.

He hockey-checked her clear out of his path while bulldozing after me. It didn't matter, I was trying to get out of the room and back into the evidence locker. While it was bigger, the sectioned-off space actually cut the room so that the front half was a really tight squeeze for three people.

Luckily, I managed to align my own body with the threshold of the door so when he came crashing into me like a battering ram, I got a fistful of his sleeves and dragged him in with me. That took the last of my reserves, and I think he knew it. My blurred vision was able to pick out each of them based on their silhouette, since little else was coming through with any kind of perceptibility.

Their clear advantage wasn't pushed, and I very graciously spat out a molar I felt rattling around in my jaw while I was laboring through a cracked rib to try to gather a full breath. I didn't recall being hit directly in the face, so that was kind of impressive but there was also a good chance that during the throws and kicks somebody snuck a jab in for good measure. The only thing my grapple had managed to do was drag the offender a bit further into the room with me.

As if on cue, the alarm cut off and I sighed a big relief. The sigh perplexed the Marked Ones, and while I didn't peg either one of them for being a chatty type, I was hoping to bait them into a bit of back and forth.

"Didn't run, even though you didn't stand a chance, I respect that." Gruff voiced, as expected, the male was trying to fight off the fact that he was grudgingly impressed. I couldn't tell you why—this was the second time the two of them had soundly whooped my ass.

"Why? Fighting a losing battle is stupid. There's no honor in losing, and I have people counting on me to get this done. That's why I was trying to get you guys in this little ass room, make you less effective."

The woman laughed, and something about it was kind of charming—it was the first touch of something human in her.

"Even with us being less effective you have no chance, so why fight if you say that it is stupid to do so when you know you can't win? Why even try to get us in here when it wouldn't change your chances?"

"Cause even though I can't kick your ass," I said, my macabre, one-tooth-down, shit-eating grin spreading ear-to-goddamn-ear, "...he can."

Patrick, fresh off of choking the male unconscious with a rear naked choke, dropped the guy's now-limp body to the ground with a *thud* that sounded like a sweet serenade to me. The female was quick to respond but Patrick was quick to not only deflect the blow but capture the limb and tangle her into a similar chokehold. He repeated the motion. I took a laborious breath and picked up my broken bat from where it had been knocked from my hands during the scuffle, and moments later we were standing in stark silence over their crumpled bodies.

It didn't last, but this time it wasn't my fault.

"Who are you? Are you with them?" a male voice demanded.

It was tempting to ignore, but the additional sound of a shotgun chambering a big gauged round reinforced my desire to answer it.

"No, we aren't." Patrick was watching the door, looking out into the darkness sparsely lit by my marbles. They were starting to fade, weakening a shade every few minutes.

"Why don't you just use glow sticks?" he asked over his shoulder flippantly.

"We have a gun pointed at us…" I reminded him.

Patrick ticked a glance to the cop, me, back to the cop and finally settled on me expectantly.

"Magic doesn't cancel out magic unless specifically designed to do so. Somebody put a darkness spell on this to take out a certain kind of light—not magical light, since they didn't expect it. Magic has to be much more precise than people think."

"Hello."

"Hi," I answered cheerfully. I carefully tied each of the Marked Ones up, including their fingers, and spoke to the knot rather than the nervous wreck of a man who'd just emerged at the other side of the now locked gate which kept me from all the evidence. I stood just in time for him to pinpoint my person with the barrel of the gun, through the gate.

"You know, even if you shoot through the reinforced gate this close the ricochet is going to be brutal, right?" I lifted both hands. Eyes dropping to the police issued shotgun. "No, we're not with them. In fact we're pointedly against them."

There was a chime on my phone, and while the leftover noise in my head from the alarm made it hard to determine what was and wasn't real, I also realized that this was like the tenth time my phone had gone off. Signing with a finger for a timeout in our conversation, I plucked my phone painfully slowly out of my pocket.

The screen was cracked and there was salt all over it, but the top text message from Kaycee read: *The Marked Ones aren't working against us.*

Well, that's fun.

"Okay, look, I don't have time to—" I started.

"Everyone in my station has gone crazy, they're trying to kill us, and they tried to get in here…" he rambled, and while I was tempted to jump in, I figured I could try to cherry-pick some information out of whatever fell out of his mouth.

"They were helping me, and then they turned too, and got all weird and creepy and tried to kill us to get to the back locker."

The black blood. They'd gotten possessed. Why hadn't he?

"Religious?"

"Huh?"

"Are you religious at all? Spit it out. Look, you're basically in a monster movie, man, and I've got all of ten seconds to get what I need to get done so we all can get out of this alive, so I am going to need you to swallow your disbelief, fear, and also lower the damned gun. Now," I rolled my still raised hand over to prompt him to be succinct. "You, religious?"

"Uh, not really…" he answered shakily.

"Okay, you got an old family heirloom on you, some kind of religious keepsake, a token or talisman?"

"Uh… No, not—"

Right then there was a pause as the deputy, who I got a feeling was more a paperwork and logistics guy, shifted some. Beside him there was a girl, barely adolescent. She was looking at all the chaos on the other side of the cage with an admirable calm, though I could tell her nerves were on edge. She had a blue streak in her hair, some punk-rock ensemble and about a dozen trinkets on her person. Necklaces, bracelets, all that.

"Honey, go back insi—"

"You make those?" I asked her directly.

The girl, ignoring her dad's directive, nodded.

"You make one for your dad, too?"

She gave another nod, while her dad shot me a baffled look about my line of questioning.

"You just make them up, or you learn them from somewhere?"

"My grandma's book, it's got cool designs."

Well, count another one for a strange, one-in-a-million happenstance offering up a Hail Mary to save the day in overtime.

"Look man, we need to get ins:—"

"Janzen?" I trapped the rest of my breath behind a reluctantly shut mouth, turning an exacerbated expression to my accomplice.

"The lights are dying out quicker," Patrick informed me, worry in his voice.

"Fine, okay—"

"—Like now." The finality turned it from worry to emergency.

That didn't mean anything good. I peered outside. At first, nothing seemed amiss—until I remembered some of the lore behind the Nightgeists: I focused not on the movement that my eye was attracted to, since whenever I tried to fixate on it, I couldn't see anything. Instead, I focused on the glow.

That's when bleak comprehension dawned on me. One Nightgeist was a nightmare, two was a nightmare compounded, but this was a good six or seven working together. It was hard to say with any certainty—instinct made me look right at them even when I knew better. I moved to stand shoulder to shoulder next to the monk, then started tearing packets of salt.

I gestured at the Marked Ones. "Take them in the back with the deputy," I said.

While I hurriedly made a flimsy line of salt at the ingress, Patrick seemed to be suspended by his own doubt.

"I'm not letting them back in," the cop in the cage said.

"Cop—name?"

"Neil."

While brushing the limited salt to quarantine off our now limited space, I give him a dose of unbelievable reality.

"Okay, Neil. Your mother was probably some kind of witch, and the only reason you're not possessed and feasting on the flesh of your daughter or throwing your own body into traffic is because your daughter, who is probably teeming with a natural aptitude for magic, made you a talisman of some kind to keep you safe because she thinks your job is dangerous. The black stuff you keep seeing but think is your eyes are playing tricks on you is known as a Nightgeist, a soul that's been trapped in an abyss of darkness aptly named the Abyss; that trapped soul has escaped, been warped by its time in that world, and is now hellbent on killing and hurting any and everyone it'll come across.

"Those two are kind of… police, like you, and are trying to help—I think—but got possessed by one of those Nightgeists because they didn't have a nifty pendant to protect them. So here's the deal: I need something out of the evidence locker, and when I have it, they'll probably all give up or chase me. But like it or not, our best hope is barricading ourselves in there, all of us, and trying to find this damn box of evidence."

Evidence that might not exist, I reminded myself bleakly.

"Got it?"

It wasn't a silent spell because he was shaking so badly it was audible, but luckily at some point he'd lowered the shotgun. The guy wasn't brave, but he was trying to put a face on for his daughter, which was admirable.

"No," Neil answered. Luckily, he was unlocking the door while talking. "Not even a little bit."

"Good man."

As Patrick carried the stirring bodies of the Marked Ones, I pushed in at the end while he locked the useless gate once again. I didn't want to tell him that an astrally-projected entity wasn't going to be bothered by physical impediments, though.

"Patrick, I need you to get them on board with us." My up-nod directed his gaze to the two Marked Ones he was depositing below the information desk. "Find out their damned names, too."

"On board? So I'm not knocking them out again?" He skeptically asked with a comical seriousness.

"Yeah, Kaycee thinks we're on the same team, I think. I don't have time to really sort it and we're kind of at the worst-case scenario here."

"You. Neil." The cop was still shaken, but it only took saying his name twice and his daughter to give his sleeve a soft tug to get him to key in on me again.

"Okay, you wear these." My aviators would help him see the core of the Nightgeists, which was the focal point of sentient energy that made these things possible.

"They're magic glasses."

I get a dubious scowl from him.

"The alarm went off for a good ten minutes, nobody came, your friends tried to kill you while bleeding black blood out of their mouths, and there's two unconscious sorcerers under your desk."

"Aren't the guys wizards?" Patrick interjected.

I scolded the inquisitive monk with my best withering glare.

"We can discuss semantics later," he conceded.

"Take the shotgun shells out, pull them apart and dump salt in with the ballistic part—are they slugs or buckshot?"

"Buckshot…" Neil was still lagging a bit, so I took preemptive steps and coaxed the shotgun out of his hand, then laid it on the desk in front of us. The light was dim, so much so that I was trying not to let panic bleed into my own mind. Careful to orientate the barrel in a safe direction, I pumped each round out without firing it. Once out, I quickly peeled the spire of the casing and dumped the salt into the cluster of balling inside, then shoved the shelling back down on top of the death-dealing contents inside.

"Do that with all of them. They don't like salt, and because this scatters you don't have to hit them directly. Now the glasses, they see spectrums of energy and power. Nightgeists will look like a weird black sphere drifting up and down. See them? Shoot them. Got it?"

"Got it," he answered.

"So, you see them, you…?"

"Shoot them."

"And they are?"

"Weird glowing balls that are floating." Saying it aloud sobered him up, and thankfully he just shook his head as if trying to cast aside the mounting doubt settling all around him.

"We have six packets of salt, make it count."

Sleeping Beauties One and Two woke up, and Patrick was casually kneeling down in front of them, eyeballing them on an equal playing field. The female woke first, and the first thing she did was, predictably, test the restraints and lunge at the Concrete Monk.

"You aren't dead," she started to say, about to follow it up with a threat.

A headache was pounding around inside my skull, and I was completely out of patience and ideas to stop the animosity. So I screamed. The others suddenly fell silent, gawking at me.

"*You* aren't dead, we aren't bad guys, and obviously there are some mixed signals. Now, I get that you guys are single-minded ass-whooping machines, but we are *all* going to die here unless we can stow the politics and figure out what the hell is going on, and the only way we're going to do that is if we get out of here alive. Together."

The male was still half-in an unconscious stupor but seemed to pick up on the happenings pretty quickly. They both chewed it over, and their mulling ceased when I pulled out my broken bat. It was easy to just exert a bit of concentration to the sigil, powering it with my own will and activating it; I say easy, but that alone took me two years to learn, and I still had yet to master it. You see, my bat was originally meant to be an instrument of simple bone-breaking. It had absorption sigils, so I would hit something with the bat and the runework would assimilate the kinetic energy. If I hit something five times, I could then unleash the force of five strikes on something else. Simple, but effective. The kicker was when I fought the Stalker in the warehouse, its claws raked my bat in half. Their claws were notorious, legend had it that they could cut through anything and as fate would have it, I was lucky enough to find it wasn't just legend, it was true. When the Stalker had swiped at my bat it captured that ability; so while it just looked like a broken bat, it was in fact capable of cutting through anything—a known attribute if they had done any research on me, and if they didn't….

I demonstrated by driving it into the metal desk cutting it like it was nothing, which saved me from having to explain it to them. Like a bound prisoner waiting for the guillotine to drop, I suddenly saw each of them as very human, despite the ink, the abilities, the conviction; I saw them as very human, and actually, pretty young.

The rumor around the Marked Ones was that they were indentured servants, sold into bondage and only able to purchase their freedom through impossible trials. The type of magic they used was extremely taxing on their bodies; they were usually used up before the age of forty, and the only reason *that* wasn't an issue was that none of them lived that long. It was a tough racket being a Marked One, and from my understanding their counterparts didn't fare much better. The Warded ones, the Goblin equivalent of the Marked, also had a pretty brutal upbringing and set of responsibilities. Think of them as the CIA and FBI respectively; we don't know much about them, we know they outrank the locals and they work for Big Brother—or, in this case, the Balance.

The surprise was evident on each of their usually stony faces when I cut them free and was amplified when they looked back at me and found that I didn't have a weapon trained on them. Instead, I was already back at the desk trying to dump my supplies and take stock.

"Neil, we need to get evidence from the back. It was a case from a while ago, on a boat."

"There is none," the girl said. "We checked, it's been destroyed, it was the first thing they went after."

"You checked?"

She nodded. "Your friend Kaycee reached out to someone who reached out to us, said that the key to your innocence was there. We are not mindless mercenaries, we are adhering to our code; we do not seek to just blindly punish anyone, Mr. Robinson."

"Janzen, please…?" Apparently, my timed silence for a return introduction didn't catch, neither did my encouraging hand signal. "Do you have names?"

"Alpha Thirteen," the male answered.

"Delta Six," she added, following suit.

"That answers a lot of unasked questions," I said. "*Except* why you attacked me."

"We aren't in a position to make assumptions, we follow orders." The matter-of-fact response was as clinical as it was justified in her eyes.

"*Nice code.*"

The lights were flickering, the last cough of life being extinguished by their much more powerful spellwork. I was about to give up and try to scheme some kind of jailbreak escape plan that would likely see all of us dead when the second half of our theory came like an epiphany.

"Neil! Homicide, downtown Cleveland; guy's name was Frank…"

"Homicide is kind of common, I me—"

"Animal attack, a *brutal* one, would have been the subject of some water cooler conversation." I could see the wheels turning for the deputy, but I needed to double-dip. Luckily with my rampant attention disorder, I could multitask better than I could fixate on something singularly. I turned to the Marked Ones and said, "Alphie, you and Sinead O'Connor—" nobody got the reference, so in defeat I graciously just pointed to Delta. "—got to get the door, and I want you to send a nice blast at anything trying to come through. *No. Fire.*"

"Fire is the most effective—"

I've never really considered myself anything of an intellectual, but I would swear to the six-armed god of face-palming that these people were all idiots sent to deliver a gangland beatdown to my last nerve. Ten minutes ago neither of the Marked Ones seemed to even know what a Nightgeist was, now suddenly he was a subject-matter expert.

"And fire takes oxygen, and oh, I don't know, catches things on fire, and kills us better than it does them. Let's just try my way on this stuff, ok? Right." It was rhetorical, but he missed it and I had to cut him off when he tried to respond. I noted that my sarcasm might have to be more on the (broken) nose with these two.

They'd broken my nose; I recalled as I crinkled my face some while trying to keep everyone coordinated. Neil started snapping his fingers in an obnoxious, generic mannerism to show he finally recalled the attack I was talking about.

It was what I did when we first walked in here and got blitzed by an ambush.

"That's in the back—it's not a cold case yet, but nobody was even looking into it."

"Back is a SUPER general statement Neil, need more."

"All the way down the middle aisle, go through the door back there and then take a left, there's a brown box taped up and it's in there."

Patrick saw the renewed hope come over me and moved to fall in step with me.

"No," I whispered harshly. I seized his attention with my stare and led it to the scared girl still clinging to her very scared father. The Concrete Monk was a lot of things, but almost all of them were unanimously good, so he took the cue and offered little rebuttal. The sentry took up a stance between the father and the girl.

"I'm going with you," Delta Six said, suddenly beside me instead of next to her partner, and while I was still a bit dubious about their motive and sore about our last skirmish (you wouldn't believe how often you breathe out of your nose), I could see there wouldn't be any swaying her. Still, if ever there was a chance for the Nightgeist to catch me unaware, it would be with my back turned while studiously thumbing through paperwork.

I mean, that also meant it would be a prime spot for her too, but sometimes you gotta pick your poison. "Be it oyster or Walrus, here I go."

She didn't get it; so few people do. I moved to the back of the evidence room just as I heard the first spell sound off, coupled by the rancorous bellow of a shotgun blast.

***

Rummaging through the files, this box in the back was loaded to the max; two rows of files on the bottom and top, with other boxes intermittently shoved into the sides and crevices of any open space. Good to see we had such a competently organized filing system that was both user friendly and easy to navigate.

"You do that a lot," I heard someone saying.

Snapping up, I looked at Delta. God, that felt weird.

"What, D? No, Daphne. Your name is Daphne now."

I could see that generated minor annoyance, probably because I just thrust that upon her and I got the distinct feeling that she'd been saying something I only caught the tail end of—an occurrence so common for me that I could read the micro-expressions people let walk over their face whenever I did it, helping me realize I was zoned out again. The extended quiet was bothersome, so I took a handful of files and started thumbing through them after activating another luminescent marble in my mouth so I could see.

"Do what?" I asked dutifully around the marble, exhaustion in my voice.

"Trust. Forgive. We've watched you awhile now, with the boy using the transference magic to the Stalker you have in your ranks; even with us. It's noble. Foolish," she added a little airily. "But noble."

"I take my own inventory regularly, and, more importantly, I take it honestly—and the result ends up I'm still something of an asshole. And despite that, I have a life ripe with good people who open their homes and their lives to me. The best way to keep hope alive that I can become something better is to extend that courtesy, respect, and foolishness to other people and give them the chance to do the same. Still, this doesn't get you off the hook for the Blind Judge. Your people really jumped the gun on that one and almost killed two of my friends."

I contemplatively shifted the marble from right to left while skimming through another passage; each file had a coinciding number to the case that would lead me to the box of evidence that should hopefully be stowed somewhere nearby.

I found the number.

I heard a scream.

Then Daphne dropped a bomb.

"Nobody has loosed a Blind Judge in this world for a hundred years, Janzen."

CHAPTER 11

Evidence

I tore the paper out of the book, staring at Daphne in a kind of bewilderment that was so laden with muddled emotion that bewilderment didn't quite do it justice, I shouldered past her to run to the front of the evidence room.

The girl was being held up by her father, but it was easy to see that this wasn't her father anymore. That telltale black goo was coming out of his jowls, and I noticed that his pupils had completely expanded, washing away any color except for daunting black. Alphie was trying to offer some of his split attention, but the first of the phantasms had pushed the door open and he was already channeling ambient energy around him to cast a barrier. It was focused defensive magic, not reckless offensive blasts, which was good, but I also knew that sustained defense wasn't exactly the modus operandi of the Marked Ones. Although they were in stellar shape, they had already fought us twice, been rendered unconscious recently and, I was confident, didn't have much in the way of sleep in the last week, which meant they were running on fumes. The Concrete Monk was suddenly scared, and that was a refreshing thing; Patrick cared about those who couldn't care for themselves, and for whatever had transpired to get them into this bind I had no doubt he was blaming himself.

"Neil, listen my man, you got to try to fight this thing…"

"Heroics don't become you, Jaaaaaaanzen," the thing cackled, and while it was one of the Nightgeists, I had an ugly feeling that this one was somehow different. "You can't save him; no-no-no, just like her. Just. Like. Her."

"Neil, this thing has got your dau—"

Neil's head turned completely around, the one-eighty twist was gruesome and yet somehow the skin-crawling, soul-chilling *snap* that accompanied the violent motion was worse than anything else. We were all momentarily stunned to stillness, and as if this grisly terror couldn't get any more horrific, the broken body of the father just turned around so that the ghastly head could stare at us all proper; looking at us with its back turned toward everyone simultaneously.

"Neil is home, but Neil is stuck—stuck, stuck, stuck. Neil pushes me out and Neil dies, dies forever and goes where I go; we go together."

His daughter, tears in her eyes, was not a victim, and I could see that clear as day. She was heartbroken, and yet instead of turning into a helpless target, there was an anger burning bright inside of her; don't ask me how I knew, or why it was so clear, but I did, and it was. The Monk smashed a fist clear into and through the table, and yet knew not to move; worse, he looked to me for some kind of cue.

I shoved the paper into Daphne and said, "Go grab the box!" She was stuck between wanting to launch an offensive and join her partner, though to her credit her indiscernible face stayed a blank slate. We exchanged a look and I prayed to whatever deity would take me on that we were soundlessly communicating, that she was aware we needed this box of evidence if we had any hope of turning this debacle into anything resembling any kind of victory for all of us.

"Maria, Neil, Maria, Neil, Maria, Neil—Zachariah!—Maria, Neil and soon—" it said, the creature from the hijacked body of what had to be an absolutely heartbroken father, enjoying itself a little too much; dangling her right in front of our eyes.

Mistake, big mistake.

It lifted her high enough to be level with the desk. High enough for her to reach the bat embedded in the surface of the counter. High enough that her petite hand was able to snare the hilt of it, and while I doubted she had the strength to rip it up, what happened next was such a surprise that a light breeze could have blown me over, even in the middle of all of this madness.

The last sigil didn't just flare up, the thing came to life like a scalding sword in warm butter. She tore it the rest of the way out of the table and sharply drove it into the leg of the once man, now monster. It gave a blood-curdling cry as it gushed blood, a spattering of black mingled with the red, and the way the thing folded in on itself was terribly awkward because of the showmanship it had undertaken when trying to steal our courage from us with the repulsive neck break.

Patrick launched into motion, throwing a devastating shoulder-check into the doubled-over walking corpse and pulverizing it into an eighties era computer, moving so quickly that he snagged the girl before she hit the ground. To my left I saw Daphne excitedly lifting up a box. The real problem was Alphie; he was barely holding on. Beads of sweat were dripping down his face from the exertion of not only manifesting a raw stream of power but cultivating it as well. This extra level of concentrated effort was rapidly depleting his strength, and I knew we had to get him some help quickly or we'd lose him.

"GO!" It was a command to all of them, all at once; Daphne was the last hold up, but Patrick was barreling to the back like a man on a mission, his free hand gathering the woman by the hem of her decorative outfit to half-encourage, half-drag her to safety. Fury pounded in my veins; the remnants of the rage from the girl ignited something in me I hadn't felt since the death of Zachariah and company…since the loss of Maria. I want to say I was above such obvious baiting, but I wasn't, I was really very easily triggered.

The trick was to show them what a mistake it was to trigger me. In my left hand I took the satchels of marbles from my belt, then shoved my right into the breast pocket of my jacket and worked my aching hand into the beautifully crafted glove left to me by my now-dead mentor, the same one whose name they'd used to try to get a rise out of me.

"Alphie," I called.

The Marked One was barely holding on, the spell no longer able to combat what was now a third and fourth Nightgeist trying to power through the door; their howling and jittering laughter was like the loathsome jabbering of any scavenger that's come upon a wounded animal; grating and despicable.

"Light 'em up."

I hadn't seen either of the Marked Ones show any kind of genuine emotion as of yet; surprise and shock yeah, maybe a touch of anger, but all of it professionally restrained.

This wasn't. The sweat soaked face contoured into a strained smile, and I felt the charge of energy change; the room started to warm, and with the momentary reprieve in the spellcasting another two or three Nightgeists managed to get through the doorway and start right at us.

Right where we wanted them.

I dumped both bags of marbles into my gloved hand. For a brief moment I ignited the gauntlet, my focus creating a kinetic net of power to contain the energy erupting from the vessels as I shattered them within it. I shook away the broken glass, a constellation of the powers once housed in the marbles now orbiting my fist and aimed my open palm right at all of them, letting loose a booming funnel of fire.

The blast had so much sheer force that it blew into the door, ripping it off of its hinges; hell it even ripped the hinges off the wall. Voracious for sustenance, the cleansing fire reached for all of the available oxygen, ripping it out of the atmosphere and using it to quite literally fuel itself.

This pent-up rage felt good to release—it was cathartic, and even as the place filled with licking wanton flames, I poured more of myself into it, channeling it directly ahead, utterly indifferent to the fact that the backdraft had brought the carnage I wrought on all of them back on us. I couldn't stop because the cries of my enemy were demanding more of me; it was Alphie who saved me from myself.

Just as the Concrete Monk had done to Daphne, he started dragging me toward the back. The haze of what I had done was hard to sort through, but with a little distance from the fire, my instincts started kicking in transforming me from being some avatar of biblical wrath to a person concerned with survival, fumbling as I chased at his heels. There was a macabre moment when I tore the broken bat from the leg of the now-dead deputy who'd valiantly tried to help us on my way out. The Nightgeist had mangled his body beyond repair—almost beyond recognition in fact. We ducked a few flaming boxes of evidence careening down from the top shelves and were forced to stop so we could hoist a fallen cabinet from our path. In the back room we found the way out; a Concrete Monk sized hole in the back wall.

Patrick had apparently realized there wasn't any alternative and steamrolled right through the damn thing to see all of us to safety. I started to laugh but was cut short as I realized the stupidity of laughing in the center of an inferno by way of a wisp of still-burning paper landing on the back of my neck.

***

As crazy as the night sky being ablaze with a menacing thicket of smoke billowing out of the collapsing building was, it was actually the creepy quiet that unnerved me. Pushing deeper into the backstreets, I herded us into an alleyway so that we could get a good view of the destroyed evidence room and take inventory. Daphne was panting, and interestingly Alphie had taken the box from her arms to check on her; not methodically either, it was less robotic and more…concerned.

The girl, fresh off stabbing her demon-snatched father, fought out of Patrick's grip and when we realized what a mistake it was to let her stand on her own two feet because the smoke-hacking teenager immediately started back toward the hell we'd just escaped, with no intent other than violence. I could feel it emanating from her just as sure as the palpability of her anger had clued me into the fact she wasn't going to stand idly by when being held hostage. Hacking out what was left of an already damaged lung, I managed to suck down enough air to talk.

"We have to get out of here, we need to get somewhere safe for the night so we can figure all of this out and get back to the others."

"You," I turned to the lip-quivering, damn-near snarling youth. "What's your name?"

"Cat," she snapped.

"How old are you?"

"Thirteen."

Something twisted in me, but I continued. "Do you have anyone we can call?"

She turned from my question to try and head toward the blazing building again; giving chase, Patrick managed to rope her up a second time and luckily, I caught her wrist before realizing it was a feint, because her other hand unsheathed my bat-dagger—luckily, it wasn't too difficult to intercept her hand, quick and clever as it may have been. Prying it out of her grip, I silenced the Marked Ones with an upraised hand while I stomped back to the mouth of the alley; the cascading song of sirens filled the night air and I realized that we were on a clock, which was nothing new, but still an unwanted bonus to compound this mess.

"We need somewhere that…oh. Of course."

At the end all I had to do was turn my head to the left and there it was: an unmistakable building from my recent past, staring me smack-dab in the face. In the thick of all this, I hadn't even realized that we were a block or two away from it, and while I didn't think I had a plan when trying to navigate us through the maze of backroads behind the industrial area of downtown, maybe I had.

Or maybe someone else had a hand in all of this.

"Come on."

"Where are we going?" Daphne asked.

"To church."

***

It was timeless, not ornately decorated, but I think to me that's what gave it an ageless quality. It looked strong, not powerful: reliable and constant. A staple of a neighborhood that was as old as the city itself. Maria and her father had gone there, and when we got to its doors, we found one of them ajar, with a soft light coming from inside.

We entered to find the place empty. Cat was falling apart, but we were off the streets and this place felt like a sanctuary. Everyone visibly relaxed; that is, until they turned to the door as it closed behind us, and they stared in unison. We could practice for the next year and not have lined our timing up that impeccably.

The Concrete Monk adopted a fighting posture (not a stance, there's a difference) and the Marked Ones, less subtle, fanned out to more effectively fight in tandem as they'd been so well trained to do—I did nothing but turn around. If the priest noticed any of them it didn't appear to register, and his tongue-in-cheek, coy smirk was directed at me.

Cat, on the other hand, sprinted down the aisle right past us and right into the arms of… an angel? Truth be told, I never really thought too long on what Justin was.

He was just a friend, a fact I realized more consciously as he gave her a hug.

Cat was a little too old to be picked up in an embrace, and yet it fit. Almost instantly she was at ease, and I wondered if this was some kind of innate calming power; wondered as I realized that I too, in fact, was surprisingly at ease.

"I am so, so, so sorry, my child. I know you'd just found him again; this must be really hard for you."

Cat was crying, but not audibly, it was muffled by her burrowing into his shoulder, but I could see her nod.

He sat her down on a pew and helped her call her grandmother, holding her hand through the phone call while the rest of us waited quietly, resting our exhausted bodies. The trauma was no doubt a factor, but I found it amusing that nobody seemed to pick-up on the fact that Justin was already aware of what was happening ... at least to some degree. After she'd told her grandmother where she was and hung up, her silent sobs returned. Father Handy stroked her hair and she slowly succumbed to sleep, the only possible escape from her grief. The other four of us maintained a respectful and tired silence. I was probably the least patient one in the bunch— the Marked Ones looked like they were well accustomed to long periods of silence, and Patrick was a monk after all. Even so, I managed to wait it out, knowing that this moment was worth it. Finally, Father Handy gently extricated himself, carefully laying her down on the pew and using the precious bag she had held on to as a pillow.

The gang mustered to our feet, despite our exhaustion.

"We need to talk," he said.

"Confession is more of a Catholic thing," I countered, trying anything to lighten the crushing darkness of our circumstances.

"Potato, potato."

"You know you're supposed to pronounce the word differently the first and second time you say it, otherwise you just sound like an idiot."

We didn't stand eye to eye, he was maybe five inches taller than me, thin and bald. Like, well groomed and head shining bald not bald-*ing*. The urge to hug him was mutual, don't ask me how I knew, but each of us seemed to just know that our barbs weren't a personal thing.

"Father Handsy."

"Really put in some overtime for that gem, hm?"

"So there I was, an artificer, of which there's like… five in all the of the continental Americas, fighting off darkling monsters doing the bidding of the Abyss because something wonky is going on with the In-Between when suddenly, in the midst of everything, I stumble across some prodigy who can not only do what it took me two years to learn to do —badly, I might add, and she can do it instantly better than I can, and we just happen to be a block from the very church where we first met when you started meddling in all this."

"Heavy handed as this implication is, I *really* must insist I don't know what you're talking about."

"You know about the In-Between, and all this shit that's landing at my feet."

"Janzen," Alphie cut into the conversation just in time because I felt an all-out tirade on the tip of my tongue and those tended to get me off track worse than the opportunity to drop an obscure fact into an awkward conversation. "Him? I mean…he's a Priest." Alphie's attempt to conceal his condescension was weak, and it was made worse by the fact that he was trying really hard to hide it. You see, in our circle, the only absolutely ridiculous thing was the fact that the Abrahamic faiths had taken off, and he was trying not to say outright that this guy didn't have any idea what was really going on.

"Alphie, trust me on this one, pump the brakes."

"Don't you think we should be trying to get real answers, like why it is your friends think a Blind Judge attacked them, rather than…" he said, motioning up and down at the priest, seeming to just gloss over the fact that not a minute prior he'd gotten the drop on four seasoned fighters on high alert by simply appearing behind us. "…You know, wasting our time?"

"You're tired, Ricky." The priest touched his forehead with a finger, and all three of my companions fell to the ground, soundly sleeping before they hit it and not at all disturbed by the fact that there was nothing to slow their descent.

"Ricky, eh?" I was unsurprised by the show. As it stood, I was currently banking that the priest was the guy the heavy hitters would still back off of. He wouldn't directly help, he was more content to offer up some cryptic nonsense about duality to me—although to be truthful, the trinket he'd left me the last time I was here was a major help, so I owed him. If I had to take a leap of faith, I would say he actually liked me.

Not cared about me exactly but liked me. Given the current state of affairs, I'd take what I could get.

"What's up, Janzen?" he asked with off-putting sincerity, which took all my bluster. It was the second time we'd stood across from each other like this, and there was one other impression I got pretty distinctly from this curious entity: he felt for me.

Sorrowful wasn't exactly the right word for his expression but it was close, his sunken shoulders making him appear as somewhat mortal for a moment.

"All of this is connected, isn't it?" I asked.

A pursed mouth accompanied a sidelong look.

"I'm never going to get in front of this with them seeming to be able to take pages out of my playbook, man, you got anything to feed me on this one? I'll even take a riddle or two."

"I think you know I can't…"

"Can't, or won't?" I asked.

"I can help with one thing."

That perked me up, and at his beckoning gesture I moved a step closer and squared myself up to him.

"Close your eyes and breathe; four seconds in, five second hold and then—"

There was a *pop* and a crack. I felt the searing flash of pain start at my nose and just haul ass all over my face. He'd set my nose, and not kindly. I lost myself to a string of curses, stomping around and holding my face in the aftermath. Calming down, I worked my jaw and nose and wiped some of the water out of my eyes.

"Dude, a warning would have been nice…"

"It would have, but if I told you what I was going to do, you would have known ahead of time and been able to try to stop me."

I rubbed my face for half a second, and then I got hit with an epiphany harder than the nose-breaking punch that made this all possible. This slick, double-speaking Socrates just helped me stumble over an almost painfully obvious realization that made my entire stomach sink.

Somebody finked. Snitched. Two-timed us. We had a rat in our patchwork ship that was so unworthy of the sea I wasn't even sure we'd even be able to set sail long enough to get the chance to sink.

"Grandma!" Cat suddenly cried. I wasn't sure when she'd woken up, so I jumped at the sudden outburst.

I turned my astonished face toward the doorway where there stood a woman who looked to be in her early-to-mid sixties. Her style was reminiscent of the flower power thing, and while older now she was still very pretty. The gut-wrenching possibility of one of the people in my tribe turning on us was eased somewhat by the sight of the emotional reunion as Cat buried herself in her grandmother's embrace, though when the woman looked upward at me all that changed.

With eyes close to the brink of letting loose tears she gasped, wrapping Cat tighter in a hug without taking her eyes off me.

Everyone was taking the three snoring, prone people impeding the walkway of a church really well.

The woman stood right in front of me, her tear-bright eyes gawking at me in a kind of awe that was more than a little uncomfortable; I was startled when I turned and saw that the priest, Father Handy, was next to me.

"You're still here?" I said incredulously, reaching out and poking him in the arm just to see if he was some kind of mirage.

"He wouldn't dare pull any of that Houdini stuff on me," she said in a light reprimand, and stepped into the authentically warm embrace that was waiting. Even more startling was the very grandparent-y pat to his cheek that was tolerated by the godling. "It's good to see you, my old friend."

She was a sage, and she was somehow juggling more than I'd ever had to and did so with an inarticulable grace. While giving respect to her… friend, it was hard to miss that she was openly staring at me with every glance, lingering a few seconds longer than would be considered appropriate.

"I am sorry about Neil, truly," Father Handy said. I seconded the condolences with a clunky nod.

"He had a good heart, and my daughter did love him very much. It's a shame, he was doing so much better."

I didn't dig into the story and given the context of how she spoke about her daughter, I was given the distinct impression she was no longer with us. My eyes lifted to the girl with the ancient-looking eyes. That was rough, and yet she was made of some of the toughest stuff I'd ever seen; while I didn't know how I knew that, I had no doubt.

"Thank you," her grandmother said, reaching out to me and giving my arm a grab. She used it to draw me closer and give me a long, clutching hug. It was more than gratitude, but I couldn't quite say what. I looked at Justin, whose fond smile was disarming, to say the least.

"You should take her home; she's had a rough day—"

"No." Cat was right up on me, and even as the two more senior and far better put together of the group stepped back, I didn't give her an inch. It might seem strange to some, but to me I was going to give her the respect of my full attention and part of that was not being cowed by a tough talk.

"You," she said, and for the first time tonight I didn't immediately seek cover after someone said that. "You're going after the people who did this, aren't you?"

I searched the faces of the other two; the grandmother was trying to maintain an expression of indifference, but there was some kind of reluctance there. Justin was attuned to everything happening, wrapping the woman in a comforting half-hug as if trying to stay her.

"I am."

"I'm coming with you."

"No, you're not."

She bristled, ready to launch into some kind of soapboxing sermon, I could tell because it had all the hallmarks of one of my own diatribes. I ignored the inclination to lean down so we were eye-to-eye; this wasn't the time to placate or kindly condescend to her.

"If you come with me, this isn't going to work, you'll slow me down and I'll have to account for you, which means my attention will be split. If you come with me, the people who did this to your dad are going to get away, and worse, we might end up dying trying to set right all the shit they mucked up."

Beyond her years, she was chewing on all this, doing an admirable job of combating the swells of outrage I saw in her that with anyone else, damn their age, would have probably boiled over by now and spilled out everywhere making a fine mess for all of us.

"You can't stop me."

And there it was, she was right; I had seen that kind of conviction, it blew way past determination and fell squarely into something so much more life-changing. She'd just declared a mission that would alter the trajectory of her life forever, and she'd done so with the kind of soul-shaping dogma that gave birth to real champions of good.

"You're thirteen, right?"

Bristling at the question with a matching sneer, she muttered, "Yeah."

I palmed my face, trying to knead some of the tension out of it only to flinch from the pain of my recently-set nose. I took the previous advice and drew a long breath, held it for longer, and finally bellowed out a sigh. I'm not tall, so kneeling made her a hand higher than me, but I retrieved a business card out of my wallet and presented it to her, with an ultimatum attached.

"This is me. I can teach you how to do this right, I can teach you how to be effective and I can teach you to help prevent this from ever happening to other people; and if none of that interests you, I can teach you how to seek out revenge. So here's the deal: if I am alive in fou—" The grandmother stiffened, luckily out of the line of sight of the caustic kid and when I surreptitiously slid a look her way, she hiked her thumb up just a little. "—five years, I will help you; but until then, you can't do shit. You can study, you can train, you can practice, but if I find out you're out there wandering the streets playing vigilante, the deal is off, and not only is it off but I'll make sure you're blacklisted from the whole goddamn city."

She was quiet for a long time, as long as some of those crazy-long lived creatures I dealt with on the daily. It was impressive for anyone who had to tap-dance along the mortal coil, even more so when it came from a fresh-faced teenager.

"Five years and you train me, you take me on, no excuses?"

"Not a one, you've got my word." I watched her turning the all-white business card that simply read *Circle Protection* with a number written across the back. She studied it and lifted her head to give her grandmother a solicitous look.

The grandmother swallowed what had to be a world of dread and just nodded, and Cat turned back to me.

"Five years."

"Five years," I agreed.

Everyone allowed the strange solemness of what passed to do so, something that had with it more weight than I had yet to know. Standing up, I muted a groan as my wobbly knee cried out; it was tough to not even be thirty and already falling apart. The woman and the priest gave each other a knowing smile and a quick hug, and before she and the girl started out, she paused and turned to me.

"Thank you… Janzen," she said, testing the feel of the name with a smile that seemed almost nostalgic. "I like that. Janzen. It fits. Try to keep your mouth from getting you into too much trouble, hmm?" Curling her granddaughter to her flank, the hellion with a spine of steel was looking more what somebody would come to expect: she looked like a tired, sad and scared child, the need to put on a face now washed away with the warming comfort that came from sharing such a small space with a loved one.

"It was good seeing you again," she said.

Again? Before I could ask her to clarify what that meant, my line of sight was blocked by the priest.

"Hey, what did she mean by that?"

"Oh," he said with a downright silly face, way too entertained by my panicked confusion, openly mocking the fact I had asked him a direct question hoping he would answer it. I was too busy trying to look around him to notice that his finger was headed right for my forehead.

I think I managed to get "Son of a…" out of my mouth before the world went dark.

CHAPTER 12

Snake in the Grass

"What was that?" Daphne asked, somewhere between bewilderment and anger. We'd woken up to a confused and frustrated parish priest who had kindly but firmly insisted that we leave as he wasn't sure how we'd entered the church in the middle of the night. He seemed happy that we hadn't stolen anything, didn't appear to be on drugs, and hadn't broken any locks or windows, but wanted us gone post haste. After apologizing profusely, we left and regrouped on the street. Ignoring her question I countered with my own…

"—What do you mean there's been no Blind Judge in our world for a century?"

"Well…exactly what I said, to our knowledge, there has not been, nor is there now any blind judge in this world." Her tone was a mix of not being sure what to make of the question—not knowing that we were told that one of these mythical monstrosities had been sent after us—and the shock of what she'd just been through. Marked Ones were capable enforcers partly because they had the unique ability to identify the signature of almost any power and pinpoint its origin. It's what made them incredibly effective at hunting down fugitives. The fact that Justin hadn't set off any of their alarms was baffling. He'd even been able to put them to sleep with just a single touch to the forehead. When they woke, they felt completely rested—like they had eaten a huge meal after a full body massage and had twelve solid hours of sleep. But the most perplexing thing of all was the story itself.

"Donovan told us that He, Gale and Xander got shredded by a Blind Judge—that's what he said, but the Marked ones say that to their knowledge there is no Blind Judge here in our world, so we're not even sure what we're dealing with. It's a very strange tale we've been told, and there are pieces of the story that are starting to come apart," I said. The thing is this; if these two aren't in the know about one of those being here, it could mean that this is an unsanctioned operation, and if it isn't a Blind Judge, it could be something equally bad or even worse. A can of worms with two really bad possibilities. Whatever it is, a lot of this isn't making any sense. I hesitated because even though I felt well rested, my mental and emotional fatigue hadn't been completely wiped away by my pew-side nap, and I wasn't sure if I wanted to divulge this last bit.

These people had fought off Abyssal ghosts in a burning building with me though, and we'd all managed to extend a lot of blind trust in the other. We'd started with the misconception that we were enemies in all of this, but time told a different tale. Playing it close to the chest was one thing, but they all had a lot of skin in the game, figuratively and literally. It wasn't right to keep them in the dark.

"The only way they knew where we would be was if someone had told them. If Frank hadn't defected, we might not have anything to go off of. Somebody on our side of the fence is playing us."

Everybody went silent. We were four separate entities, each with our own agenda. It wasn't like we all belonged to one big happy family. Patrick was a freelancer; a kind of monster masher that was capable but didn't usually get involved in this kind of thing. Alphie and Daphne were bound to those they served, regardless of whether they liked us or not. They had a duty to see those obligations through—they didn't owe us or our people anything.

"We should get the car," Patrick said, breaking the tension. I handed over the keys and sat down in the middle of the sidewalk to start digging into the box of evidence to see if there was anything we could mine out of this to help us figure out what was really going on and save our asses. Unexpectedly, Daphne offered to join Patrick and the pair of them set off.

Alphie and I watched them leave, and then I started scouring the contents of the box. We hadn't broken bread or bullshitted over a beer, but we'd burned down a building together so that was something.

"Can someone duplicate a Blind Judge?" I said.

He drew a harsh breath between pursed lips. The question felt above his pay grade, but it couldn't hurt to ask.

"Not the Unet, but there's been a rumor about the Tribe of the Masarou…." The enforcer didn't quite trail off but pivoted. "The House of Unet judge has a unique architecture, and equally unique power source, so from what I know it's impossible to duplicate."

"And the other side?"

"Well, the Masarou—"

"The goblins?"

He nodded, having the courtesy to dumb it down for me. "Goblins use pieces of specimens from the Abyss and the Veil, stitch them together and then reanimate them. They harvest all that stuff. They keep a lot of creatures on hand so that they can make more whenever they want to, though it's supposed to be forbidden. If I had to guess I'd have to say no, I don't think they could duplicate it, but they could certainly make something similar…without question."

"Ok, that helps. Now Donovan said it was the other tribe that made them in the first place…."

"Donovan, the exile of House Unet?" Abruptly interrupting with a flat affect and a very controlled voice, it was easy to see that there was a lot more to that question than just the question itself.

"I'm guessing. He's a gnome, a Tinkerer."

"Yes, that's the one. Well he would know. He was among the most respected in the House for a long, long time before becoming an outcast. My understanding is that before being ousted he was one of the key architects of the Dreadnought, so I can't imagine him not knowing one when he saw it."

"What's the Dreadnought like?" I asked as I came across photo albums in the box. Those didn't help me, but they did remind me that Frank was a person once. It's weird, when you deal with death so often, you can kind of forget that each one of these soon-to-be-forgotten people once had whole lives. They leave behind an entire world all their own, and the effects of their departure probably hit a lot of people really hard. Frank was handsome enough, he seemed to have fun in these snapshots, and it looked like he had a big family to boot. With uncharacteristic reverence I put the album aside, and while it wouldn't serve what I was trying to accomplish, I made a mental note to track down his family and pass it on.

"It's a construct, a magical golem that's…" he trailed off. The source of his dawdling was tough to get a fix on, so I just waited him out. "It's impressive. Resistant or outright impervious to magic, not only can it defeat it, but it can absorb it and redirect it. It's said to be made of an unbreakable metal, the same used to forge Excalibur."

"Weakness?" I said, uncharacteristically ignoring the mention of Ex-freaking-calibur.

He gave me a contemptuous look that reminded me that, come the terminus of this, we might not be on the same side of the fight.

"Anything man, anything at all? I'm way up a creek, without a paddle or a clue."

After a moment's pause, he answered, "It takes three people to control it, so it's not as… quick to react as the Masarou Judge, because it's a team that's regulating the thing. I don't know if I would call that a weakness though. Even at half speed they're incredibly fast, nearly indestructible, and the only way to beat one is to beat it down until the hinges come undone. I don't know of many things that can take on a twelve-foot-tall metal monster that's impervious to pain and doesn't get tired, do you?"

"So it's either a patchwork beast made up of the most lethal killer creatures in all the known worlds, or a big-ass indestructible terminator being run by 3 powerhouse magical types. Excellent."

It was such a beatdown of bad news that I couldn't even get excited that I found the one guy in all of modern America who still had kept a journal that he wrote in daily; it even had chapters dedicated to the turning of his coven, the plan to usher in a quasi-apocalypse with that black-souled Goddess from the Abyss. He even described in horrific detail how they planned to gut Maria and use the budding power inside of her to create a portal that would hold a threshold between our worlds open. Carefully reorganizing the rest of the content, I saw the car coming around the bend.

"So you and Daphne, eh? I saw that look…" Cheesy as my grin was, it had nothing on the exaggerated nudge I offered up.

"Who?" he asked matter-of-factly, and I realized that I had named her without anyone else present.

"Uh… I mean Delta, I just… It seemed like you cared about her as more than just a partner."

"Oh, that." He seemed…not exactly sheepish, but maybe ashamed? Seemed a strange reaction to me, but their life was a militant one and I had to wonder if mere feelings—let alone fraternizing or dating—were even allowed.

"Forbidden love? They frown on that kind of thing?"

Alphie gave a little smile and shook his head. "It's a life. A life with purpose, and it isn't easy, but it's not awful. And no, it's nothing like that, I mean I do love her, but she's my sister. We're not supposed to emote much, and most of our past they 'trained' out of us. But I can't shake the feeling of responsibility that I have for her."

I knew there were a million ways to go with this—it was a potential bonding and an unanticipated, revealing intimacy. The dip in his admittedly hard-to-gauge tone when he talked of "training" would have gotten by a lot of people, but I had an ear for that sort of thing; still, I wasn't sure if I was the right person to speak on it. Finally, I settled on what I knew best.

"So she's single?"

"I'll actually kill you."

While not proud, I used the momentary distraction of levity to covertly pocket the journal that would serve as evidence for all of this. Nothing against Alpha, but I knew the type; we could be amicable enough, but if the order came down, he would take my life in a moment.

Not only did I know the type, I ran a business with one.

We both couldn't help but smile while we poured ourselves into the car and headed back to Kaycee's shop to reconvene with the rest of the group to try and make sense of this mess.

***

Kaycee's magic emporium was bustling with life. Inside we had the whole cast and crew of our hodgepodge tribe. Max was dutifully going from person to person, regardless of disposition, stature or temperament getting his obligatory pets. The fearless little pitbull curiously ended up beside Sam who seemed the keenest to dole out affection to the canine.

Max was never a great judge of character—the dog basically picked me instead of the other way around, but that's for another time.

The car ride had been tense, though to be fair, that was expected. There was a clear divide between all of us, despite what we'd gone through. A parting when it came to sides, and whether we liked it or not, there was a good chance we could all end up opposite one another if this came down to a fight.

Alphie and Daphne's departure was awkward and reminded me of a far blunter version of how Grove conducted himself. When Kaycee came outside with Max on her heels, her affable manner had been replaced by a more businesslike affect. Tail wagging, Max circled Alphie and then dodged when the sorcerer reached down to pet him, preferring to barrel into Daphne's leg which made her laugh. Max settled beside Kaycee, giving me, his owner and provider, a disinterested once-over. Daphne deliberated going over to give the goofy dog some affection until Kaycee cut her off with a terse "Bye."

She was not normally abrasive, but was less amicable than most times, since she thought they might pose a threat. I shrugged helplessly while watching the two shift from unsure, socially stunted soldiers to the cold-eyed, hard-bodied maulers they were.

I'd forgotten they tried to kill me, so there was that too. Their stares drilled into the unmoving magic shop proprietor before both promptly turned away and started down the road.

Kaycee, Patrick and I stood there until they were comfortably out of earshot.

"Glad that wasn't awkward or anything," I said.

Kaycee's flat look fell on me.

"What? I like them."

"They tried to kill you."

"Nobody's perfect."

Patrick chuckled at the exchange. Kaycee tried to steal his own bemusement by way of the same glare she'd used to control me, but it had no effect—he just laughed.

"Can you get Grove, and Xancer if he's up to it?" I asked.

Kaycee looked ready to muster the resolve to try to stay, notwithstanding the indignant twitch she made at being asked to go and fetch someone. She seemed ready to insist on involving herself, but I firmly shut that down.

"Call Donovan, too, and then if you could give us some privacy, please."

Premeditated consideration kept Kaycee from outright leaving. She wiped her hands on an apron that just made them messier before holding me in one more stare—a stare that was somehow sorry and scornful all at once.

Told you I had a way with women.

She slipped inside quietly, giving me a moment of solitude. I shared the silence with the Concrete Monk who, true to his M.O. remained steady and still, standing next to me while somehow merging into the background. It was an enviable talent that he had, this ability to show support by proximity alone, as if he exuded some kind of calm that penetrated the consciousness of those near him. I don't think it was as simple as saying that he was at ease or even at peace with himself; maybe it was also because he was at ease with, and in the world around him.

It was hard to say, and I spent too much time thinking about it. My wandering thoughts were scrambled when I heard the shop's bell chime. It sounded off sweetly for the soldier and baritone for the Rougarou as they came inside.

Xander's heavy heels were dragging uncharacteristically, but he managed to remain upright with Grove beside him on standby to offer a broad shoulder should he need assistance. Their faces turned to me, attentive and resolute, and the realization struck me that these powerful, capable, good men were looking to *me* for orders. I felt like an impostor for a moment—*how did I become this person, don't they know better?*—but I locked that shit down and reminded myself that nobody had asked for any of this, and we each had our role to fill regardless. This was mine, and there was no room for self-doubt or deprecation.

Donovan shut the door of our own shop across the way, carefully locking it behind him, and then whispered some kind of incantation to wake the rest of my runework for extra measure.

"What's up?" he asked after joining our small group.

Discretion was not my forte but given the circumstance I didn't have a plethora of other options. I didn't want to just turn this into a witch hunt all of a sudden—no pun intended—but moving forward with a rat fink traitor in our midst wasn't going to fly either.

"We've got a snitch inside" I said. Impassive faces stared back at me, so I drove the point home adding "somebody is betraying us."

That hit the mark. Xander snarled, and I caught a pensive look from Grove who I could tell wasn't exercising doubt but caution. It was subtle, but I could see the difference. Usually we were in step with each other, but I couldn't quite sync up with whatever it was that he was mulling.

Donovan didn't blink and immediately said, "It's obviously the Stalker. We should put her down."

I was all for intuition, which is why I wasn't all that big on evidence, but there were two issues here. One, I was wrong so often they might as well rename mistakes "Janzens," and two? I was the antithesis of my mentor. On the one hand it was good to see some remnants of emotion—even humanity in him, but on the other, it kind of robbed me of one of my best thinking resources; an overly pragmatic asshole was a lot more helpful than you might think.

"Well hold on," I said.

"Do we even have any evidence—anything to go on?" Xander wanted to know.

Apparently, someone had clued him into what was happening, since he'd been unconscious for this latest episode. Dipping my hand into the pocket of my old leather jacket I managed to get my sore fingers to wrap around the spine of Frank's journal when Grove caught my eye.

"Gone, they destroyed it." I said, lying seamlessly because it's what I used to do daily. "They got there before us and ambushed us."

That stole the air from the room, and we found ourselves once again in a sullen silence.

Xander's face flashed with discomfort and frustration, and he turned and stormed back to Kaycee's to confront the stalker. As the door flew open, I caught a glimpse of the scene inside. The Stalker was casually petting my dog, a contented smile on her lips while she watched Johnny B. bring to life several laid-about dolls and action figures with the simple strumming of his guitar.

"He's a bard!" I said, lighting up at the realization. My awestruck smile was short-lived as Grove elbowed me out of the way, moving to impose himself between the mastodon of a doorman and the entrance to Kaycee's shop.

"*Xander*," Donovan snapped. He had a way about him, diminutive yet commanding. Bristling, the doorman looked at each of us with a predatory eye.

"We don't even know if it's her," I said.

Donovan's tone was icy. "Don't be an idiot Janzen, this isn't the time for your juvenile notions of loyalty or your flawed belief that there's good in everyone."

"Nor is it the time for you to be playing armchair shrink just to get your way. Check that shit at the door, Donovan. I know you'd miss my flawed juvenile sensibilities if I were gone," I said. "And even if it *is* her, how about we try *not* tipping our hand, hm? I'm a little tired of being one step behind here."

It was early, everyone was deeply fatigued, and this thing was about to get a lot more complicated. One, if there was no Blind Judge, that punched a massive hole in this whole theory, which I didn't feel comfortable bringing up because I was getting all kinds of uncertainty coming off of Grove. Donovan was still holding on to some semblance of civility but was rawer than I had ever seen him. Xander was about as expected, and Patrick seemed more interested in staying firmly on the sidelines. In fact, the realization that the monk was still there was a kind of testament to his ability to pass as low-key and inconspicuous.

I felt like if this thing was all going to come together, by the time the bow was tied it would be around my casket. Kneading my temples to ward off an oncoming headache, I thanked myself for only acquiring a single concussion in this most recent melee.

"We need to regroup," I said. The bit about the Marked Ones being thoroughly confused about the supposed appearance of a Blind Judge I kept to myself. It's not that they just dismissed the possibility—they did so emphatically, and with real surprise at the very notion. Seeing as only Kaycee and the monk had met up with them at this point, it was probably better to keep my mouth shut on all of that. There was so much out of place with this thing that I felt like I would need a sounding board to bounce everything off of—even after I wrote it all down and saw it in black and white.

I touched Grove's arm to get his eyes on me. "Take Xander over to our place. Set him up where we have Gale."

That noticeably calmed the Rougarou. I knew it couldn't have been easy to manage him when he came back to consciousness and wasn't allowed to go over and see her, but as expected, Grove had his ways and held him off. Turning around, I shuffled to intercept him when he attempted to go inside.

"Around back, big man. Down through the sewer."

"And that traitor bitch?" he snarled. I thought Donovan's reaction had been visceral, but it was only now that I realized how wrong I was. This was raw and relentless, and I was wearing a face full of spittle to prove it. Leave it to Xander to add some perspective to my inner monologue.

"Xander," I said, wiping my cheeks and then sighing. "Go, see to Gale." My exhaustion took some of the anger out of him, and to be fair it was tough not to be a bit deflated. We were no closer to figuring any of this out then when we started; and even if I had any kind of answer, it all seemed futile because of what we were up against. Grudgingly, and with Grove's assistance, Xander got moving. Grove kept his eyes on me a beat longer than usual, letting me know that there was something to be said, and that now was not the time or the place. They vanished into the alley.

"You want to risk your life being overly trusting, you go right ahead, but this isn't about you anymore. It's about us, all of us, and we're trusting you to do the right thing, Janzen Robinson."

There was something in the way that statement was delivered that made me more mad than reasonable, which is why I fired off an unfair dagger in the wake of his own condescension. "Why don't you let me do my job, Donovan of the Unet."

I watched the first human expression I'd ever seen on his normally impassive face. That one hit the mark—and it hurt—but before I could muster the decency to apologize, he'd turned on his heel and started back toward my store. I thought to caution him against being so cavalier with his whereabouts, but I must have insulted him soundly enough for him to have forgotten about that.

"And what's your verdict?" My tired eyes sought out the wallflower with a front row seat to it all. He was contemplative and choosy with his words, so I tried to make it a lot easier. "This is heavy shit, so we can call it square and consider the pizza a wash. Your call."

"Yeah…because you have such a crack team firing on all cylinders ready to take up the fight that you don't need me to stay in any longer."

Hearing someone who defied the seriousness of a situation with some offbeat humor made my heart happy. Laughing felt good.

"You still need my help?" he asked. It was a damn decent thing for him to do, standing beside me when we kept coming across such monumental headaches.

"Yeah."

"Then I'll see you tomorrow." He shoved off the wall into a swaying walk, and the shepherd of the homeless cocked a half-wave at me before starting down the road. He dug out a crumpled bag of sunflower seeds, tossed some in his mouth and started to whistle on his way.

Kaycee met me at the door, halting my momentum and blocking me from coming inside.

"You should rest."

"Not yet." My bleary, blood-shot eyes were fixed on the Stalker. She was within arm's reach of the children, and my unfaithful mutt who was well aware of where I was had yet to even dislodge himself from her lap.

"Go home."

"Kay, look, I ha—"

"Did you ask him?" Dani, Kaycee's oldest kid, suddenly appeared out of nowhere, nearly bowling us over with excitement.

Kaycee nudged me a little too hard in a still-soft spot.

"Huh?"

Dani wasn't deterred.

"Mom said I could get my own Max if…" she said, tugging and twisting her shirt into knots while she stuttered through it.

"...If I asked what is, uhm, the biggest uh challenge to owning a Max." She eyeballed her mother, who'd coached her up on this and was mouthing the script that they'd both agreed on and obviously rehearsed. It was adorable.

"A Max?"

"She means a pitbull," Kaycee clarified.

"Oh, well… People tend to get out of your way pretty quickly, which is a bummer for Max, but I dig it." I looked to my surrogate sister, where she was waiting for me to take the question a tad bit more seriously. Dani laughed, so that was a win, but out of respect for both Kaycee and what she was trying to do here—install her daughter with a valuable life lesson—I elaborated.

"You have to remember that if you get a dog like Max, people are going to think the worst of them right off the bat. For so long, people have said that these dogs are bad and that they'll just end up hurting you. Constantly working against this frustrating bias, this crummy prejudice is probably the biggest challenge of having one—kinda like…"

"Like you," Dani chimed in brightly, which brought me back to an ugly adolescence spent hustling on the street. Surviving amongst monsters, constantly trying to keep myself from becoming one, and pigeonholed into the unfair assumption that we were all the same. "'Cause mom said you have bad tattoos and a stupid face, and you used to always be in trouble."

"Not what I was thinking exactly, but yeah, like me I guess." There were some refutable, albeit true, quips in there that I wanted an opportunity to come back at, but she suddenly stole the spring from my step with her next insight….

"And Sam!"

The announcement of her name garnered the Stalker's attention. Her alien eyes softened for the child some, before returning her rapt and almost innocent gaze back to the sideshow being put on by the bard (was nobody as excited as I am about this?).

"She's super nice even if everyone says she's a monster."

"Yeah…" Dani got a knowing nod from her deceptively innocent mother, the cue she needed to be getting back to the playroom.

I sat in stupefied silence.

"I'll go home and rest," I finally said.

Kaycee gave my back a big pat on the way out, and the bell gave me a lowly and almost embarrassingly plain ding on my way out. That's the thing, there was nothing really distinct or special about me. I'm Not trying to sell myself as some kind of shortchanged hero here, it was just the fact of the matter.

And right before the door closed, my wily mutt managed to muscle through and fall into step by my side. In spite of myself, my smile was as sincere as the life lesson my friend just force-fed me.

CHAPTER 13

The knock on my door was crisp and commanding. Not demanding, that would be sharp and repetitive. You might think this isn't important, and that's because your life has never hinged on the cold read you just made on someone during some back-alley deal you shouldn't be making in the first place. Especially not before you're a teenager, but starvation is a hell of a motivator.

This knock belonged to an authority figure. Grove was sound asleep, but Max had groggily managed to muster enough energy to open an eye. I rustled the blinds open and got a glimpse of the wonder twins standing outside, inked up and dressed down. I pulled a theatrically grumpy face, and despite themselves each started to allow the shadow of a smile.

I retreated from the window to shrug into my clothes and gear up. I double-checked all of my Artificed accessories, grabbed my armor-like leather jacket and finally strapped my metal, heavily ensorcelled baseball bat across my back before setting my bat-dagger into its holster. Eat your heart out Bruce Wayne.

As I opened the door, Max slipped out like a fish and almost bowled Daphne over. She was trying her damndest to fixate on me and my weaponry but kept dropping her gaze down to the dog with muted hopefulness.

"Oh my god, pet the damn dog," I said. "We're probably gonna have to all fight to the death soon, let's get it in while we can."

Everyone was trying to make sense of the muddled mess of it all when Max, ever the moment maker, reared up and put his paws right on Daphne's stomach, stretching his head up to demand attention. She giggled, an adolescent sound; it made me wonder about the working theory that people ceased emotional development once they'd been burdened by trauma. She cradled his massive head in her suddenly small hands; they were riddled with thick, gnarled calloused and deep grievous scars, but they were put right to use stroking his velvet-soft fur and scratching behind his floppy little ears. Her laugh was juvenile, innocent and joyous. Despite her joy, she offered the goofy dope of a dog over to her brother, who shook his head and held his ground. In his defense, this wasn't an ideal situation, but his terse headshake was met with open defiance as she rustled the dog's ears between her fingers.

"I've got two-day-old coffee, but it's better than three-day-old coffee."

"Why don't you just make a new pot?" Alphie asked, genuinely perplexed. "Never mind," he said, wisely cutting me off before I could try to come back with some inane witticism. "You need to hand Gale over to us." In line with his firm tone, Daphne gently removed Max's paws from her, and her posture said that she was back to business, albeit somewhat reluctantly.

"Who?" It was my turn to seem honestly confused.

"This isn't a joke."

"Good, because your delivery was flat, and the set-up was ju—"

"*Janzen*," Daphne cut in. Her brows were furrowed, not finding any of this amusing.

I was glad she interrupted, because truthfully, I didn't have a lot of energy left, and this schtick could be as exhausting to me as it was to everyone else. Honestly, they looked as taxed as me.

"I can come in her stead, but she's unable to. That's the truth. And what is this, a formal request?"

".. If you go in her stead…." Even their skepticism seemed reluctant. "You should really just give her to us."

"Would if I could, and I already figured standing in wasn't a really wise thing to do but I am trying to stay in character, so no— won't tell you where she is."

Alphie looked from me, to the door, and back to me.

"Yeah, 'cause I am stupid enough to keep her inside my own shop that's openly advertised on a card I hand out freely." The best lies have a lot of truth in them, the kind of thing that can fool anyone or thing: a mentalist reading micro-expression, an outdated machine or even another liar. They seemed a little doubtful that anyone would be that dense, and this incredulousness is what I was banking on. People too often didn't appreciate the predictability of stupidity and underestimated it. Plus, I had a hell of a poker face.

"Let me in, then."

"No."

The nonchalance was all that kept it from seeming defensive, it wasn't even bitey.

"You guys said your piece, we get it, there's a summons, I'll be there. When?"

"I've already put you down once, Janzen." The climate went from classic tension to outright combative, so much so that Max gave a kind of mewling, unsure sound before idly pawing at Daphne's leg while she tried to keep me frozen in a glacial stare. Me? I played it coy, and kept my focus fixed on him.

"Look, you want a cool one-liner to try to bait me, I got a baker's dozen, but I don't want that, and neither do you. Plenty of reasons in life to fight without going out and looking for one, so just tell me when and where and I'll be there."

Chewing on which route to go, the pair of them shared a look that considered all options. I got the impression this wasn't going my way, so I readied myself—and then the door opened.

Max barked, and Grove racked a round into the old-time rifle with the axe-blade addition on the bottom side of the barrel. Music to my ears. Grove wore an expression that answered any unasked questions about his willingness to engage.

And from down the street? Whistling, well a kind of bastardized, disjoined whistling punctuated with an over-selling of seed spitting. Patrick, The Concrete Monk, made his way to

Daphne's side while Grove circled to my strong arm Alphie's weak side.

"This looks scenic, what's going on?"

"Alphie is deciding if he wants to kill us before we have an opportunity to sort this shit."

Sometimes hearing an option you're not yet entertaining wasn't enough, sometimes you had to share what an ugly outcome would look like should you keep being so stubborn.

"At seven tomorrow night, beneath the old courthouse. Both the House of Unet and the Masarou Tribe will be present to hear a formal charge against your friend Gale. As a stand-in for her you'll be charged with her rebuttal and subsequent defense, as well as subject to whatever punishment they settle on should she be found guilty."

Desolate, out of the way, the perfect place for an execution via gigantic golem.

Grove's spine stiffened, and Patrick's concern was clear as day as he eyed me sidelong.

I was trying to make sense of all this myself. Given that my only suspect seemed to have found a friend in my surrogate sister, the best thing I had for a lead was unconscious in my cellar, and the henchmen of the big bad looked as if they were about to be let off the leash and set after yours truly. Truth is, even with the intervention this could be a brutal throwdown.

"Insert some clever rejoinder in here and kick rocks, I got to get some affairs in order."

I signed for Grove and headed inside, my perfect-timing-having hired help in our wake; I gave the door a hard slam just as I heard Daphne half-heartedly call my name, as if trying to appeal to some sensibility in me.

Or to tell me I left my dog outside.

I ushered Max inside with some embarrassment before pausing to aim a mock-glower at each and slammed the door shut a second time in as many moments.

***

Kaycee called down to the cellar through the Styrofoam cup from her side of the street to let the bunch in the basement know that the proverbial coast was clear. I waited some before heading down, the other two in tow as we navigated the less-than-sturdy stairwell.

"She still in a coma?"

Xander nodded, though Donovan felt the need to make some kind of pointless correction for accuracy's sake. It was annoying and reminded me of myself.

"She's in a hibernated state to rehabilitate from her wounds, a magical failsafe to ensure her survival."

"Oh, So a coma" I said, cutting Donovan off before he had enough air in his lungs to sound off on some other pompous nonsense.

I must be so annoying.

"I've got to stand in for Gale tomorrow night. She's being formally charged or something. Both the House of Unet and the Masarou Tribe are going to be there, so we get the whole cast and crew. Yippee."

If I hadn't seen it myself, I would say the look exchanged by the Tinkerer and Doorman was scripted. Hackles up, concern in thickets, and an eye toward the respectfully wrapped yet still comatose Gale.

"How bad on a scale from one to…."

"Whatever smartass thing you're going to use as worst-case scenario—that one." Xander's gruff voice was shaken; whether from fear or fatigue was hard to say, but it was disturbing.

"This is a new level for them; got it. Well," I said, sighing out more than just air—I felt my shoulders sink. It was the death rattle of my certitude. "How do we do this?"

"I can go with you, but that's it." The Tinkerer stood; the trinket he'd shown me earlier carefully tucked beneath the collar of his shirt. "You're her stand-in, so I can represent you."

"And us?" The Monk's voice startled me, having forgotten the brick-breaking karate-kid was right behind me.

"We'll talk when we go across the street. We still have to deal with Sam."

The silence was deafening, and the befuddlement that spurred it came from the name I'd given her. Grove could have helped, but he was directly behind me so as to see what the two beside Gale would say. He probably had a good idea as to what I was going to say. Sarcastic tidbit, piece of actual information, self-deprecating zinger, or some pithy combination thereof. I decided if I didn't die, I was going to go out and try to get some depth and new material.

"The Stalker guys, her name is Sam. We have to deal with her, she's the only source I can think of. I mean, it's obvious as hell, but maybe they just banked on me being an idiot."

"That's a pretty sure-fire bet." Xander snorted, entirely without mirth, his shoulders slung as low as mine had been when the gravity of this all had first settled on me.

"You're a bad checker player about to try your hand at chess against the masters of the game," Donovan said coolly.

"Out of my depth, Don? Let's just say out of your depth. It's a wonder this thing didn't just kill her."

"Well…" Xander hesitated, and the withering look that Donovan shot him gave the now palpable tension a name: secrets. What the fuck.

I wasn't about to play this game with them, and instead of bickering any further, I figured I'd lay my hand on the table and give them my final offer. "Tell me or I tell them where she is," I said…how's that for bold.

"I would—" Donovan started, but I shut him up with a wave, and dared the Rougarou with a look.

"Spill."

"It's said that Gale has a spell she set on herself that will kill whoever kills her. It's a legend from the Veil… what she used to do there."

"… And that is?"

"We can't."

"Guys"

"We literally can't." Xander pulled his shirt collar down across on his impressive chest to expose a brand on his left pectoral muscle, and Donovan followed by turning over his right wrist and tugging up his sleeve to expose the same brand. This was magic beyond my level, oath-keeping magic to keep Gale's secrets from spilling out of unworthy vessels.

"Christ on a crutch, all right. Enough. But, *theoretically*, maybe that's why someone didn't finish the job?" I tapped the expanse of my forehead as if the physical jostling would bully my brain out of inaction. The schemer in me wondered if the clever girl just twisted a half-truth and used it to her advantage, but instead of trying to dissect that I pushed on. "All right, Donovan you're with me."

"Grove," I said, turning to the soldier. "Take Old Yeller and see what we can come up with in the way of a plan. Head out there now and do your recon," That rare glimpse of indecision wasn't hard to unsee, but I offered up assurance in the form of a devil-may-care smile. "You got this man. If they're going to get us, let's not make it a walk in the park, a'right?"

Steady yet unsure, as paradoxical a space to exist in as one can imagine, he managed to embody these contradictory postures perfectly. I gave a single nod, and he matched it, then turned and gave a gesture with his head to the hulking Rougarou.

Xander was moving with a bit more spring in his step as he followed Grove up and out of the cellar, not that it would really tip the scale in our favor, it just meant that his renewed strength might make dying take a bit longer.

Patrick broke his comfortable silence. "I'm with you, or…?"

"You're off the hook man, this isn't for you. We've entered the suicidal stage of this, and we're gonna need someone here after all of this is over."

The Monk was silent as he chewed on this.

"They win, there's gonna be a lot more bad getting out in the street and that's where you'll be needed. Really, the needs of the many…and all that" I said, channeling my inner Spock.

"I always took you for a Star Wars guy," he returned.

"I'm just asking you to live long and prosper, my friend. I mean it. This has the sound of a game that's gonna be less Street Fighter and more courtroom drama. You're needed out here." I spoke respectfully, and because I meant it as much as I wanted to make sure that my appeal hit the mark I reached out and offered him my hand.

Patrick the Concrete Monk, champion to those who were so desperately in need of one, clasped my hand. "You're a tough kid," he said as we shook. "And I wish you luck."

"You're like *thirty* seconds older than me," I said, laughing while letting go. "And I'll need it."

And just like that, all that remained was the three of us. My mentor, a comatose Gale, and me.

"All your friends are much more likable than you," Donovan said after a moment.

"I know," I said. And despite myself all I could do was start moving toward the stairwell. When there was nothing left but to move forward, you moved forward. "I know I've earned my enemies, but I haven't the slightest clue what I did to win over so many great friends."

Always forward.

***

Kaycee's store was a comfortable, cozy place to me. I'd only gotten there after leaving ample food for Max, as well as the cellar door open. He'd taken to sleeping beside Gale and there was no way I was anything less than a hundred percent sure that his vigilant proximity was helping. Max was always helping as far as me and mine were concerned. Plus, I'd attached a note advising that Gale was to take care of my dog if anything happened to me, so all my bases were covered.

Donovan wasn't really an impediment in all of this, and with Grove and Xander trying to situate some kind of game plan for when this inevitably went bad, it wasn't like I had anywhere else for him to be. Kaycee's shop was very specifically arranged in a circular design that seemed merely aesthetic but was very much intentional. Each cupboard, bookshelf, display, and chest had been meticulously organized to achieve a particular effect. The bell announced our arrival, to which Kaycee was quick to react as if she could immediately read our ill intentions.

Donovan was thrumming with power, which was uncomfortable enough and had a contorted effect on the bell; it sounded his chime, but a bit cleaner, and menacing.

"You two, you need to look at thi—"

"You're getting sentimental, Kaycee." The Tinkerer chided.

"And how the hell would you know, pipsqueak?" Chastisement didn't go over well with Kaycee, no matter who you thought you were. Donovan might have been a big deal in his own in-house hierarchy…

…But this wasn't his house, and nobody came at Kaycee with mockery in here.

Then the shit show began. The half-elf stepped dead-center in the gnome's way, as Sam emerged clothes askew, with a shirtless Johnny B not far behind. Life's just not fair.

Some guys get all the luck.

While Donovan was only mid-tier when it came to power, he was amped up and I wasn't exactly sure that Kaycee could take him. What I was sure of, was that this had the potential to devolve into a slugfest in a very crowded space, with a bunch of physically wired people who were emotionally drained and mentally exhausted—and that that was the last thing we needed.

"Kaycee," quietly but forcefully I called her name until I saw her turn her attention back to me. Again I made a note of how wearing that had to be on everyone who was forced to do it to me on a daily basis. "You gotta trust me, Kay."

Her silence was palpable, a little less long-lived than any other time she'd drawn into herself, and she emerged from the silence with an extrinsic stoicism. That nothingness reminded me of Gale actually, which prodded me to set my feet and make my way forward. I heard her shut Donovan down with a concrete *"No"* when he'd tried to make his way around her. Dejected but not defeated, he turned into a silent spectator. Johnny was out of his element and seemed perfectly unaware of what was unfolding, but Sam keyed into the happenings and set herself in a stance that was unmistakably wary.

"One of us wasn't enough Janzen, need another set of slave teeth for your trophy case?" She was defensive, and not just in her biting words—there was a scathing flush of power coming off of her. The dark crevices of the building seemed to be coming to life, and it wasn't the first time that I was reminded that there was more to a Stalker than just the fearsome strength and uncanny speed. I lifted my arms up and out in a peaceful-looking gesture.

"You need to appreciate our situa—"

I'd gotten close enough, she bolted toward me as I collapsed down, my open palm just barely able to smack down on the circlet in front of my feet; with a surge of will through my focus, I enacted the runework which sprang to life and revealed what this entire place really was.

A cage.

She hit the invisible wall with such ferocity that, even though she was still in her human form, the air passed all around me; a frightening reminder of the first of her kind I had come up against. Originally, I'd built this as a panic-room type thing for Kaycee and her family, but the reverse could be true of it as well.

"You honorless RUNT!" she screamed at me. For good measure, she swiped at the translucent energy keeping her prisoner, rocking the building itself. My attempt to placate her was interrupted by a respectable right cross—apparently the karaoke king took umbrage with what I had done. Spinning with the momentum, I bit down on a bloodied lip and stared daggers at him. He was angry but reconsidered; once in a while I can offer up a bit of menace, too.

"You get *one*. I'm done getting hit without getting my own in. It was this or an ambush, and this way you get the chance to prove you're not involved in all this by sitting your ass right here." My tone shifted to congenial, even downright conversational. "And if you want to help, you can link up with Grove and help us set this all up. We're trying to get this done without a dozen or so people dying." That last bit had the stink of regret fueled by the fire of an angry, sore-jawed, second-hand hero. Kaycee even shrank some.

"You got a plan?" the punk-rocker said, looking from the once-lovely lady to me; Sam was fighting off a transformation, given the looks of her; fingertips bloodied, feet starting to turn, and her pupils had narrowed to slits.

"I've got the makings of a plan," I said.

Apparently, my routine had run itself out.

"You're going to have to trust me too. Gale did. Kaycee does, now it's your turn."

They both looked at our host, who backed my claim with an acquiescing, tight nod. The reprieve went as quickly as it came as another jarring hit rocked the place down to the damned foundation. Sam, snarling, had eyes on only me.

"I'm going to kill you after this."

Stepping forward, right into the limelight of her wrath, squared up and chin high, I held her awful gaze: eyes I'd seen, challenged, and come out on top of with a win.

"If that's the price of trying to save your life, sure, have at it. Better than you have tried."

It was obvious the musician had torn loyalty, keeping an eye on me while casting a few looks back at her, he finally landed on fumbling after me. Kaycee wasn't at all happy about any of this, and honestly Donovan wasn't thrilled either. If you can't make everyone happy, make them all miserable, that's my motto.

"I need you to leave town, Kay," I said.

"So, your brilliant plan is to run off all your allies and lock the rest up? Then you'll, what, talk them into submission? You realize I have a family?"

"I'm the stand-in for Gale at an official charging, where both the Unet and the Masarou will be present… And I understand exactly half of the words in that sentence."

If I thought I'd ever seen her shocked before, this time made each of those look downright trivial. Donovan was suddenly solemn, and an almost sympathetic nod confirmed Kaycee's suspicion that this was every bit as serious as it sounded.

"You….They're going to charge you with disrupting the Balance Janzen, I mean… That's…"

"I kind of glossed a book over what that entails, so let's just skip it, shall we?" I raised my fists in mock excitement and gave them an unenthusiastic shake. "I do love surprises."

I hate silence: it's like the antithesis of a mix of screeching tires and fingernails across a chalkboard that somehow married and produced something so much more awful than each as a standalone. She was truly distraught. This wasn't some errant beast or able-bodied sorcerer; these were the keepers of the balance. This process erased and eradicated people, they were the end-all-be-all, the masters of the Blind Judges. Cautiously and caringly, I took Kaycee by the shoulders and made sure she was not only aligned with me, but that she'd returned from her vacant, horrified stare to make eye contact with me and really hear me.

"You guys have to go. I doubt you're in fantastic standing, and this isn't going to help." I had a kind of quiet suspicion that her husband, Jay, was not exactly compliant. Don't ask me why, but in a world where everyone acknowledged the Balance and at least played ball, she tended to be strict with her adherence. Disoriented, she managed to make her way through all of what was said and just faintly nod.

"But what…"

"Donovan is defending me. If anyone can speak their language, it's him. And look, no matter what the case against us may be, we have the distinct advantage of being on the right side of truth in all of this. So…" I said, pursing my lips and giving a little nod, "we've got that going for us."

Kaycee was reaching for something—not physically, but I could tell that she was trying to navigate this mess in her mind to come up with some kind of shotgun, save-the-day solution. Wearing what I hoped was a reassuring smile, I continued to comfort as best as I could. "If you're out of here, I can concoct one of my madman plans and try to keep a step ahead of them. I mean sure, they're like undefeated against me thus far, but you know what they say about dogs…"

"They poop in the house." Johnny said.

"They're dumb?" Donovan deduced.

"They have their day," Sam said from inside of her invisible prison with an irritation that matched my own.

"*Exactly*, and it can't rain all the time." I tried, after the objective failure of my first go around.

"It does in the rainforest," the bard blurted out, though it was choked down with a withering look and a backhanded smack from Kaycee.

The buffoonery had alleviated some of the suffocating sourness in the room and it sapped the foul mood of my shaken surrogate mother, who I pulled into a hug. I felt her resistance, but eventually she stifled the need to try to fight this, and just wrapped her arms around me.

"Janzen, you listen to me." She snatched my jaw before she'd even manage to fully disengage from our previous embrace, at which point I immediately screwed up my face but didn't dare wrest myself from her. "Do not let them cow you or back you down. You're every bit as smart as those pretentious bastards in the House of Unet."

Donovan stirred as if he was entertaining the thought of intervening and announcing that he was in fact a member of that group, but Kaycee just gave him a dirty look and kept on. I swallowed my propensity for swatting away the compliment as it was defeatist and served no good purpose. I had to dig deep to find my inner warrior poet—the one who believed he was in fact every bit as big and bad as the enemies at the gate.

"You're as clever as any of the tricksters in the Masarou too. Trust nothing and nobody but your instinct, trust what we see in you and what you see for yourself with the outer and inner eye—you hear me! Promise me."

My attempt to promise her was cut short by a little jerk of my jaw.

"*Look at me* and promise." Her eyes were lined with wetness, but she was not willing to let a single tear fall. I knew what she meant by that, even if everyone else was stuck scratching their heads. We watched one another in a new light, and with an unforeseen serenity I found my center, and willed myself to a calm that concealed a confidence that I didn't know I had. I nodded and let her know that I wasn't going into this half-cocked, and that if it came to it, I would make them earn every fucking inch. Satisfied, she looked to the gnome. "And you… do your prickly best—you understand me?"

Even Donovan was able to find some pretense of decency and concede with a nod.

"Good. Now drive me to my kids' daycare." She told him. I think the gnome expected me to come up with some kind of saving pursuit, but I gleefully gave a shrug that left him saddled with the job. "My things are upstairs, Janzen. Take whatever you need."

Kaycee and I were very, very careful in what we said to one another. All of it had a kind of meaning known only to us, and all that we said in this world was binding, like a signature. My shock bled into confusion and finally just a kind of stupefaction. Kaycee had some heavyweight stuff tucked away in this place. The veneer came down from my surprise to display something more suitable, like appreciation. She gathered herself and her belongings from the hook beside the entryway before walking out, accompanied only by the sound of the bell.

"We'll meet there. I'm guessing you're going to stop and get some stuff yourself?" My question took the momentum from

Donovan, whose suddenly expressive face seemed perfectly awe-stricken.

"Anything we have would just ensure our death was a slower affair, so no."

Odd… not the way I would play an inevitable end, but everybody's different.

The door closed, and the sharp chime of the bell died slowly behind him. The silence was suffocating as the now-dressed rocker sidled up beside me, his long arm looping over my sunken shoulders.

"We're fucked, ain't we?" he quipped.

"Proper fucked yeah."

***

Tomorrow came in an instant, even if I didn't sleep a wink.

It wasn't cold out, and it wasn't raining. That's how I always imagined this kind of thing would be. I was part of that generation that seemed lost square between all sorts of greatness. Middling in mindset and temperament, just across the board kind from painfully average—at least to everyone else.

I scratched my chin taking inventory of myself and my clan, looking at the desolate building where the next step of my fate would be decided. It had that kind of archaic aesthetic that was built into it by design—I think to give it a more dramatic affect; keep it a bit more enduring and intimidating. It actually looked regal, which I think was ironic since it was always the common people who ended up kneeling at this makeshift altar. Maybe that was the point.

Judgment. This is where we came to be judged by those who deemed themselves our betters, our superiors. Judged by way of strength or riches and not merit.

The boiling rage that centered in my chest was interrupted, probably the only thing that kept it from boiling over. Donovan had crept up beside me, on my right. I'm not very tall… in fact I aspire to be average height, so the gnome's own height deficiency wasn't really noticeable when he stood next to me. Once again, he adopted his quiet mask; that inquisitive, non-blinking stoicism which was a kind of cold comfort to me, though I wasn't sure why. He eyeballed me with a sidelong look. The gear I was wearing was pretty standard, though there was a gizmo or two he wasn't familiar with. That's what he saw, too.

"Are those fidget spinners…?" He sounded crushed, like I had annoyed him to the point of utter disgust. I beamed proudly at him: on my left arm there was a kind of bracer wrapped around my forearm with three fidget spinners all locked into place with an ugly looking latch. What they lacked in aesthetics, they more than made up for in effectiveness, after all, I had no time for pretty on such a tight clock. Of course, having a Stalker on my ass wasn't exactly conducive to high caliber presentations either.

His abhorrence mellowed itself to something a little more benign. I knew the look well; it was acceptance. My entire life was spent doing things my way: I have the hard-headedness, resilience, constitution and above all, the character to live my life in whatever fashion I see fit. I start off with people rubbing them raw and then move to outright antagonizing them. It just happens… but with those that ride it out, I like to think that a grudging respect starts to develop. Once they hit that acceptance, that's when the friendship begins. We walked up the stairs together, closer to shoulder-to-shoulder than I'd care to admit if I somehow found my way out of this. I found satisfaction in knowing that even if I was laying myself at the feet of the executioner, I was doing it on my terms, with a friend by my side.

The place was in shambles, and that tickled the anarchist in me; the lobby was ripe with an unholy mess of vandalized statues and all kinds of trash. It was a middle finger to the architectural imprint of authority written over every inch of this place. It was dusky and the lighting was poor, but the spindled silhouettes cut a menacing backdrop. The dim ambiance made it hard to discern the second story, although it felt like it was thick with prying, furtive eyes. Donovan and I walked further inside: he with a kind of confidence I was trying hard to replicate. Actually, I was a bit unsure about how he was navigating it all so well. Even with the cognitive map I had from coming in earlier to scope it out, it was hard to not stumble a step or two…I gotta get me some of those night vision glasses for next time.

Moving through the lobby, we followed a walkway which sloped downward until we got to the mouth of the next opening. What I saw next stole the air from my lungs and ripped the faux-confident grin from my face the instant we looked through the doorway.

The room was a massive half-sphere, and at the center of the dome was a platform that I had no doubt was designed for us. There was a podium on each side, one for the accusers and one for me, the stand-in. To the right was something that seemed so out of sorts that even I—a man who had fought with the impossible, braved the bizarre and crafted magic items—couldn't believe it. The House of Unet had a dais where three of them sat, their knotted faces displayed free of any glamour or artifice. Most of the time it was easy to forget that almost everyone I was associated with had some manifestation of deceptive magic running at almost all times. But this group was almost painful to look at: scrunched faces with wrinkled noses and thick furrowed brows that seemed somehow capable of raising themselves even higher at me like they're not just insulted by the sight of my person but the stench as well. They were shorter too, and plump. Fattened from their status no doubt. I would imagine that people in a position of power hated the caricature of being big bodied. but if the shoe didn't fit….

It's what was beside them that made me just marvel. The metal construct was a flawless piece of ingenuity, an engineering feat of magic and metal created by the Unet. A featureless golem exuded an elemental kind of dread. This emotionless entity had been manufactured for murder, and its undefeated streak expanded farther back than I could even conceive. Maybe the deepest reach of the Abyss had monstrosities that could tear it to ribbons, or even the Veil might have a few cavalier godlings that could undo it with a word, but here? In this shared world? It was an apex predator: it was in fact the undisputed hunter champion of all apex predators. Those blocky arms had magic-eating qualities carved into them, so intricate that even the basic base design of each ringlet was beyond my comprehension. The legs had the same rigid stout quality as the arms, and just beneath the facet shielding of each limb were three-pronged shafts that acted as what I imagined were toes and fingers. This thing would be a nightmare for anyone or anything, and I guesstimated it stood a dozen feet tall and had to weigh several tons. More so, the glyphs all could defeat, assimilate and redirect magic of almost any kind. You'd basically have to get into fisticuffs with the gargantuan, and the mystical metal was probably reinforced many times over which made such a task inherently unfeasible. We live in a world of the impossible, and this thing was unimaginable.

Its Masarou challenger stood directly across from it. I stood there, completely out of pithy remarks; they'd managed to take that from me for the second time in as many seconds. My axiomatic mindset made me believe that neither of these titans had any glaring weakness, which was so god damned frustrating. This Frankensteinian thing spat in the face of what was natural order. I identified several attributes of some of the most legendary monsters from all chronicled time, and a few even older. Where one was forged and shaped with a mind for magic, I could see that this thing specialized in cannibalizing its own.

Its three-prong tail belonged to a Sucant, a kind of insect creature that feasted on the superstitious who dared try to venture deep into the Earth. Each barb was armed with a different venom: one that could wrack every inch of you with unimaginable pain, another that could weaken you to the point of paralysis, and the third prong? I forgot what that did; not the first time I lamented not taking my studies more seriously. I opted to go with very bad—that somehow it was the worst of the three.

The arms were reminiscent of a primate, and I had heard from somebody at the Last Love that the legend of the oversized ape actually had a kind of origin that wasn't all mythology. From what I understood of an actual gorilla it was something like six times stronger than an average man and this thing was probably ten times that. The thing could probably shot-put me clear across the city if it chose to.

I recognized the claws too, they belonged to an old nemesis. Blotched with blood, the pernicious talons were so sharp they actually bloodletted the wielder. That reptilian head was new, but I'd wager it could see in almost any spectrum which meant that there wasn't any way to hide from it. I'd read of a Drake creature that had several kinds of diabolical breaths; so this thing could bellow out a stream of fire or a current of frost that would capture and kill you in a matter of moments…It's important to have options after all.

It appeared kind of docile at the moment, which I would guess came from the collar it wore around its neck, its creepy eyes detached and glazed over. The controlling faction was a different hue in skin tone, they had a greenish, almost brackish look to them without the phased glamour having to be called upon. Ironically, while the two sides seemed to be at a perpetual state of enmity, the two hostile parties had very similar features. All of their conflict, this eons-long strife, basically boiled down to skin color. It felt perfectly ridiculous, for all of the one second it took me to parallel what we've been dealing with for the better part of… ever. It's ironic that prejudice could live on, even now, in them and us. To the credit of the goblins, at the center of their own three-person tribunal was a woman. She had a bosom and looked less severe with a notched nose and bushy eyebrows. Her feminine face regarded me first, and almost as one everyone else turned to regard and gauge me as well. Her look felt a little more penetrating than the rest, but I figured it was because she'd been the first to set her eyes on me—that or the fact that I'm incredibly good looking compared to the males of her species, which wasn't saying much.

Before the proceedings began, there was one more interruption. I didn't see a door, but I did hear one slam, followed by a second one after which two respective parties emerged: A male and female dark elf. The Warded, they were called, and they took up sentry positions at either end of the table that held the Masarou goblins. At the same time, I saw the two human Marked Ones—Alphie and Daphne, or rather Alpha and Delta—take position flanking the Unet gnomes. Though I recognized them, I knew enough not to jeopardize their standing with the House of Unet by doing something stupid like yelling how's it hanging guys.

For me?

"I should do a magic trick," I felt rather than saw Donovan's teeth grind. "You know, know your audience?" My default was epigrammatic. I had leaned on sarcasm all my adult life and well, here's me being true to self down to the bitter end. All of them turned to regard us. The gnome shifted, and I buckled in for some kind of berating at my antics and instead the look I got was something reminiscent of melancholy, which in earnest was about the bleakest thing I could have seen at the moment.

"The tribunal first calls the Accuser, One … Donovan, disgraced member of House Unset, to testify against the accused, Gale Houdini."

Never mind.

CHAPTER 14

Falling Pieces

…"It's an average thought wrapped around an awful idea, Janzen." Donovan had reminded me of a more severe version of my old mentor Zachariah. I mean, Zachariah's haughty detached English attitude manifested feigned indifference like it was a factory setting, but Donovan's actual indifference was the logical next step. They weren't exactly alike though. Donovan was strict, brutally and relentlessly honest, and wasn't warming up to the idea of us being anything other than student and mentor. We'd been working together for a while now, maybe half a year, and I had never brought anything to him that was up to snuff. He'd soundly shut down every one of my ideas until now.

"Really? So you think it's an improvement?"

The gnome didn't even have the damned decency to blink. Even my misses didn't warrant an inkling of thought.

"Average," he reiterated. "Average is why you'll keep losing people."

That straightened my spine. I was half out of the chair with a balled fist when he took to moving on with his sharply introduced point.

"You can't be average; you have to be better. For them. Or else the ones we love will have to leave us." It wasn't that I was jarred out of an emotion, it was how violent a shift in the spectrum it was. I'd had fire in my blood—an eruption of adrenaline coursing out from my chest, with violence on my mind—and just before it peaked there was a to-the-bone, cold hard reality dumped all over me. I'd stood across bullies better than twice my size, had crossed steel with paladin warriors, and recently fought back an ambassador of the Abyss while somehow coming out on top. I didn't freeze, almost ever, but this stopped me cold.

"We? Love? You mean to tell me there's a Mrs. Awful Son-of-a-Bitch…"

"Not exactly," the gnome softly finished, and I would swear the ghost of a smile passed over his alien features, his callous disinterest abruptly abated.

"Well what do you know…" I said, dropping in the seat across from him. Watching the way the small-fingered man fidgeted with the outline of my concept was fascinating.

"I loved someone once, I am not so different from you in many ways."

An old interrogation trick told me to mirror his silence. That was a particularly tall order when standing across from a slow-aging race renowned for their sparse speech habits. Thoughtful pauses were Donovan's thing, but despite the uphill climb there was no way I was going to pass up an opportunity to glean some insight about him.

He was almost immaculately ordinary if that could make any kind of sense. In fact, he was so commonplace that I realized for the first time that despite being almost a foot shorter than the average man, I'd never once heard someone remark on his height. He wore the outfit of a midwestern, middle class, middle-aged father. There was something about his face, as if the glamour or maybe the man himself wasn't sure how to go about emoting. There was a solemnity in the strife he was reflecting on, and maybe entertaining sharing.

"Love can make an amazing man settle for average, and that averageness can cost him that love in the end."

Now that he'd broken his silence, I tried to think up some kind of masterfully worded, baiting retort. I wasn't sure I understood what he was saying. Was the woman average? Was his job average? His life?

"Once love has a man, he'll never be sensible again."

Backpedaling in a conversation wasn't wholly new to me, I had a storied career of shoving my foot in my mouth and immediately ending up on the losing end of a thorough ass-chewing. This was new; this was like bomb after bomb, as if the six months of such stress-inducing strictness wasn't all for naught. Donovan had just shared more with me, I would comfortably wager, than probably anyone outside of Gale.

"Maybe more than an average idea," he said, and I found that the last bastion of angst I could have against him, the one port in this storm into which I could dump all my toxic anger, was being washed away. That last stronghold, defeated by the fact that he, a Tinkerer, was saying I may have had an above-average idea. "You just have to know, if this absorbs too much energy it'll blow up, so I think your idea for using it as a magic lock pick is probably dangerous. Fastening it on a rune-protected trap door might assimilate all the energy from the spell and allow you to go in unmolested, or it might be too much energy and blow the whole door away. You try to neutralize a protection ward but end up with a massive explosion—which I guess would be fitting for you. Plus, it's going to have to spin for these runes to work in concert correctly." A lot of traditional spellwork had to involve movement with the runes, which is why many traditions still celebrate ritual dance with magical objects.

"Still," he continued, "that's an interesting way to counter energy, interesting runework to steal and siphon power. Subvert it rather than challenge it. Crude," the gnome trailed off absently, a phantom smile still trying to stick at the edge of his perpetually downturned mouth.

"But clever," I ended the sentiment, echoing words he'd said previously. I got back to work on my design while the Tinkerer took a period of reflection, the magnitude of the moment not lost on me despite the simplicity of it.

***

"...And from what we could glean they had planned to use the great lake as a conduit to a spell, a spell powered by the blood of a Wanderer, to breach the In-Between and move within the worlds, though for what end I cannot say."

I snapped back from my pensive stupor after dwelling on the singular fond memory I had of this traitorous prick. I wasn't able to catch the majority of what he was saying, but I could see that he was laying the blame of it all on Gale and calling her out as some kind of coordinator of all that had happened. There was a reason he insisted on us being alone, I was sure of it now, and while I wasn't one to stand on ceremony, I had to let my anger simmer while he power-talked through all this endless fiction. It was thorough, rehearsed and wholly believable.

"We all know the reputation of this Gale and, given her background, it would make sense that she might try to return home by any means possible. She used the local riffraff as pawns, setting them to do her bidding while she waited to watch it all unfold. She has breached the In-Between once, she would not hesitate to do it again, and we can be sure so long as she is able to roam free that there is no assurance she won't eventually succeed."

There was some commotion in the tribunal as the two respective factions spoke among themselves, then the Masarou Tribe fell quiet. The lone female goblin in the delegation, a surprisingly lean and graceful creature, flowed to stand, and while I should've been keyed in, focused on the intricacies of the trial I was knee-deep in, I wasn't. I was looking over at Alpha and Delta, watching firsthand their faith in me erode. It shouldn't have hurt, but it did. I turned back to the nauseating back and forth going on between the aloof presiding bodies and set my jaw.

"Any other witness to this claim? You are a Disgraced outcast; we can't simply have you give testimony at this proceeding and take it as truth."

My smirk was dark, deep, and satisfying, because that scored as clean a hit as I had ever seen put on Donovan's person. His fidget was minute, almost imperceptible, but for a man who coveted control and lived by that law, it was a pretty revealing tell.

With a terse nod, the dark elves set to motion, and with a deceptive strength given their lithe frames they carried over an enormous, tarp-covered oval. Once comfortably settled and steadied, they pulled the tarp away to reveal an inverted dome-like mirror that gave a distorted reflection that was uncomfortable to behold. I tried not to let my eyes rest on it, but the moment I did I realized I could see everyone in the room. Not just see them, but observe them with immaculate detail, even getting a sense of their true selves. It was hard to put into words—not an ideal thing if you're the orator of a story but try to stay with me.

Donovan then said a series of names, most of them I couldn't quite discern even after reflection; I caught an Abigail, I think.

The mirror's ornate perimeter shimmered with energy, the living green pulse of magic that I'd come to know as the In-Between; it was a magic all at once its own and felt like a living thing with raw overwhelming omnipotence written all over it. The fringe of the mirror's lip became more and more constant, until the green had engulfed it entirely and spread into the bowl proper. My peripheral vision was trained on the two castes of the tribunal, and neither seemed all that thrilled by this intervention.

Soon enough, I saw why; it was her, the dark goddess of the Abyss who had marched an unbeatable army to the gates of my world and almost passed through with the aim of catastrophic devastation. She was tall, lean, and uncomfortably good-looking: majestic and lovely, in truth she looked like royalty, but that shifted when our eyes met. She morphed, and I hated her more than ever before in that instant.

I stared into the mirror which now housed the vessel of Maria, the host-body an obvious ploy to try to rub salt in an open wound since she was so confident her victory was all but assured.

"Mr. Robinson," she said. My sharp stare was blunted by a spell-breaking blink. The gnomes all seemed irritated, and the goblins confused, and when I came to, I was at a loss.

It was the familiarity of another feminine voice, firm but not unfriendly, that brought me back into the present.

"You may respond to the witness," Delta explained, despite the reproachful look aimed at the back of her head from the House of Unet. It was a small token, but it was appreciated.

"Does Disney know about this shtick? I mean, they kind of got the evil-bitch-in-a-mirror gimmick on lock—" I choked, my entire body suddenly wracked with pain. I doubled over and then outright collapsed, and an awful surge of energy erupted up from beneath me. It felt like an eternity, but I knew it was the exact opposite, and when I managed to claw myself back up by way of my podium, I saw the smugness I had tried to throw their way on display thrown back at me in spades. I was up the creek, no paddle, in shark-infested waters.

I was outnumbered, outgunned and the antithesis of a fan favorite. Despite the jolting rip of pain they'd used to buckle me under, they seemed inclined to hear what I had to say, so I waved it off.

"I would remind you, Janzen Robinson, that you have taken upon yourself accountability for this egregious happening; we do not wish to hear your take on humor and would instead insist that you keep to the point at hand." The Unet gnome speaking to me was seated in the center chair and given my stunted understanding of how this all worked, I assumed he had the most authority. My deduction of the hierarchy notwithstanding, I could see that Donovan wasn't all that keen that the Abyssal queen had adopted such a pointedly antagonistic attitude.

There was a brief silence before the female goblin turned to her to ask about her recollection of that night. The goddess in Maria's body had eyes only for me, and while it was a gut-churning, heartbreaking and anger-invoking sensation all at once to hold her stare, I would be damned if I didn't do it.

"We all must know our limits. We all must respect the law of our lands, else the balance will be gone, and none could be expected to survive what would happen if all we built was thrown into disarray," the witch said in Maria's voice. She turned to regard each respective party individually while speaking. "When Donovan of House Unet—"

"Disgraced," the presumed leader of the gnomes interjected, and while I saw a hint of anger rise up in her at being interrupted, she handled it with a showman's grace and kept on with her thought.

"Right you are. Well, Disgraced or not, it seemed he understood he had a duty beyond self, and when the terrible plot to break our precious borders progressed, he knew not to whom to turn, for while Disgraced you would not hear him out." It wasn't chiding and it seemed the point connected. Grudgingly they acknowledged that their previous biases may have made them less than receptive to any kind of claim made by the Tinkerer. It was all a lie mind you, but it was layered and carefully constructed, and right now it was being feasted upon by both sides.

"And with the proud goblins similarly predisposed against him, he set off to try to solve this all on his own. It was during his search of the Abyss to see where a vulnerability may be that we found one another, and once I had won his trust, he told me this troubling tale. This is my home, and I know while it might not be much to all of you, we are quite taken with the way we conduct ourselves. Had Gale been allowed into the realms guarded by the In-Between, there's no telling what was next; did she plan to try to breach into the Veil and return home? Was she seeking a way to bring destruction on the world you're all in now? I did not know her aim, and it's dangerous to try to discern the designs of somebody so unpredictable. As it is with the Accords, I knew I could not allow them to enter, so I gathered my own personal forces to combat them once they opened up the rift. And they did with ill intent, and at the expense of the very woman whose image you see before you."

She was gaining traction with her monologue, and while neither party seemed particularly inclined to care about some random human, that last bit was aimed at me—it hit too, but more important was the reveal on its heels.

"An unwitting Wanderer, one of the strongest I've ever come across, was massacred in a macabre fashion on a slab of stone. They used her blood and body to not only breach the In-Between, but to tear it asunder." She made a theatrical ripping motion, her joined hands moving apart and a wisp of magic following each as if to better illustrate the hard-driven point. "I lost some allies, and nearly my life, but luckily, we could thwart them. I pleaded with Donovan to bring this to your court—despite the history between you." Words matter, and there was something in that statement which made my eyes narrow and reconsider everyone in attendance. "And so here we are. This grievous slight on our ways cannot go unattended."

"So you're to tell us *Gale* was able to give you all this trouble, and push you to such a brink?" The gnome at the center asked, pressing his point of curious skepticism. "She is a considerable power, but from what I recall of your prowess—which is no small thing—she wouldn't warrant the full of your attention."

"Right you are," she said. She wasn't even going to play at having a hiccup, she responded as if the man had just given her a rehearsed launchpad to another talking point. "And that would have been the case should she have been alone, but there was a host of middling wielders. There was a Rougarou, one Xander, and of course some meddling half-elf that came to her aid. It was a concerted effort, and honestly, a well prepared one. Had Donovan not surreptitiously come to my aid, I wouldn't have had a chance."

Everyone simultaneously turned to the accuser, my former mentor and almost-friend.

"When trying to scry to see where they were going, what vulnerability they planned to exploit, I was able to give her a warning; if not, they would have caught her unaware, and with their combined force they could have very well overtaken a respectable piece of the Abyss and moved from there. Any breach is an offense, but this is beyond the pale."

The delegation seemed satisfied. After talking amongst themselves in a litany of tongues I didn't understand, they stopped their chatter and almost as one, the darkling bitch in the guise of my dead friend Maria, Donovan playing his part as Judas, and the two lofty ruling bodies turned their attention on me.

"And my understanding is there is no witness to speak on behalf of the accused, as well as an utter lack of evidence?" the Masarou woman said. That much I was able to catch—their English was a bit garbled, but not outright guttural. She seemed to have a pretty good command of the language actually. I couldn't tell if her sneer was an expression of utter disdain or twisted cruelty, so I just considered it one and the same.

The gnomes hardly gave the goblin the time of day and looked ready to be done with the whole affair. Court was about to adjourn, a death sentence ruling about to come down on my head harder than a guillotine blade, but before they could drop the proverbial gavel I reached into my jacket and slapped Frank's journal down on my podium.

The journal that exonerated me and Gale and detailed each step of the coven's inner workings and its descent into an Abyssal cult.

I looked at Donovan, stone-faced. "Chess, not checkers."

CHAPTER 15

Hung Jury

There was a lot of rumbling, and from what I could pick up (as it seemed to happen all at once), the gnomes had some kind of direction they wanted to take with this new development. Meanwhile, the goblins were angered not only about being interrupted, but by the fact that they felt relegated to an afterthought in the wake of the verdict their counterparts had started to make. Evidence was the key, because as regimented as these two bodies of power were, they had to keep the code. The code was everything…the *Balance* was everything, and the blow that I just struck peacocking about some evidence that I had, changed everything. The basic premise of the case was rattled, and the foundation had shifted dramatically in an instant. It went from a one-off case about some mid-level power trifling with the Balance and needing to be made an example of, to something much more nefarious. This was a long-standing vendetta between two castes, with the gnomes often looking at their goblin kin as second-class citizens. The tension was palpable, and I felt a bit out of my depth, so for once, I shut up.

I watched it all unravel, my once-uncomfortable podium now a kind of front row seat. See, you wouldn't think an honest defense would be problematic, but it would if this kangaroo court was just a mockery of itself. It would if this was a carefully scripted incident that was now going off-book.

What I had was evidence, as Frank had taken to not only documenting the type of magic that had been gifted to the cult leader, but remarked about the secret rendezvous that Jackie, their leader, and this darkling creature had. After each communion with that Abyssal entity, she became terribly apt in a number of magics that the cult had never before entertained, let alone collectively studied or dabbled in. It was all carefully chronicled: Jackie's ascension, her growing madness, and her increased prowess and power. It would make sense: the mirror-trapped Abyss Queen would need a competent spellcaster to navigate the other side of the portal she'd attempted to open so as to build a bridge between the Abyss to our world. The devil wasn't in the glass dome, glaring at me with as much ugly as can come from a face designed after my Maria, it was instead in the details.

"It didn't have to be this way," I said, somewhat sadly. Something was changing in Donovan, and he—like the woman in the mirror—only had eyes for me.

"You don't think I hadn't planned for this contingency, your next, the one after, and a dozen you haven't even thought of you impetuous nothing?" His cold control started to wane, a visceral hatred brewing up from beneath his stoic mask, and it was then that the amulet he was wearing started to come to life—not the circular one that housed the power of Gale, the one he told me contained her energy because it would help suppress her presence and keep her hidden. It was another—one I had not seen before. The Masarou goblins stifled themselves, grumbling down to a strained silence. Apparently, they'd noticed the stare-down going on between me and my mentor. We stank of anger and had ill intent written over every inch of us.

"Temper is the only thing you can't get rid of by losing it, big D. Here's a suggestion: be better."

While my ability to effectively get under the skin of everyone I have ever met had never before yielded a benefit, today was the day. Donovan's snarl was the dam breaking and giving way to a flood of anger, and his emotional charge made the man seem insane. His elbows went up and then out at the shoulder, then his index and middle fingers came down to his chest. His fingertips touched the rim of the amulet, and Donovan gasped with a renewed breath of power.

The gavel from the House of Unet came down again and again, and while I hated to distract myself from whatever destructive concoction Donovan was about to damn us all with, I tried to signal Delta and Alpha to get themselves out of there. Luckily, they reluctantly started to do that very thing, moving further from our raised dais to watch what was unfolding.

"Donovan Unet, this is your LAST warning: you will calm yourself; you will center yourself, you will obey the decree of this court. Have you not already embarrassed your once good name enough?"

There was a pause. I'd read too many comic books not to know that something awesomely awful was about to happen, but what came next managed to make even me reconsider my plan to try to antagonize him into making any kind of mistake. He was mad but in control, and with a surge of will his joined fingers became bathed in fluorescence. A blur of hand motions simply willed a glowing circle into existence, suspended vertically in the air between us. His fingertips brushed complex sigils into the air around the rim of that circle, and it crackled with green energy. I could feel the power radiating from it and realized that it was a way to, on the fly, manipulate currents of energy and harvest power in real-time and wield them instantaneously: a magical workbench.

In the backdrop was a profoundly confusing scene to try to keep any kind of track of. The Masarou goblins were furious, and the Unet were protesting that Donovan wasn't really one of theirs. Right when it seemed to come to a head, the female goblin's shriek cut the air. The scream shattered the dramatic pause, probably a glass or two as well, and most importantly, gave the green light to their plan B. Reluctantly looking back at Donovan who'd just made his own violent intent clear, the female goblin exploded into motion; She spun on the goblin jurist to her left and smashed a wickedly curved blade into his chest. I couldn't help but think of

Caesar and Brutus—I had a really strong suspicion that the two of them had worked with one another more than once to be seated on a council like this.

The remaining male goblin became fleet of foot. He made a nimble leap off the dais, landing in a roll before springing up and making a beeline for the exit. The Warded seemed stunned still, what with all legal structure falling apart right before their eerie eyes.

A chorus of cries came up from the gnomes. The Unet Blind Judge, the hulking metal monstrosity, had suddenly lurched forward—and nobody was at the helm. It easily seized the table that the elders of House Unet were seated at, and viciously slammed it into the unforgiving concrete wall behind them. Once. Twice. By the third time there was nothing but a pool of blood and body parts, cruelly misshapen and suddenly, shockingly dead.

It was a most undignified death.

The Dreadnought went upright at some new command, and it was then that I saw Donovan piloting the gargantuan construction. He was under an excruciating strain, his attention split between making sure that he had me dead to rights and watching the female goblin scramble to get to her own Judge. I realized it wasn't a magical workbench at all…it was a control panel.

"She's gonna make it," I teased while retreating from my podium. "Better keep both eyes on that one, yeah?"

The amulet was a furnace, blazing with the power emanating from it. It was the battery for all of this, because creating, channeling, commanding and just having this type of power was way out of Donovan's depth. Right when I had the thought to bolt, my attention was pulled by the sound of relentless slamming and screeching. That caught my eye, and it would no doubt do the same to the Tinkerer. It seemed the black goddess smoke screened us for another attempt to make it out all on her own.

"So, you went from royal reject to the footstool of a sadist. If you wanted to be treated like a bitch, I could have thrown a few paddles and whips in it. I mean, I'm not about that life, but if you've discovered yourself, who's to say we could—"

"Shut up, you disgusting idiot." Donovan cycled through a handful of emotions, each ratcheting up the ladder of irritation. When he was annoyed, he still acted almost indifferent, but if you got in there and annoyed him with something that had teeth to it, he was going to lose some of that control. I just needed to work him out of his wheelhouse and then aim his rage in a specific direction.

"Don't go all soft on me now Donovan, I ain't about to die on my knees. Especially by some second-rate traitor. My only regret is that someone as small as you are is one to d—"

The control panel buzzed with more energy, the amulet glowed with a ruby sheen, and suddenly three sigils appeared. Each of the three floated and shifted within a caging circle. The matching network of insignias at the center of each respective circle all lined up, and then, by lining up the templates front to back, a surge of power actually filled the whole of the phantasm weapon like the barrel of a gun. I felt the power climax and eyed how big a jump it would be for me to try to dive down from the dais. Instead, with one last defiant middle finger to the pint-sized fucker I dared him on, ready to meet my maker.

His fingers worked like a fountain pen, scrawling runes to life before my very eyes. There was a pause, perhaps spurred by some remnant of his humanity, and I met that vulnerability with a devil-may-care grin, gaming him to go off. Donovan pushed on the floating spellwork and let loose a spout of fire which became three spires that snapped out tornado-ing around themselves and locking onto me. Wondering if he felt bad about killing me, or if I was just a throw away—collateral damage in whatever his bizarre hidden agenda—I waited for the strike.

Except there wasn't one. The vortex of flame heading straight for me, deviated from its course mid-flight, and went right into the open palm I had thrust out in front of me.

There was no spectacular impact or explosion with an astounding concussion of force and a wave of leftover heat. Instead, the vein of fire fixated on the center of my hand, piercing it and then funneling into me. All of it, until the magical attack seemed to have just evaporated from the air. The golden lines shimmered and dissipated, but that wasn't his concern, not even in the slightest and for the second time today I saw the maddeningly controlled man be anything but. He was laboring to breathe and watching me, attempting to grasp at an understanding; and wouldn't you know? It was astonishing. I was alive, and I was rewarded.

Cinders belched and crackled all around me, and a foreboding wisp of smoke wove around me like a long-lost lover, and there I was. Standing upright, smirking, watching, and waiting for Donovan.

He stared at me, breathing heavily, then surveyed the room along with me. The male goblin who'd almost gotten away was dead, a black scythe embedded in his back. The female dark elf was down too, and it looked pretty… final. I'll spare you the details. I'd imagine the finality of her gruesome situation is what prompted the sudden vanishing of the male member of the Warded pair.

Inside my left palm was a fidget spinner, carefully inscribed by my own tools, and at the center of the glove was a thin pillar where I could lock them in. When Donovan made the move for such a crude and direct attack he was bluffing, a braggadocious thing to show the kind of fighter he'd become; it was a chest-puff to boast about the kind of energy he'd harvested. Me goading him into using it wasn't out of character, but given the shared company, he'd had no choice but to implement the use of it and smite me—or try to.

"It's not my fault you're so easy to read," I said.

Donovan looked skeptical, a toothy smirk residing just as easily on his face as his dead-eyed neutral expression once did.

"Shitty people ain't hard to read Donovan, even smart ones."

The Kansas City Shuffle was an old hustle. I pointed an accusing finger at my pint-sized enemy while my other hand set to work. My fingers carefully dislodged the locking mechanism that kept the fully charged fidget spinner fixed to my palm, freeing it for use.

"Another minute and I would have killed us." Donovan's nonchalance was feigned, he had no interest in dying. It was true too, if he kept funneling power into the sigils the fire would have eaten all the oxygen out of the room, and it would have blossomed into an inferno and burned us all alive. Or, more likely, the fidget spinner would have been capped in its ability to siphon magical energy and exploded with enough ferocity to only kill us two. He did figure out where he'd seen this idea, though, and the man wasn't far off when he noted that if my energy-thieving gauntlet-slash-fidget spinner combination had taken on any more magic, we would all be dust.

"I'm good with that."

"How can you even entertain winning against the Great Mistress?" His dubiousness was condescending as he gestured to the mirror-locked woman wearing Maria's face. "Against me, a master Tinkerer? What about them?" He swept his arm toward the monsters in the room. "Two of the most feared Judges ever? You can't be serious, Janzen." That's when I took in the whole of the arena. The murdered House of Unet, the Marked ones still unsure where they fell in all this and doing their best to be quiet, off in a corner, looking incredibly human. The bloodied bodies of the male goblins were slumped over in two places, with only the female being left as she started to slink over to the beastly Judge of her tribe. The remaining dark elf with the long, wicked scythe was fixated on me, though to what end I couldn't yet say.

All in all it was an impossible climb, the hazardous trek riddled with powerhouses I couldn't hope to compete with but holding onto a defeatist mentality wasn't going to keep me upright. What kept me upright was gumption, defiance, anger, and some good old-fashioned ego.

"Still thinkin' small, which I guess comes naturally for you." Being short myself, I had an arsenal of these, and I never got to use them.

His next move was going to be to barter for my imprisonment, give me a bunch of empty promises about how it doesn't have to be this way, that they can take care of me, us even, all I need to do is slow down and think—

"Janzen, really, think about what I'm offering you in this current set of realities." True to form, he actually started on that very thing…You see, I'm smart too, and we're not in Kansas anymore Toto. Let playtime begin.

With a sigh, and tightening my fists, I hung my head.

"What's he doing?" The mirror-bound Matron couldn't tell, and while the she-goblin got to unleashing the living Judge that was a hodgepodge of monster parts, she stalled to watch Donovan. She was exercising caution, but the apprehension was about him and not for him.

"Janzen, this is the most logical action you can take that has any hope of seeing you and your friends safe." The first skirmish was to feel each other out, and I had already witnessed a handful of things I had no hope of actually contending with.

I did have a good curveball though, and they saw it when I abruptly wound up and let loose, sending the fidget spinner soaring over to the dome in a blur of a throw. The creature from the Abyss only got the chance to press herself against the countenance of the mirror and glower at me as it struck true, letting loose a volatile explosion. It was concave too, and that sent it skyrocketing into the back of the auditorium and splintering right in half. There was a gasp, an unseen cackle of power, and an almost poetic clap of thunder as if to bring it all home.

Donovan and his Blind Judge stood to my right.

To the left there was a now-distraught female Goblin, the remaining dark elf and of course the Marked Ones.

Donovan, the last remaining member of the House of Unet was on his feet. There was a moment where he and the last Masarou goblin stood and beheld each other in this weird hypnotized, longing stare, and despite every other moment where I'd felt like I didn't belong here, I realized this whole thing had absolutely nothing to do with me—or Gale for that matter.

"Nothing changes," Donovan said. The ground trembled as the Dreadnought delivered itself to Donovan's side.

"We kill them all," the goblin hissed, the towering monstrosity looming in her wake.

"And then cleanse the city." Donovan looked to his goblin cohort with desire, and Ja'Sune seemed to delight in the shared sentiment. This was the hidden agenda. The female goblin was Ja'Sune, the love of Donovan's life, and they were willing to do anything to be together. Even this.

***

"They're never a sensible man again, eh?" I'd already started backing up, and with some very expressive hand signals and gestures I managed to convince Delta and Alpha to do much the same and caught a glimpse of them ducking out a side-entrance beside the overturned table.

Donovan gave me a look that softened despite himself. Ja'Sune had a read on her long-lost man and lovingly took the reins from him. "Mortaus," She gave a commanding touch to the thigh of the scythe-wielding sentry beside her and the Judge. "Kill this man quickly, and if you can salvage his body, perhaps I'll allow Donovan to make him decor."

"See? And everyone says you're an ugly, short-sighted, unqualified, mean-spirited bitch." Pause for effect, stiff-upper lip, and deliver. "You ain't *that* mean."

I left in a dead run up the hallway that led me down into this coliseum-styled courthouse. Donovan just watched me go with those lifeless eyes; as his head turned, so too did that of the golem in perfect synchronism. They had a long overdue reunion to get to and couldn't be bothered by me. If the elf was on me, I couldn't tell, and you know what? Even if he was, there was little chance I'd hear him coming.

So I ran.

***

As the coliseum-like expanse was disappearing behind me, I realized that I hadn't noticed the downhill trek I'd made to get in here. What I did realize was that I was in an uphill climb now, and that I could use that to my advantage. Grabbing at one of the three satchel-cases on my right hip, I dug out a handful of marbles and dropped them. Dark elves had exceptional vision, but they used them in different spectrums. Heat was one, and seeing a magical signature was another—you get the point—they were exceptional hunters, like everything from the Abyss.

A moment later I heard a slapstick sort of commotion behind me, because these particular marbles that I had dropped didn't have any divine power or elemental energy—they were just a good handful of regular old marbles, quietly rolling down the inclined carpet.

This wasn't what they had been meant for, but when in Rome…

The fleet-footed elf found himself abruptly off balance and crashed to the ground just as I came out of the hallway and back into the foyer of the condemned courthouse. I risked a glance back at the dusky passage I'd come out of, and the living shadow was starting toward me again, the glint of his scythe signaling his hateful approach.

A quick eyeball of the dimensions of the passageway told me that this must have been the way they'd brought the Blind Judges into the courtroom, and that settled it. I took out a handful of marbles that had destruction written all over them—literally. Acting panicky, I sold my despair by almost fumbling my backpedaling while throwing both handfuls at the elf. He leapt with powerful grace, twisted midair and kept coming as soon as his feet touched the ground again. The next handful was scattered with a twirl of his long scythe before he resumed his pursuit of me.

I got my shield up just in time to catch the first offensive, more deflecting than intercepting, my head not yet turning to regard my assailant who sailed overhead landing somewhere behind me. Extending an open hand, I pushed some focus into the three rings I was wearing on my reaching fingers. They momentarily illuminated, which triggered the marbles to them; first was an eruption of kinetic energy, then a flash of freezing, and finally a cat 5 whirlwind.

It sounds impressive, sure, but the blast radius of each was no more than a few feet. It wasn't meant to be an offensive weapon, anyway.

I felt an awful wound open across the length of my back, the pain so sharp it stole the air from my lungs. Crumpling over, I caught myself by the very hand I'd been concentrating on. Luckily, it worked; the explosion ripped the drywall and veneer off the hall, exposing the structure. The ice froze the studs and the violent gusts of wind, mixed with the brittleness created by the cold, caused the whole causeway to collapse.

I suspected the commotion was the only thing that saved my life. In my peripheral vision I saw the quick-stepping dark elf beside me, scythe raised high overhead, and the only reason he hesitated to detach my head from my neck was the realization that I'd just sealed the Judges and company away. Dark elves were fast and deceptively strong, but the trick was to get inside on them. The ground hadn't finished quaking from the collapse when I wrapped an arm around his ankle. I dropped my shoulder and head into the vulnerable joint of his knee, then pushed with my upper body and pulled with my arm. The dark elf stiffened in sudden awareness of what was happening; he swiped, but his strike was ungainly, and he failed to break his fall. We both went down, but while he was supine, I hoisted myself into a guard mount, straddling his hips like an eager prom date—except instead of following it with a blundering kiss, I summoned my shield and dropped it into his face.

He was no novice unfortunately. I got a hit out of it, but his hands flew up to grab my wrist before we devolved into grappling.

I didn't have time for this. I had a pair of Blind Judges a few minutes from finding a way out of their makeshift tomb, an entire city about to get caught unaware with no solution to speak of, and if I survived all of this, the repercussions of being party to the bloodbath that killed the Unet and Masarou leadership was sure to be biblical.

I shoved him away hard and growled as I pushed myself to my feet. I tried to buy some space by throwing anything within reach from the condemned building. Chairs, a table, a lamp; the stalking dark elf was suddenly very patient in his defense, his well-timed strikes neatly destroying each impediment.

"Fine! Let's do this."

I ripped my metal bat out and let every sigil of energy crack to life. The artificery was carved in three distinct columns, two runes on each column, and the bat's rubber hilt was so well-worn you could see the imprint of my fingerprints on it. This was a tried-and-true companion, a lifesaver when I first happened on the Marked Ones before. Twirling it in my hand to re-familiarize myself with old faithful here, I beckoned him with a smirk and a gesture with my other hand and invited him to dance.

We rushed, we roared, and we both swung.

And at the end only one of us was standing.

***

It wasn't me; I came to on the ground.

Coughing out debris was a sensation one didn't forget. Grove and I had talked about it before, his being from a particularly nasty improvised explosive device in Mogadishu and mine of course from when the Stalker and I dropped a building onto one another. You coughed, but it was a body-wrenching, throat-seizing cough because it wasn't lubricated. It was just pieces of dirt and sandpaper scraping against each other.

Mortaus, the dark elf, was standing about ten feet away with his back turned to me, his long scythe still in hand. He twitched when I coughed; I suspect he thought he'd killed me. Apparently, if you cut an elementally charged bat in half it releases all of the stored energy it had inside of itself.

I heard that steady thrumming sound that told me I had a concussion once again.

Shit, *so close*.

I threw the lower half of my bat aside. It clanged against the marble foyer floor, disturbing some of the dust I'd chugged down. The top half of the bat was in the dark elf's hand, and he still hadn't turned around. I ran through my inventory: I had two pairs of gloves, the fidget spinners which were for energy assimilation, my shield, my bat-dagger, and one remaining satchel of marbles. I was having a tough time gathering myself, and unfortunately when it comes to concussions you didn't actually get better at them with experience. It wasn't like drinking, where if you hit that sweet spot of functional alcoholism at least you could fake being a contributing member of society to those who didn't know you (or have to interact with you for more than five minutes).

I knew all of this to be true by way of experience.

I got to my feet grudgingly and noticed the rather respectable circle we'd cleared out when the bat-bomb went off. My blurry vision drew a bead on the elf long enough to focus, and when the slinky assassin shifted to face me, I saw why he'd taken his time.

His face was a wet massacre. Ribbons of flesh were torn away, black ichor oozed out of a dozen superficial but impressively ugly cuts. He was madness incarnate; beyond his ruined face there was hatred in his eyes that few could evoke in someone so freshly met. What can I say, I'm talented.

"Bro," I said, then hacked out a wad of bloody phlegm for emphasis. "You look like you got hit with a sack of what-the-fuck."

My aim was to aggravate him, and I was spot on as usual. He hurled the remainder of the bat at me, which I barely managed to duck under while tucking tail to run. My pivot was so messy I had to catch myself on the ground to get steady again. I was almost outside, and that was where salvation lay. I needed to get out of range of his vicious weapon. Given how effortlessly it was skewering my gear, I figured the blackened material it was made of had to be Stalker claw or some kind of *bad-ass* named steel only available in the deepest recesses of the Abyss.

The revolving door took a really hard push to get going; I fought with every bit of my strength to get it to go even an inch or two, and then it came loose and flung me outside. I climbed to my feet and hurried down the ornate stairwell, only to watch my adversary hit the revolving door like a battering ram, his enhanced strength amplifying it all.

He spun a good two or three times.

There was nothing wrong with the door, it worked fine.

Almost as important as how funny it was to watch that long-limbed fuck get all tangled up in such tight quarters was the time it bought me—it gave me enough of a break to get to my duffel bag. I heard rather than saw him manage to make his way outside. I could *feel* his second, scorched hand take hold of the shaft as he flew toward me, taking a leap halfway into the stairwell and coming down on me with enough conviction to cut me clear in half.

I tried not to panic, I tried to make this moment into many; I reminded myself not to be the problem, the urgency, or even the mission, but the *now*. I knew I had it when I felt it, the weight of its hilt so faithfully familiar. Instead of trying to rise to my feet and fend him off, I dropped to my knee and rolled onto my back, meeting the black-bladed scythe with a sword of my own, a sword that caught the steel shank, challenged it, and ultimately deflected it, leaving a sizable chunk missing.

Cold raindrops pelted my face, and yet for the first time, I wasn't the miserable one in all of this. I found my feet, the paladin Bhalore's sword in my hand and my shield activated on the other arm. I stood between the dark elf and my city with a renewed sense of hope.

For the first time I saw that I had this darkling champion on his guard. He was confused, hurt, but most importantly… he was scared.

I drove it home by adopting a solid fighting stance and bade him on with a bloodied grin.

CHAPTER 16

Monsters and Men

"...Again!" The worst part was that he said it with such an infectious, booming laugh. Bhalore wasn't tall, but he was big. I mean he was a few inches above average, but the only reason he's towering over me is because I was, once again, flat on my back.

I was a month outside of twenty, so I'd grown into my body, and I was pretty regular with the gym and training; in fact, most of my ragtag group had taken to training me, and I tagged almost all of them at least once or twice which I crowed about as much as possible. It was something of a badge of honor, making the progress I had in such a short amount of time.

The only hiccup I had in earning the set from every team member was Bhalore. My frustration must have been evident, because the jovial man wore a satisfied expression—like the cat that ate the canary—and without any complaint or quip, he just moved to the far bench and sat down. Bhalore was a devoted Christian, which surprised people since he was middle eastern. He was thick-bodied, not fat but not chiseled either. Bulky I suppose, but it didn't diminish any of his speed. Bhalore wasn't just fast for a guy his size, he was fast for a guy built for speed who trained to that end every day.

"My red-faced owlet, what is it that's vexing you?"

He called me an owlet because he called Zachariah an owl. Bhalore's baritone voice was like warm honey, just unfairly great. It went with anything, and everyone was a fan of it. Bhalore could recite the alphabet and I'd experience it as a lullaby. Pulling myself upright, I looked down at the array of bruises that were already starting to develop.

"I can't hit you."

"Not yet, no." He smiled.

"Come on man! It's been six months! Six months and I ain't even skinned you—not once. This is a waste of time…who uses a swor—" I stopped myself, which never happened; I wasn't fearful, but honestly, I didn't want to slight what Bhalore did for me and meant to us. My intermission of discretion was blessed by his all-knowing, ear-to-ear grin.

"What then, you want I should let you hit me like the others do for you so that you won't flail about like a prepubescent child who hasn't gotten his way?"

That hurt on so many levels. I was a street kid, and proud of it; we were tough, and it meant something. So to be called out on that was a matter of pride, but the realization that this attitude may be so tiresome that other people actually eased up on me so that they wouldn't have to tolerate my whining was a hard pill to swallow. I suddenly felt very small and hugged my knees to my chest. My head started to sink. Maybe that was why they hadn't taken me on a mission yet. Had all I earned as of yet been given to me because of my griping?

I snapped out of it in time to see Bhalore come off the bench, and with a bewildering grace place himself cross-legged in front of me, his sword laid across his lap. His dark eyes had so much light in them, which was a fun thing to try to explain about him to anyone else. His shaved head made him look militant, but the smile he wore allayed any concern of him being too much of a disciplinarian.

"I will not coddle you Janzen. I will not hand you a gimmie either." He was gently unapologetic and wore a sort of bemused expression. "I think soon enough you'll need none of that. I think, soon enough, you will become the sum total of all the pieces in your life…. And that, my dear friend, will be quite special."

"Yeah?" I hated dwelling in sincerity for too long, but this guy made Mr. Rogers come across as abrasive, so it was hard to just fire off some sarcasm and call it good. "Then why can't I hit you?"

"A fight, a battle, a duel, it's all different. If I gave you a hundred things to think about while fighting," he said, his gnarled fingers snapping while circling in the air around him. "Then you'd be great. You'd be able to manage it, you thrive in that you know. But this?" The snapping stopped, and his strong hand fell to the hilt of the plain sword he was never without. "This is different. This takes focus and patience, and you can't overcome your impatience without focused effort. You need to experience yourself in the present, in the now; you need to learn that and apply it in a fight. Once you can see and think of only me and my motions, and tune out the distractions, you'll fall into your own, and that will be a sight to behold. What you do not yet see, the river knows."

A quizzical brow bade him elaborate, which he did with a hearty chuckle.

"It means you'll get there eventually, owlet. Eventually."

"What if I use your sword this time? It's got to have a bunch of magical properties, some kind of strength enhancement… I mean, is it the sword in the stone—Excalibur?"

There was a long, amused pause. "You do know that those are two different swords?"

I scoffed and rolled my eyes theatrically. "Yeah, obvi." It was my turn to pause. "They are?"

He laughed, clapping me on the shoulder through his rolling amusement. Most big guys who did that never realized their own strength, they could bowl you over into a whole flight of drinks or an unsuspecting bystander, but not Bhalore. Bhalore was so mindful that somehow he managed to stay connected with himself, his surroundings, the goings-on and how they not only affected him but how he could affect them as well. I admired that, and because of the pandemonium that lived in my brain, I was a little jealous that I couldn't ever emulate it.

"This is the sword of a good man Janzen, nothing more or less. There's a story of a retired soldier who would not fight for a new king in a land long since forgotten. He would not fight for he believed in defense of his nation, not the subjugation of others. Labeled an outcast, disgraced and dishonored, they pushed him outside the protection of their great city.

"Years passed and the old man, unfazed, kept to himself, farming and living a simple life. Even as his own wife left him, he kept to his truth. When his children named him a coward, he fashioned them weapons and wished them well when they pledged themselves to this new king. The king promised a return to prominence, he vowed that the nation would have no equal and that all would bathe in the glory of their conquest.

"Well, blood begets blood—and don't ever forget that Janzen. The reach of the new king went too far and made enemies of a dark force that came to visit its vengeance upon the kingdom even after it had mercilessly crushed their invading armies. This dark force bled into their streets, stealing back the spoils they had taken from others, killing indiscriminately and destroying the innocence of those whose lives were not immediately forfeit."

Composing himself with a sigh, his knuckles whitened on the hilt of the sword as he turned it upright. It was an unremarkable piece really—nothing much in the looks department— but it was cool that it was so old and still functional, and I found myself not only drawn to it, but comforted by it as well.

"A few escaped the city, and begged for refuge from the outcast soldier, who obliged. Of course unlike them, he knew it wasn't over. The dark forces had not been sent simply to visit damnation and make ruins of the once-majestic kingdom, but to salt the very earth itself. Gathering food, supplies, and fashioning them a cart, he sent the survivors southward.

"One of his sons who was still alive asked why he would not come, but he already knew the answer. This enemy would be relentless, and they hadn't the time to escape… not without a sacrifice."

"Evil, the father said before disappearing to hold off the darkness, must always be met. It must be challenged by good people willing to take arms and make the hardest of sacrifices if that is what is asked of them. The lesson was twofold, for the evil the old man spoke about was within his son, and through his son passed to these people who had come for them and would come again."

"That was some three thousand years ago. Since then, this blade has found its way to those who would wield it for the righteous, and for the righteous it will gift them with the calm needed to navigate battle. It cannot be broken by evil, not so long as a good man wields it."

I considered it. "So does it take a good wielder to use it, or does it just help the wielder be a better person?"

The paladin stood, offering a big hand to help me to my own feet before we paced our distances to set at each other once again.

"Yes."

And we charged….

***

…The ricochet of weapons clashing reverberated down my arm and rattled my teeth; our weapons sang the song of steel as we passed each other, both spinning around to set after one another once again.

Normally, this fight would have been over before it started, but Mortaus's grievous wounds were depleting his stamina, robbing him of his preternatural speed, and most importantly, the pain was infecting his mind and disabling its ability to function. I'd thrown punches with broken knuckles, walked on blown-out knees, fought with brain bleeds. This was the benefit of being the underdog—when the fight got to the final stretch, you had nothing left to lose. You weren't even supposed to be here. As for him? It was likely that he hadn't seen a worthy rival in a long time, having occupied such an elite guardianship. He'd been handing out ass-whoopings for so long that he forgot what one felt like. That pain clouding his mind, invading his focus, and ruining his chances in this fight was an alien distraction; for me, it was a default setting.

He was still fast, and our first few exchanges had me on the defensive. That didn't matter, I absorbed more than just tough shots from the scythe: I was analyzing. Veterans of combat see stuff other people don't; Mortaus couldn't lift his right arm above the shoulder, he relied on routines and attacking in predetermined patterns, and now that his injuries were slowing him down his swipes weren't just impossible blurs. Each had a signature, and after a couple more slashes I abandoned my fighting stance and put myself upright.

The rain started to fall heavier. It wasn't cold enough to hamper either of us, and while we stared one another down I started to review not just my opponent but the logistics of my cockeyed plan and how it fit into all of this.

From inside the condemned courthouse there was a muted smashing noise which drew our attention. It seemed Donovan had ditched trying to think his way out and set to pulverizing the walkway till they could work their way clear.

I lifted the blade up to my face, the pommel at my chin and the cross guard across my eyes. There was an old prayer once whispered by Bhalore that I found coming from my lips, something that surprised me almost as much as the next bit.

"If you lay your weapon down now, this can be over. You can leave and salvage what life you can. I won't chase you down, I'll let you go back to whatever hellhole you crawled out of and leave it be."

The incredulous look I got wasn't wholly unexpected, but I maintained my serious vigilance. He chuckled in a way that was unmistakably condescending and shifted the grip on his weapon so that the blade rested flat against his back, shoulder to shoulder.

"You have lost this fight, lay down your weapon." I wanted to add *I don't want to kill you* but that wasn't true, and I wasn't going to lie while holding a sacred sword. I wouldn't call the feeling regret—I wasn't going to try to justify my inclinations. I hunted monsters, I put them down, I kept them in the darkness where they belonged, and in order to get better, I had to adopt a lot of their proclivities.

With a dancer's grace, Mortaus shifted into a toe-heavy stance until he was ready to explode into motion. Flying full tilt at me, the scythe came free in a helicopter spin; it was a feint, he'd done this once before except now he was starting from the middle of the offensive set instead, thinking it would be enough to trick me.

It wasn't.

I didn't bite at his first feint, so when the blade followed in the next predictable strike, I was able to catch and tangle it with my sword. Its dulled, seemingly unremarkable steel met the ferocious challenge of the onyx steel at the base of the cross-guard. I twisted my wrist inward to lock in and trap the scythe's blade, then lifted my sword-arm skyward, bringing his trapped weapon with me and badly exposing his flank which I crushed with a brutal chop of my shield.

I followed it with additional blows to his ribs until he crumpled to the side in shock. One of his hands dropped the scythe but the other was clinging for dear life, an instinct rather than a cognitive function. My sword arm swung back down in a half-circle, launching the bladed end of his weapon into the street where the arcing claw betrayed him and buried itself deep into the pavement. It didn't matter, my now-disengaged sword came back up and a pommel-heavy hand smashed right into his face. It took him off his feet, a macabre portrait of blood splattered everywhere. Even more poured out of his nose, and his shallow breath told me he was still alive, but unconscious.

I didn't like how long it took me to convince myself not to finish him off.

The rhythmic cadence of smashing became more predominant, a steady soundtrack reminding me that this fight was far from finished. I unfurled the fist I was making with my shield arm, which triggered the reliable keepsake to fold back in on itself. I dragged Mortaus's surprisingly light body into an alley, but not before binding him thoroughly. There was a pun to be made about loose ends, but I wasn't really in the mood to make it.

I went back to my duffel bag and dug for my phone; not my phone, but a burner I bought for this sole purpose.

"Is it done?" I asked.

There was a tense silence before a terse, "Yes." They asked if my paranoia was just that or was I actually having to eat that big of a shit sandwich.

"It's like I feared, yes. We're even now."

I hung up. I managed to outfit myself with the rest of the bag's contents, all the while wondering how I could account for not one, but two Judges in my plan. I was taking a one-in-a-million chance going after the Dreadnought, but the living Judge was another thing altogether.

No sooner had I thought about it when I recognized that I was in complete silence, a silence that was supernatural in nature. I paused in unpacking the bag, glancing back over the slope of my shoulder.

And there it was, that beastly Judge, its eyes glossed over. Its indomitable will was being contoured to obey someone else. Should have guessed the collapsed corridor wouldn't have kept it contained. It was more agile—scaling a wall and bursting through a roof wasn't out of the question for something so acrobatic.

I wasn't ready. I had another ten minutes of preparation at the very least left in my suicide strategy, and that was *if* I rushed and half-assed work that most certainly should not be half-assed.

"We told you Janzen." The beast's throaty tone was not a voice I recognized, but I could guess at the original orator. "This was futile. The call for war is here; we must kill the old way, and with it the broken worlds it has built. Stay down and this will be quick. I can make it painless; I owe you that much. You have done more than even I could have ever imagined, but you alone aren't enough to challenge all of us."

The voice told me to stay down, so my knee-jerk reaction was to stand up.

It told me it could make it quick and painless, so I activated my shield and drew my sword.

It told me I wasn't enough alone, but I heard the low beat of the opening notes of *Juke Box Hero* by Foreigner making its way to me across concrete and asphalt… And I knew that it was right, and that I wasn't alone.

***

The beast's head ripped back, its snarling maw spewing the street with acidic saliva, and it seemed that while so small a thing shouldn't have bothered the beast, it was frantically clawing at its own head. There was a sharp *crack* in the air after the Judge's roar, and it took me a second to realize the percussion of a fired shot actually belched out *after* I saw the reaction—someone had really reached out and touched this thing. Not many people in the world could make that kind of a shot, and there was no doubt in my mind that Grove was abstaining from self-congratulations and was casually, like so annoyingly casually, racking another round with the bolt action rifle he'd built for just this type of situation.

The music ramped up, it seemed to be coming from all over, and I couldn't pinpoint its point of origin. Not immediately at least, but after a scan of the skyline I saw Johnny B above an empty diner shredding on that weird guitar, bellowing and belting as the song demanded. He was in an outfit so ostentatious even 80's rockers might think it pretentious—and he was *owning* it. The music was exhilarating, and not because I was living, for the second time, a dream of fighting with a soundtrack attached to it all, there was magic infused in every chord that breathed new life into my broken-down body.

The monster's incessant clawing kept it busy until it dug deep into its own eye socket and ripped out the ruined eye. Amid the blackened, bloody muck of the discarded organ was a bullet—a bullet inscribed with very, very basic artificery. Grove had carved the bullet himself with a rune for fire. Between the power of the spent powder, the concussion from the primer and of course all of that energy being absorbed into the sigil, the round wasn't only a sharp stab into the eye, but a raging inferno once it found itself embedded in flesh.

Crude, but clever.

The beast's rage boiled over as it drew a bead on the shooter and singer. Of course, that was the point.

A blur of motion caught my eye, and when I homed in on it, I saw Xander, in his true Rougarou form, in a fluid sprint toward the edge of a nearby building. The baddest man on the block took soundless flight, looking majestic; the water dampened his tawny pelt, but the ethereal light from the moon made it all seem so poetic. Teeth bared, claws at the ready, this power-ball of constricted muscle came down like the hammer of Thor. I *felt* the crushing, claws-first clash. Xander drove the monstrosity into the ruined pavement before using its abused body as a launchpad to leap away.

And as cool as that was, and man was it cool, it had nothing on what I saw next.

The Concrete Monk came off a second-story ledge over my own head, timing his arrival with Xander's exit. Normally, throwing a punch into a thickened, ape-like skull wasn't an ideal attack, but this wasn't just anyone. This was Patrick, master of the Five Forms, *Something* of the Last Gate—who hit the thing with such a humdinger that I swear the echoing shock of the haymaker actually cleared the pouring rain outward. Like the sheer force blossomed out and made a dry spot in the middle of a tsunami. He wasn't in his usual street clothes, but instead he was dressed in a plain, homely cotton outfit, all white. That hit was enough to stun the towering titan, and with it disoriented executed a fast-snapping kick to the other side of the cranium.

"We only got one more of those rehearsed, man," he said, his centered voice restoring what I needed most in all of this. Hope. The Concrete Monk stood there with all his coy, off-centered charm. This morning I'd given him an out, I'd even reinforced why it was the right way to go. I did it, because truthfully, I was sure this wasn't going to work. I didn't want to sabotage the city by robbing it of an actual hero. But here he was with a smile on his lips. "We'd best get to work."

Despite a perfectly coordinated attack from some of the best in the business, the monstrous Judge roared back to its feet. Xander latched onto its back, glad I think to have a hide he could actually rip into; Patrick was dancing back, staying out of the way as the two tangled. Another shot rang out, but this was about to turn into an all-out brawl.

Even more concerning was that the brutal drumbeat of mythical steel on very ordinary pavement just kept coming. Donovan wouldn't be kept from this fight much longer. I sprinted to my bag and dug into it, my hands quickly finding what they were looking for: a smooth, flat metal plate a little bigger than a softball, carved into a simple rune with a hinged piece to act as a handle.

I slipped Zachariah's old glove on and closed my fist, finding comfort in his reliable work. I couldn't focus on the fight, but I could hear the succession of gunshots more frequently and with far greater clarity, meaning Grove was closing in on the battle as it turned against us. Xander was only holding his own because Patrick was surgically taking out the Judge's legs whenever it was in a position to strike the Shifter. That strategy wouldn't work forever, and the deadly three-pronged tail of the abomination had now begun thwarting any backside attack by snapping out at anyone or anything within reach.

They had started to work their way down the road past the condemned courthouse. I could still hear the music, and it alone might be what gave me enough courage to hold on to this insane conviction of mine. I activated the glove's fire artificery and palmed the metal rune until I felt the steel start to sizzle.

The metal made the rain scream, turning water into steam, and that was when I knew it was ready. My breath came in shaky gasps while I tried to solidify my resolve, but it was one of those things where there was no easy way to see it done. I reached up with my spare hand and ripped my shirt open, sending buttons scattering into puddles.

Shit-shit-shit-shit was all I could hear in my own head. I lifted the glowing branding iron to my chest.

"Shit."

And I drove it home, directly into my chest, the white-hot flash of pain taking over my every thought as well as scarring my skin forevermore. Agony dug deep into my bones, and because of the need for the mark to be as perfect as possible I couldn't flinch, so before I lost consciousness, I made myself pull the stake in some more to make the wound clear and true. The edges frayed; a bit more went black. I didn't completely check out, but I felt my body sag and hands go weak, and I heard the *clank* of the brand as it hit the ground—I hadn't felt myself drop it, nor felt it tear away from my screaming wound. Small blessings. I looked for the bag, which was just out of reach but might as well have been miles away given the agony of stretching for it, but I finally got a handhold and dragged it over; I was so weak I couldn't even open the jar.

Fine. I smashed the jar on the sidewalk and gathered a handful of the transmogrification goo—with bleary eyes I searched my hand and picked out the glass shards, because I couldn't risk altering or damaging the rune I'd burned into my body. I wasn't even sure if this was going to work, or how much more pain I could tolerate, but right before the black could take me, I slapped it into my wound, and then fell, face-first into the muddy, bloodied gutter water.

***

The fluttering curtain of my eyelids kept me from making any sense of what I was seeing. I knew there was a blueprint for how the fight should go, but the architect of it was having a hell of a time sticking to the plan. Xander looked badly hurt by the time I came to, gasping at the air as if it was the very thing drowning him. Music was heavy in the atmosphere, and when my bleary gaze found Johnny B I could see his hands were bloodied. He was also on the street, but on the far end, even farther back than I was.

At the heart of the fight was Patrick, serene and indomitable. The boogeyman of boogeymen. He was losing ground, torn to shreds, tiring, but he delivered grounded strength behind every kick, fluidly deflecting instead of absorbing blows; there was an art to the way he turned a parry into a punch. It was captivating watching the way the burly man moved, and it wasn't as if these were impossible acrobatics or nimble escape tactics...these were well timed, patient and deliberate movements that took a tremendous amount of focus—and faith in that focus.

The Judge's three-pronged tail had come down in a succession of stabs that forced Patrick's retreat, but their real aim was to bait the monk into a tighter corner of the street and when its limb swung a left hook from his other side, he had no answer for it. He sailed across the street into an abandoned building with a horrific *smack*: neither the brick wall nor the man gave, the collision had stolen his breath and consciousness, maybe his life. He slumped to the ground, expressionless and still.

I pushed myself up to a haggard kneel; my inner meditation made it difficult to key into my own body, but I knew I had to get going. I also knew I couldn't forfeit my concentration, or all of this would be for naught. I'd just gotten a foot beneath me when I saw Xander doing his best to try to attract the beast's full attention, though to what end I wasn't yet sure. Pride was a funny thing and trying to go at this thing by his lonesome seemed stupid, but I had never credited the Rougarou with an abundance of intelligence. Of course, as the Bard started to let loose on *Blaze of Glory,* I could see the writing on the wall. Grove was driving headlong into the damn thing; the Karaoke King was belting out his swan song which admittedly was a big boon to me as I managed to get my other foot beneath me. I rasped a *no,* I even pathetically reached as if that would somehow stop all of what I was seeing from unfolding.

It couldn't…it wouldn't.

The truck smashed into the Judge, not budging it even an inch. Xander leapt away too late. It all seemed to happen in an instant, but my consciousness made me relive it for several lifetimes inside that moment. Johnny found the trigger, the truck exploded, and the street was clear of any and all menace; and there I was, stumbling down the soaked street, bloodied, burned, and again without a tribe, a family…without my friends.

Even in my anger I forced myself to hold my focus on that which I was holding inside of me—a bead on my own endgame.

For once I didn't curse timing when the Dreadnought arrived in front of me. At the far end of the street that my friends had just torn down was the source of all of this misery.

Its chestplate slid down, and nested inside was the maestro of all this madness: Donovan. There he sat, plugged into the thing's internal controls, and at the center of his own chest, the ruby amulet that seemed to make it all so easy. Its magical amplification allowed him to pilot the Dreadnought all on his own, though I suspected that in his arrogance he'd designed the thing for that very purpose. The amulet just gave him the edge, its power bolstering his already impressive talents making him as close to unbeatable as it got. The man didn't even have words for me, he had laughter.

This wasn't a time for talking, anyway. I launched into an inelegant sprint; my legs unwieldy as they seemed unable to understand what it was that I wanted them to do. I could still hear that laugh with a metal tinge to it as it echoed out of the Judge's chest. The golem lifted an arm aiming to smash me, but at the last second, I slid, baseball-style, between the Judge's legs. While sliding, I threw as hard a right hook as I could manage, roaring out all the animosity eating away at me as I did.

The Dreadnought was hit with a deafeningly loud blow that sent it staggering stupidly forward, lurching over on itself. My leading foot from the slide stopped when it hit the cleat of the legendary Cleveland Browns Running back, Jim Brown, towering in all his eight-foot-tall bronze glory. I clawed at the statue for shelter, sliding between its legs and stood behind it; carved into its bronze surface was the same emblem I'd burned into my flesh, the symbol anchoring my consciousness to it through the medium of the magical goop.

I wanted to say something catchy, and even if I only entertained it for a half-second; there was a fire burning behind the beastly Judge reminding me of the people who were relying on me in this moment, as well as those who'd sacrificed themselves to give us a chance at this. People never took the time to understand how much had to go right for the little guy to even have half a chance, and how many good men and women had to lay down and die so that a rebellion could hold on to hope.

I didn't waste the moment.

I raised my hand a second time and charged, the football great mirroring my movements in front of me like a massive metal puppet. My head pounded, the throb growing so severe with every passing moment that I wasn't sure how much of this I could take before giving in to the cold comfort of unconsciousness again, but for now I surged ahead. A bumbling right hook connected, and the following left to the body managed to sway it some, but when I moved again to keep pushing, it seemed the better-made construct was already in motion. My next swing was caught by a countering arm, and the one after was swatted away, though I did manage a forward snap kick before Donovan could try to concoct an offensive of his own.

Stumbling back, I tried to push the tempo but then something happened—there was a blink where I couldn't see the fight as I was, but instead saw through the eyes of what I would assume was the statue I was fighting to control.

What the heck...

... Did I just say Heck?

That hesitation cost me, and when my mind righted itself, it was all I could do to try to block the blow by crossing my arms over my head like an **X**. That hit scored, and a second one right behind it was even worse. As bad as they were mangling my avatar, that strike rattled me beyond the body; it was a hit to my true self, and it doubled me over instantly. Bloody spittle and some kind of unclear white stuff flowed freely out of my mouth, and I could only manage a glance as I saw the exemplary Jim Brown receive an awful kick to the solar plexus, a shot I felt light my own side on fire.

It didn't register but I must have slid a dozen feet back, and just as I finally ceased tumbling over top of myself, I felt the cold kiss of bronze beside me.

The fight was over before it even started.

***

The rain was heavily falling all over my face, the taste of bile backing up from my stomach and creep-crawling into my throat, complemented by that tasty tinge of iron which could only mean a kind of bleeding that I hadn't the mind nor care to try to pinpoint. All of that, and the Unet Judge just kept coming. It was an almost mocking serenade, each thundering step reminding me of my failure, growing more vivid by the moment, telling me of the life-ending scene about to play out.

Then, the rain stopped.

The Dreadnought's foot was suspended in the air. I was in pain, but it wasn't as present as before, it was almost an afterthought. I didn't take long to figure it out, though, and with a toothy smile I couldn't help but hurl a bit of cynicism at my momentary savior.

"I know you can't actually help, so how many pep talks are you going to make me listen to before you just go ahead and let him finish this?"

My newfound causticness dissolved before it hit its stride, because the person who came back at me wasn't at all who I was expecting.

"How many more are you gonna need, *Janzen*?"

Hers was a voice that could take the anger out of a rattlesnake, she could calm a hurricane with a look and take the snideness out of any smartass.

That wasn't Father Handy.

I shot up, and even if I was yet to lay an eye on her I exhaled the name that was as close to sacred as it got with me.

"Maria."

***

"Maria." I fumbled my way to my feet and turned to regard her. Her projection? No, it was her. It had to be her. I would *know* if it wasn't her. Immediately, and shamelessly, I was crying. I saw that while she wasn't sobbing, she shared the sentiment. I was suspended by… I don't know what—shock, disbelief, and maybe just the fact that this kind of good wasn't commonplace in our world and I wasn't sure if I should trust it.

She abated every worry, concern and doubt with a sigh that said so much: resilience, annoyance, and beneath it all, affinity. I ambled forward and wrapped her in a crushing hug that I couldn't hold long enough. I hugged her off her feet and spun her around, which gave me time to not only appreciate what may or may not be happening, but also to enjoy the world being at a stand-still all around me.

"Holy shit, Maria, you look great."

"You look like a fool, trying to badly pantomime every attack."

"Really? I was trying to like go for a Hugh Jackman thing."

Only I could exacerbate the dead. "I can't believe you're using this moment to make a Real Steel reference, Janz."

"Worth it."

"You'd lay down your life if the punchline was worth it." She shut down my retort with a pleading hand, my signal to stop.

Standing before me was the spirit of the woman, the quintessence of her being, but I knew that Maria, as I understood her, was gone.

She drew a breath and waved her hand in my face, an attention-grabber and a reminder for me to refrain from opening my mouth. "I am well, it's beautiful on this side, and it is really me. You need to let me talk now, okay?"

I nodded, albeit with a downtrodden expression on my face.

"What you're doing," she said, but paused and slid her fingers down to my chest, where my maimed chest still bore the weight of what I had done. "You… Oh, Janzen." She didn't shy away from the wound, but she seemed hurt by it. "You can't be *you* and the construct at the same time. You have to give way to it completely. If you can get *there*, you'll be able to move it like it's your own body. The Judge is a supremely powerful machine, and it's relentless, but Donovan was arrogant and introduced a very human element to that formula."

My confusion was obvious. I looked from the downed Jim Brown mirroring the fetal position I'd been in to the juggernaut that was halted on its path toward smashing us to death.

She swatted me. "Him, he's the human element. No matter how smug he is in there or how powerful, if you rattle him around enough, he's not going to be able to take it. Be quick, be ferocious, and beat the hell out of him. Give up to the construct, and that's when you'll have your window. You won't have long—the bronze won't hold up—but if you can pry him out of there, you can do this."

I tried to stammer something, to find a witty rejoinder or give some kind of assurance that I understood what she was saying, but I was running on empty. "I… I don't know Maria, I don't know how much fight I have left, or if it's even any good. I mean, look at this…" I gestured at the wreckage of the half-ruined avenue, the suspended fire reminding me that I was not even sure what was left of my companions, and of course the fact that she, my greatest failure, was right in front of me, wasn't as big a boon as you might think. "I couldn't even save *you*. I'm shit at this hero thing."

Slap.

I wasn't sure if this was an astral projection, a metaphysical manifestation, or some kind of spiritual sabbatical where all and none of the rules applied at once; but whatever it was, I was fairly confident that it wasn't supposed to sting as much as it did. I didn't just *look* wounded, I actually was.

"Save *me*?" She scoffed. "Janzen, you couldn't save me because I saved *you*. I saved *all* of you. You weren't the hero of my story."

"I was." There was a pride, the right kind of pride, written all over her as the woman straightened her spine and stared me down. There was no escaping eyes like that. And for the first time, I saw them for what they really were—fierce.

We sat in the silence for a moment following the truth bomb she'd dropped on my head, eventually closing my eyes to just breathe. Perspective could be damned sobering when you took the time to listen—not with the intent of talking—but to absorb what was being said. "Did you really see me as some damsel in distress? I wasn't some hapless victim Janzen, and as my friend you should respect what I sacrificed."

I felt a small twist in my chest when she said the word *friend*, and just as quickly rejected the feeling and felt ashamed that that had been my initial response.

Maria set her hands on my cheeks and lifted my head back up so I could see her warm eyes again. "If we'd had more time, I think we could have been best friends and I like to believe you're the kind of man who would be grateful, and appreciate that, as much as I would have. Despite everything, I'm glad we met and that I got to know you. But we weren't a love story, Janz, and I think you know that." A little smile touched her lips, like she could tell that I'd only recently arrived at that conclusion, but at least I'd arrived.

"We weren't a love story, and you weren't the hero of my story..." She pulled me into an embrace and kissed my cheek, then pressed her cheek against mine and said softly in my ear, "... you're the hero of this one."

When she pushed me back I half-expected to be catapulted to the now, to be thrown back into the madness of it all, but I wasn't. I turned to survey the landscape, to stare at this invincible giant that had convinced us we were doomed. Except now when I stared at it, I felt that tinge of impetuousness, that devil-may-care brazenness which made me such a pain in the ass; when I stared at it, I did so with obstinate defiance.

"Janzen," she said, commanding my attention, and when I looked back, I saw her center-stage flanked by Zachariah and Bhalore. There was a wildness to the fierce, full-mouthed smile she was aiming at me.

"Kick his *fucking ass*."

CHAPTER 17

Touchdown

Stomp.

He was probably three strides away, so I had plenty of time to figure out this whole *oneness* thing she was talking about. If that was even real. Maybe it was just the concussion—they make you kinda wonky—but a second inside a moment in the same time/space could clarify, or make things seem downright outlandish; in this case it did both.

Stomp.

I shut myself up, cleared my head as best I could, and tried to recall what it was I glimpsed when I saw through the eyes of the construct instead of trying to muscle it into some kind of obedience. I wasn't trying to win a war with it anymore, there was a fight to be had ahead of us so there couldn't be one between us as well.

Stomp.

My cheek burned a bit, and I remembered Maria, the hero that brought us all together under one banner.

When my eyes opened, I realized that I was seeing through the bronze statue's eyes. I saw the Judge towering overhead, its foot hiked up with the intent of pancaking what was left of me into the gravel. Not the death I'd fancied for myself, and truth be told I might meet a worse end on the road I was currently traveling—but this wasn't it.

I got a hand under me and used it to hoist my padded bronze shoulder under the Dreadnought's raised leg, then wrapped my arm around the limb to capture and lock it in place. I hauled myself the rest of the way up to my feet with the mechanical leg locked on my shoulder, which made the much more cumbersome Judge struggle to keep itself upright. It tried to throw a haymaker from the same side as its trapped leg, but I dodged it easily and the blow only glanced my arm. When it cocked back with the other arm I drove forward, lifting its leg so that I turned the whole thing over and sent it careening into the very gravel it had tried to mash me into.

While holding the advantage for the first time, I knew I needed to be very mindful of what tactic I employed next from my arsenal.

So I kicked it in the side—once, twice, three times. The fourth time my leg got caught by the mythical steel plating this thing was molded from; not only did that send an explosion of agony across my shin but it caved the bronzed limb, and I realized in my own agony the very real danger I'd put myself into by sharing my consciousness with it; It felt like I'd actually broken my own bone. Still, as this wasn't my body proper, so winning was a matter of managing my pain threshold and mental state. For a moment I saw my real body sprawled out on the street, pushed in the cleft of the sidewalk. It looked lifeless, but I was still connected to it; my anchor to this world. The sound of the Judge smashing road and nearby cars to pick itself upright from the rubble returned some sense of urgency to me.

Donovan's arrogance had him piloting the Dreadnought manually instead of remotely as it had been designed to do. His little nest in the control center was how he circumvented the issue of needing three practitioners and using the amulet to supercharge his efforts was ample compensation for the missing operators.

His steel was better-made, his endurance was superior, and it seemed my infused consciousness was going to make me pay for every pound of flesh, so I had to make this a completely concentrated effort. Never been called a precision machine before, but here I was, executing a surgical strike on this monster.

I charged.

It seemed Donovan had developed something of a plan himself and lifted a lumbering leg to try to kick me off, but I had anticipated that by now he'd picked up on what I was doing and easily slipped to the side. Making the legendary running back proud with a stuttering side-step, I lifted one hand to stiff-arm the upraised leg and keep it from interrupting me as I dropped my opposite shoulder into the golem's midsection and drove it back. Our momentum stalled once the lifted leg drove back into the pavement, but by then I sent a crushing uppercut to the center console followed by a knee. I kept the fight close and dirty, where it would seem nobody would want to be because of the menacing size and power of such a structure, but now that I wasn't restricted by the mortal bounds of a flesh-form, this was an ideal attack. I could endure a clunky swing of the arm, which I did by tucking into myself like any boxer knows how to do, and I could deflect any lifting leg-limb by pivoting inside my workspace from left to right, just like any mixed martial artist understood.

Another right, then left. I could feel my fist giving, it's what I imagined throwing broken hands must have felt like, but I kept it up. That flawless facade of magically crafted steel hadn't given— not yet—but I drove forward, bearing through the pain and beating on it like a war drum. I was a hair's breadth from my limit, my sapped soul unable to swallow the agony that came with every punch, but as I pulled my battered hand back, I saw it.

I'd made a dent. Not just a dent, but a cleft on the plate that protected the gnome piloting this monstrosity. Our expressionless faces regarded one another, and it was here that I saw we finally had a mutual understanding of one another.

***

The Judge's sluggish movements were easy to predict—the problem was that even when I managed to catch its lumbering straight-jab it was still painful as all hell. My bronze-glossed feet couldn't get enough purchase on the sidewalk I'd driven him into, so in effect the blow gave him back the precious space he'd been so hard-pressed to win. When close-in, I could use his lack of limb mobility and steal the advantage of his reach and also situate myself in a place he couldn't really hit.

The Dreadnought's featureless face didn't give anything away, but I knew that inside, Donovan was frustrated. You see, if a caster were here, they'd send a spell, which the ornate and brilliantly designed sigils that ran all across the Judge would just assimilate. Not only would their magic be useless, it could in effect super-charge the golem and make the Judge even stronger. House Unet had crafted a destructive, lifeless hunter that was the bane of the Veil; there was no magic wielder who could hurt it and no beast that could damage it enough to put it down before its own claws and teeth betrayed it.

But this simple, heavy-as-hell statue? All I had to do was suck down the pain, grit through it and try not to lose consciousness; it had no real answer to the hurt-bombs I kept raining down on it. My mangled fist radiated agony, but as this was a mind over matter situation I wouldn't be deterred; and I could *smell* the proverbial blood in the water.

"Janzen!" someone shouted.

Out of sheer instinct I lurched to my left, and that was the only reason I wasn't split in half. The Masarou Judge's three-pronged tail slashed down; its lethal stingers embedded into the ground I'd just been occupying. I barely had time to get my bearings; the voice that raised the alert was coming from an alley, so there was some shred of hope that my friends had survived the blast.

Excellent.

The grotesque creature we thought we'd put down was badly wounded, but far from out of the fight. It was missing a leg, and upon closer inspection the tail was badly burnt, and it seemed its prongs were struggling to move with the menacing independence they once enjoyed. Normally this would be good news, but the cruelly contoured and mangled face was starting to stitch back together. Slowly mind you, but fast enough that I was able to pick up on it after only a few seconds.

Bad. Very bad.

Fighting two of them at the same time was a new ballgame. They could use angles, and fight in concert—there was no telling what would happen to me if the statue was hit with that tail, if that cocktail of venom could actually still hurt me in this metamorphical state or not. I mean, everything about science would tell me *no* but I just got friend-zoned by my first (and dead) client. At this point, there were a lot of questions that I had no answer for; and my dumb ass had decided not to ask them before projecting my consciousness into the bronze statue of Cleveland's Hall of Fame running back Jim Brown.

Oh well.

The Judge was compensating for its missing limb by moving much the way a gorilla did, with the same amount of ease whether standing upright or prone, navigating around the missing limb admirably.

Donovan's dented golem lifted its metal arm up in a signal to the other Judge, pointing at my unconscious, human body prone and unmoving on the sidewalk some hundred feet behind us.

It was another stark reminder of how bad I was at thinking all of this through, but then again this was my Hail Mary plan. All they had to do to end this was destroy my human body. I mean, they could kill me while I was in here too of course, but that would be tremendously difficult—I would fight them until the statue was nothing but slag, but my human body?

All one of them had to do was stomp.

***

The initial sparring—if you could call it that—had allowed me to deceive myself into holding onto a tiny bit of hope. I used my speed advantage to dance from opponent to opponent landing a couple of sound blows, but between their ability to coordinate, their prowess and their timing, I was quickly running out of steam. Every hit sent a flashfire of pain through my entire consciousness, which stalled movement, and more than once ended up with me barely evading a potentially deadly sting by taking a powerful blow from the Dreadnought.

I was losing.

Part of me entertained the idea of taking a hit from one of those venomous stingers to throw them off and maybe maneuver for an advantage, but I discarded it almost immediately. Given that this statue contained my consciousness and that my mind ruled over its matter, I couldn't shake the suspicion that because my own mind associated those things with death, that if it landed a strike, I would—in a best case scenario—be thrown from my Jim Brown body back to my own beat-up one; or worst case I'd die.

I realized a moment too late that the slash by the disfigured patchwork beast was a feint. She hadn't intended to land a blow, she was trying to bait me into one of the frantic, unaimed leaps I was using to get away from it. I felt my back hit something solid but moving, and before I could get my arms up, the Dreadnought's limbs closed around me. The bearhug was brutal, and as bad as the pain of it was, the realization that I just bought a front row ticket to my own execution was the real kicker. In terms of raw power I was screwed, and honestly the way I heard my metal brass giving way, whining as the superior construct started to crumple me, the agony of it all was taking not only my mind's desire to breathe, but my will to fight.

I was suffocating, and that fire I had in me was expiring. Donovan had turned on us, Gale was comatose, and the only semblance of government our mad world had was just shredded to ribbons right in front of me. She was about sixty feet from me when I waited for it, that spark of fury, that stroke of genius, that *something* I could do to get myself out of this.

A shot rang out and I heard the blinded beast let out a cry so sharp that it snapped me out of quitting and right back into the fight.

Its remaining eye had just been ripped into by hot lead.

There was Grove, about twenty feet down the road, his face slightly marred by a burn that wrapped around his neck and down his shoulder. It was gruesome and would have robbed most men of their consciousness and will to fight.

But he wasn't most men. He was my friend, my brother in all of this, holding the line with me. He racked another round into the chamber, immune to the shrill, spine-tingling shriek that came from the monster now running full tilt at him. That was spirit and good old-fashioned gumption; that thing you only hoped you'd find inside yourself should you ever have to dance with the devil.

That thing Maria had when she died giving us our chance.

***

....I spat more blood than saliva on the god knows what-infested wrestling mat we'd bought secondhand from the local high school. Above me stood Grove, studiously examining the way I pulled myself together after another failed exchange. My entire life had basically been spent kneeling before subject-matter experts; it was a little tiresome, honestly. Above our cheap dojo was a wood sign with the words *Bleed in training, sweat in battle* burned into its surface. I was tough, there wasn't a soul alive that wouldn't attest to that, but the only thing equal to my toughness was my laziness, and today was a day I was filled to the brim with *I-don't-give-a-damn.*

This is bullshit, I told Grove.

Since the end of summer I'd been actively learning to sign in ASL, and found I took to it. It was a shame I didn't have any real talent for outright spell-weaving, it would probably be helpful as hell. It was a dangerous practice, but a person could wield magic with intricate hand motions in a crunch, and that could be very helpful.

Which brought me to my point.

"I'm an artificer, man." I ripped the headgear off, my matted hair now long enough that it brushed the top of my eyebrow. "This stuff is good to have a warm and fuzzy on, but like every day? There's a hundred different ways to get this job done."

I'd barely gotten to the glove strap when I was forced to put a hand up and defend myself from a jab, Grove pushing the issue with physicality. It pissed me off, and I let him know by absorbing the shot, rolling with it and then firing back at him with a momentum-charged right cross of my own. This wasn't for sparring; I was angry, and I put more than a little of that emotion into it.

Grove didn't retreat, he stepped into it and threw his helmet-cushioned crown right into the front of my face. My sloppy punch sailed harmlessly off the clip of his shoulder and back. He'd staggered me; he was in my workspace—what a fighter usually calls the area between his own arms—and as I reeled backward, he gave me a brutal body shot with his left. It was adding insult to an injury, not really his style.

I went back down on that musty, unsanitary, downright disgusting ugly mat where this all started. The only thing that surprised me more than the final cheap shot was the sound of Grove's voice.

"That's not what it's about, Janzen."

In the shared silence afterward I heard every pop and release of cartilage, muscle and bone from his war-battered body as he knelt to meet my eyes.

"Someday there's gonna be a problem right in front of you, and there won't be anything you can do except go *through* it." I understood the implication without him having to give it a voice; that there wouldn't be a way for me to quick-talk, side-step, or pawn off an issue. That I wasn't going to be able to manifest some kind of miracle throw that ended up saving the day; that sometime—maybe soon— there would be an issue I couldn't weasel my way out of. Grove's gloved fist gave the center of my chest a light jab. "And when that day comes, I don't want you to forget this. The suck." Without pushing the issue, my slightly deflated friend started to untie the wrapping on those well-worn gloves.

Disappointed, the man I'd come to call friend and brother stood up and started to walk away.

I hit him in the back with my sweaty helmet. He turned around in time to barely duck another punch, and we trained for another hour. We trained until my blood felt like fire, till my heart was hammering so hard I thought it might come out of my chest. We trained until both of us were sure that so long as we had anything left in us, we would stand the fuck back up.

Bleed in training, sweat in battle.

***

….I threw my head back to smash into the Dreadnought's face. The shot sent a clap of pain throughout my entirety, but it also jarred the Judge so that when the top of its head was rocked back, its big, stilted arms slid up. I saw my window and took it—I dropped down through his arms and into a forward roll.

I felt the sidewalk smash to pieces as Donovan came after me, shards of sidewalk spraying in every direction. I had to get to Grove—I was in a panic that had driven me to hysterics. Even with my escape there was no way I could close the distance, she was already on him, rearing up with each arm out wide ready to slam them together and crush him.

And just then, in came the Concrete Monk like a comic book avenger, throwing every bit of his mortal body into the beast's massive, mauling palm in the form of a snapping kick, an immaculate and masterful strike. On the other end, Grove used the silver blade affixed to his gun to take a big chunk out of the other incoming hand.

And then singing filled the air. "*Mother... Tell your children not to walk my way.*" Danzig's titular hit single *Mother*, one of the songs that served as a genesis to the American punk movement… as most accurate-*ish* shows depicting the eighties would lead you to believe. It was perfect too, it had a grungy kind of resistance to it; it was a song of defiance.

And I'm a sucker for that.

I caught a glimpse of Johnny B as beaten and burnt to hell as the other two but still in some kind of good spirits. He grabbed ahold of my limp, real body's arms and dragged me out of the gutter and away from this predator who was looking for an easy meal. Once I was deposited snugly behind him, the preternatural voice belted out the chorus as the ornate axe-guitar swung back around his badly beaten body before he deftly seized it out of the air with nimble fingers and immediately took to making it screech by running knowing digits up and down the neck.

No such thing as a free lunch.

***

We'd turned the tide of the fight, and now I was beating the bricks off of Donovan. The metal Judge wasn't designed for this kind of fight, and since I wasn't going to throw a spell at it or try to cut through that impenetrable armor, its defensive measures weren't doing anything for it.

The problem was that on the other side of the street, the guys were barely holding it together against the other rapidly healing Judge. Who, unbeknownst to the group, was inhabited by the consciousness of Ja'Sune, the star-crossed love of Donovan's life. She'd used the tail to corner them, and though they were holding their serve as best they could, the unsure footing was becoming more and more treacherous. They didn't have long.

Just as I was about to abandon my post and try to get them out of there, one of my strikes landed on the battered, creased plate of metal protecting Donovan and folded it open. It was a real opening—an opportunity to get that scumbag—to rip him out of his protective shell and face us properly. The next right was thrown with such vigor that it bent my bronzed limb back and sent a shot of pain like I'd never felt before roaring through me, making itself heard in every inch of my mind.

It got bleary from there. I felt the construct try to make a move to get out of the corner I'd pushed it into. More by way of stupid stubbornness than sense I threw the left with the same recklessness. That hit too, and when it hit, the entire plate exploded off the golem. It spun like a dreidel in the air, and that was the last thing I remember before it all went black.

CHAPTER 18

Slap.

That hurt. And it stung afterward too. Not like the sizzle of a slap's sting but that burn that you get when somebody slaps a bruise or a sunburn.

My head was swimming, and it was like being in a pool filled with tar. I was groggy in a way that let me know that every time before now that I'd thought I was groggy, I was wrong. I vaguely made out some singing. *Taylor Swift maybe?*

All I could think of was that if they ever made a movie about this, Johnny was gonna cost us a fortune in rights, but then again, I don't think Tay-Tay would let us bump her bangers anyway so moot point.

Hey, I'm a work in progress.

"He's alive!"

"Fat lot of good that does."

Through my fog, I saw Patrick as he danced just out of the reach of a downward swipe from the monster's tail, and Grove trying to get back on his feet after he'd been swatted through a window by the beast. Judging by the broken frame behind him and the pool of glass underneath him I'd guess that probably hurt—a lot.

Movement drew my eye, and I looked over to find Donovan's treacherous ass climbing out of his destroyed vessel. He'd taken a beating but wasn't as broken as I'd hoped. I knew it was because of that necklace, it glowed with a green energy that was a hypnotic pulsing power. It was amping him up somehow.

Grove collapsed, and the last dodge effectively cornered Patrick with us. By now the other Judge had healed even more substantially, although its leg was still a bit club-like, but most of the important pieces had come together enough to make it as deadly as it was before.

I thought of something snarky to say now that I was cogent enough to get a good lay of the land, but I didn't. They deserved to die with some dignity.

There was a blur, and what light there was around us seemed to just dim… as though the night suddenly got deeper. The creature noticed it too, aware that something was amiss, and growled low. Suddenly it whipped around, turning away from us entirely, and I caught an almost imperceptible blur of living darkness. The Masarou Judge cried out in pain and was stunned in disbelief. There was a massive gash across its back, black ichorous blood oozing out of the wound and hissing in the rain. Somewhere I know that Ja'Sune felt that.

Across from the infuriated Judge, and in front of our rag-tag group, stood the most unlikely of allies.

Verrakh the Stalker was in her true Abyssal form, sleek and powerful, taunting the Judge with a beckoning onyx claw.

*****

"…I know you heard me come downstairs," I said to a quiet room.

Sam was sprawled out across the magic shop's rug at the center of the store. There was another beat of stillness before she slowly peeled herself off the ground. There was something softly feminine in the way she moved, and it was messing with my concept of what a Stalker was. It was nighttime proper—the prime of night, when all the best kind of shadowborn badness is at its best. She gave me a capricious once-over, the tip of her tongue finding a canine as she deliberated.

It was finally time to talk, so she took the meeting in her own way, moving in a dancer's prowl around the barrier cleverly concealed in the store, the magical fence we'd used to cage her.

"A good host will lead the conversation," she said.

Oh, right. I crossed the room to approach her invisible enclosure, arms crossed. "Are you still working for her…your old Queen?"

At first, she barked a laugh, but after a gauging look at me, she recognized the earnestness of the question. She paused her pacing steps to center herself on me. "That's for you to decide," Strong but still svelte-framed shoulders shrugged, but the contemplative, slow-blink she fixed me with seemed to find something worthwhile enough to field a little more. "I don't really think we have time for us to go over the nature of my *service*."

My narrowed eyes let her know that she was walking a fine line, but all she managed was a coy smirk before she started her prowling again. I moved past the unsettling, almost threateningly true observation, and fell back in step with her.

"I'm being played, I just don't have a read on the who or the why."

I wasn't sure if she was mocking me with her exaggerated pursed mouth and head nod, or if she just hadn't quite gotten the hang of emoting as a human.

"That's insightful; I'm not used to your kind being this present. You're usually so bullish and stubborn, petty and motivated by such basic comforts. I'm surprised that you've survived this long."

"Hey, we humans aren't all bad… I mean—"

"I was talking about men."

Oh.

"I want to trust you, even if I haven't the faintest idea why."

"So that's your sell, what's the catch?" she continued, as if unimpressed with my half-stepping.

"Well…I've got a plan, and I need you."

"You want my help? After your treatment of me?"

"This was beyond my control, this all—" I said, gesturing widely.

"This was without honor. You are a slayer of one of our oldest, you are looked upon as a great hunter. A warrior. Since I have been here you have treated me like property, partnered me with the elf, made decisions about me without consulting me, and now you are sneaking down here in the dead of night trying to whisper some kind of confession to me so that I will help you."

That was a lot to unpack, and this time it was my pace that staggered as I was blown back by the fact that she was madder about these collective grievances than her current imprisonment. I'd long since learned that these beings from worlds so unlike our own were incredibly alien to us, and if you lost sight of that you might have unnecessarily done what I did to her.

Deeply disrespected her through sheer carelessness.

I started at the beginning.

"Can I ask you a few things so maybe I can better understand what I've done?"

Again she held court as to whether or not she was going to let me plead my case, and that's when I realized that if she was in fact innocent, I had just—in a roundabout fashion— condemned her along with myself. If we lost, there was no way her turning to our side and helping us wouldn't come up. I had taken away her choice.

"What is this about an elder?" I asked.

When she huffed, I could swear her flared nostrils released a blossom of smoke.

"The *Cura'sha* you killed was old, and still would go on the Great Hunts. He often brought back the biggest kill for all the males, some of the catches even respectable for a youngling female hunter."

Another gear shift. While I was most often incredibly dense, the reason people found me so frustrating was that when I was tuned in, I was deceptively insightful. Women played the dominant role in their societal structure, and I would guess that she was on the high end of the pecking order in her own right. That also brought to light the fact that the Stalker I'd killed was probably far from the best they had in their arsenal.

"He was also able to *vuuntai*: he could change prey's perception of him to elicit more fear."

The look she gave me was a challenge, daring me to say something about the way they operate, their culture, the rawness of their wild traditions and powers. I didn't, it wasn't my place.

"In his—you call them funerals—he spoke of you as a champion, a worthy opponent. He grudgingly respected you."

The urge to ask how he spoke was pretty significant, but that wasn't my place nor was it the point. Whether through some kind of spiritual traditionalism, or actual magic that allowed them to commune with the dead didn't matter—hell maybe it was just during his reports back to the Abyss, who could say.

"I did not mean to do that Sam."

"That's not my name."

That was another gut check. I'd renamed her without even thinking about it, hadn't even asked, because she was one of *them*.

I asked her her name, and the name she gave was throaty in a way I had no hope of replicating, although I tried. She stripped out some of the throaty grit and we organically came to a compromise on what we could call her, a name that was her own.

Verrakh.

"And now that you have my name, you may ask wh—"

My foot cut through the sigil keeping her contained, breaking the confines of her imprisonment. There was a long silence, and if I told you I wasn't afraid I'd be lying. My gear was scattered all about, and even if I was armed to the teeth there was absolutely nothing I could do in this close of quarters.

Apparently, I'd barely beaten up an old man, and I'd had to cheat and use a few friends and a building to do it. A fight with Verrakh would be over before I could think to start it.

She was old, like a firsthand edition of the Bible old, so I didn't immediately panic as she took her time with all of this. No, the real panic started to set in after four or five minutes of absolute silence and stillness, and my hard-beating heart was gumming up my ears so that I didn't even hear Max pad his way down the stairs and with a sluggish enthusiasm—something only a pitbull could manage—bury himself into Verrakh's leg and flank.

She snapped to the present, smiling sweetly and kneeling down to give Max some long overdue affection. She spoke to him in her native tongue, then paused to look at me. Curiously enough, a suddenly inquisitive-looking Max did the same.

"Why trust me now?" she asked.

"My dog does, and if he's wrong…I don't want to be right."

We stayed up a while and discussed the plan. She agreed to pretend to stay locked up until we left. I packed the jar of transmog goo and the diagram of the rune she'd need to carve for me of the statue. Verrakh had a better command of old tongues than me, and her spellwork was better than my artificery, so between the pair of us we'd managed to work out a pretty reasonable design for the sigil that would connect my body to the statue I was having her vandalize. With our combined insight into the arcane, and the transmog goo slapped on, we had a chance to kickstart this war and steal a battle before it all went to shit.

Though she didn't divulge after the reveal, she let me know in passing that her tribe had been subjugated to this dark deity … A creature actually not native to their Abyss, but wielding magnificent strength and old, forbidden knowledge.

I wished her well, and I told her if she did that much, I would do all I could to make sure this fight never ended up at her doorstep. When I left, I strongly suspected I'd never see Verrakh again. It was a somber thing really, and I hated it. In my experience, whenever I had a feeling like that, I was never wrong.

***

….Verrakh brought the fight to the Masarou Judge. She moved in a blur, navigating the stabbing tails and clawed swipes with uncanny ease. That cut to the beast's thigh bought her some time, and she pressed the offensive before it could heal enough for the Judge to manage to get both legs under it. Then the tide was going to turn quickly, and not in her favor.

Johnny had pulled me to my feet, and my raspy breath was more a product of shock than fatigue. Trying to remember what it was like in my own body was bizarre. Patrick joined in the effort to help me stay upright. Grove tried to watch the fight but eventually relented and looked back at me, joining us in something of a makeshift huddle.

"Donovan's necklace…."

If not for a whooping screech from Johnny, we'd all be dead. There was concerted power in that voice that launched a counter-spell at a bolt of lightning that was surging directly at us. Patrick caught the brunt of the seismic clap of power in the aftermath, it hit him in the back and staggered him into Johnny and me, but as he continued to fall, his head ricocheted hard off the cement sidewalk.

Grove was thrown down the alley, and before I could check on him, I saw the source of the blast.

Donovan, mad eyes alive with crackling energy, was walking toward us. It was hard to imagine him as something menacing, but the bloodied gnome with that radiant green pendant and mad smile on his face was a complete departure from the even-keeled teacher I had known. There was something vile, crooked and deceitful leaking into him that was changing him.

"You're a cowardly piece of shit!"

It was my eloquence, in a pinch, that impressed even me. I threw a punch, and Donovan caught it mid-flight. The fact that he was physically handling me was startling as hell. It was almost surreal the way the stout armed once-friend literally whipped me ten feet across a walkway into the corner of the closest building. This was *brutal*. The supernatural were pretty much universally faster and stronger than us, and that included gnomes, who were the seeds of the whole dwarf mythology actually, at least our understanding of them on this side.

… There's probably a better time for that story.

Around the third tumble I stopped flipping over on myself and groaned as I pushed myself up to a knee. I could barely make sense of my blurred vision when I got enough clarity to see the big body sprawled out on the street, a mess of blood and gore. The graphic scene was made infinitely worse by the fact that the water was carrying the pooling blood even further than it ought to.

It was Xander.

He was dead.

How my people, my tribe, my pack had survived the blast made some kind of sense now. Xander must have cast his body over the rest of them, and undoubtedly used his remaining strength to bring them in closer so that he could absorb the brunt of the explosion. I had no time to react because the Tinkerer was on me, and I just managed to get both my arms up to block a side kick that sent me skating back over the slick pavement. My forearms felt like somebody had just come across them with a baseball bat. That didn't track—even if he was stronger than me it wasn't by such a margin that would be considered inhuman. From my understanding, gnomes and goblins topped out at about the power level of a professional athlete; elves were the ones who could be many times stronger or faster.

It was the stone. That thing around his neck was the key to it all, and he'd been possessive of it from the start. He was channeling power somehow, as a conduit…like a Wanderer.

"Why don't you just know when you're beat?" he said.

***

My back slapped against a wall, and I ducked beneath the leaping spin kick he was quite fond of just in time to hear it take a sizable piece of the wall out with his heel. Brick and mortar debris rained down, but I planted my far foot and pivoted back toward him with a punch to his face.

It was like hitting cement. I was reminded of all the stomach-churning, nauseating pain that I'd experienced fighting the golem and I almost heaved. Normally a hit like that would crush Donovan, or almost anyone else for that matter, but there was a weird glimmer of that green effulgence around where my hit landed. That sheen was a kind of sentient energy, and immediately I saw it for what it was.

The barrier. The In-Between was keeping him safe. Behind him I saw Verrakh moving with the night and doing her best to stay just out of reach of the Judge's lethal tails, and now she had both of its arms to contend with as well. The missing limb had grown back, and while she was dragging a leg from where Verrakh struck, it was serviceable.

Not good.

"Give up."

An open palm strike from Donovan sent me skidding backward. I could barely get my breathing in check after having been hit with what felt like a mallet.

"You turned on everyone," I said, my voice gutted. "People who saw you as family, who did everything for you." I fought against the tightness of my throat, not all from the fight. Just like the wetness in my eyes wasn't all from the rain. "You killed Xander, he was your friend."

"*Friend*," he sneered, the sheer contempt in his voice so intense that I could feel it wash over my skin. "Let me tell you abo—"

Grove's gun cracked Donovan's head, my quiet companion wielding the weapon like a baseball bat. The blow made the Tinkerer stumble, and I didn't hesitate. I charged, throwing everything I could into the tackle. After a dizzying impact in which we rolled into one giant, jumbled mass of short limbs wildly flailing about, I ended up on top of him. I watched his eyes go wide as I lifted a gloved hand skyward, making a show of drawing in all the ambient energy I could; that kinetic force swirled violently around my hand and was about to reign down on him.

There was another eruption of energy, and I was thrown back once again. I hadn't seen the how of the attack, or even orientated enough to know where it originated from. At this point my entire body was bruised, internally and externally. Donovan pushed his way upright, his madness making him look outright rabid.

"I'm going to rip the life out of every one of you. You and your *friends*." Stiffly squaring himself up, he sprawled out some to adopt a wide-legged stance. Behind him was the Judge locked in battle with Verrakh. Grove was trying his damndest to stand up again, but he was badly hurt. He was burned, gouged, bleeding from a dozen grievous wounds and riddled with road rash. The last hit he'd taken had broken his gifted gun in two, although he still had a death-grip on the barrel with the silver axe-blade beneath it.

He was determined to die on his feet, and I was too.

Donovan was in the process of preparing some sort of spell, conjuring up an endgame attack, and something happened…it wasn't working. He was a Tinkerer and needed a conduit, or a force so powerful it could divine one.

A conduit like the amulet, hung on that precious necklace.

The necklace in my gloved hand.

I reached for its power, feeling it out. The landscape changed instantly, and energy reverberated throughout my battered body. It was a living energy, an energy capable of magnificence. It didn't resist me either, in fact it felt relieved to have me with it. It was foreign, yet familiar, and it wasn't long before my suspicion was confirmed as to what a Wanderer's stone was. It was a stone, made from the life force of an actual Wanderer.

In this stone's case, that Wanderer was Maria.

***

Verrakh was fighting a valiant fight, but she'd run out of real estate. The Judge was shivering with anticipation at the prospect of visiting some violence on someone else—even after all of the day's brutality. The theft of the stone swayed it though, and the beast momentarily lost focus to steal a glimpse my way, trying to gauge what was happening.

The healed eyes still rimmed in gore made for a spectacularly horrific sight.

Verrakh erupted forward, a suicidal gambit to try to score a last fatal blow. The Judge's senses were too finely honed—it was an amalgamation of every top-tier predator in all the worlds, already a compressed spring of readied muscle. It was ready to meet her challenge head on....

And then Johnny B did his best impression of Grove, launching his bladed axe end over end scoring a hit to the Judge's knee. His guitar's sculpted shape showed what it really was, a magically concealed battle axe with a bite so fierce it looked like the whole of its head was buried in that gnarled flesh.

The beast stumbled to a knee, and when it tried to launch with the other leg, the Concrete Monk was there, a mask of blood from the head wound he'd suffered earlier covering his absolutely determined face. He didn't have the thing in some masterful jiu-jitsu grip, but a desperate one instead—one that managed to hold on long enough so that when the Judge tried to rely on that leg, it was the final trip-up needed to send the beast careening.

Verrakh made up the ground in an instant, avoiding two lashes of the tail before swooping low enough to catch the big gargantuan on its descent. One of the prettiest uppercuts I had ever seen found purchase, the claw-first strike punctuated by a scream that Johnny, Patrick and Verrakh seemed to let loose all as one.

It cut the monster's head clean off, and the Judge was dead before it hit the ground. As Verrakh brought her arm down we saw the last stinger embedded in her midsection.

The moment caused a sudden stillness. We bore witness to what she had done, almost all by herself, and even as she shifted back to a human vessel I knew not to look away. She was a wildling, a queen, my friend after one of the strangest nights of my admittedly bizarre life, and she had just given her life for all of us.

Johnny was on her before she could fall, but her build was deceptive. In order to transform into such a colossal creature her body mass was much, much denser than ours. I would say she was an easy six, seven hundred pounds.

Patrick was torn between attending to the scene unfolding between me and Donovan, and what had just happened with Verrakh—but my people trusted me, and with a look, I directed him to our fallen friends.

I had it from here.

***

Sirens were starting up, their song usually an epilogue to any incident, but not this time. Nobody was walking away from this. Donovan snarled, his eyes turning from the dead Judge to the catastrophe on the street, and then to me.

I was literally thrumming with power. It was intoxicating. Every wild concept I had ever dreamed up was waiting at the tip of every finger, but I knew this wasn't me. It wasn't really Maria, either; it was something else, but a piece of her was in it and I reveled in that. The shock on everyone's faces when I pocketed the amulet was priceless, but not as much as in this moment.

A little bit of laughter escaped me, and I realized I sounded as insane as Donovan.

"Get out of here," One of the loose teeth in my mouth finally gave, and I spat it out. I walked toward Donovan and stripped off almost every piece of artificed gear I had. I veered closer to Grove, keeping an eye on the gnome as I did. Soundlessly accepting my free hand and helping himself up. I gave him my bag of marbles, my fidget spinners, my destroyed glove, and even the dagger-bat I had come to rely on a little too much. He was about to make a thing out of it, reading my intent as plain as if I'd written it out in crayon.

Something passed between us in the look I offered him back. We didn't need to say a thing. Despite the bitter pill of my decision, he really was an exemplary soldier and followed my unarticulated order without hesitation.

"We trusted you," I said to Donovan.

He now had my undivided attention, and I could see him try to muster up some sort of courage to meet me head on. I watched his once-analytical mind, now ripped to ruins by the Abyss and whatever else he'd been dabbling in during his time spent exploring the darkness, trying to convince himself that he was smarter than me and that there was still some kind of an out. As the disfigured wheel in his head finally stopped turning, I watched a second thought come into his hateful mind.

He was faster by a considerable margin, and make no mistake, he was also stronger.

I sidestepped his clunky haymaker, burying my own counterpunch a good six inches into his gut as if my aim was to blow a hole right through him. Before he could even come to understand what it was to be so abruptly robbed of oxygen, I pivoted into his guard and threw an overhand punch swimming above his shoulder and smashing down like a frothing, angry wave. That was something he wouldn't think of because he'd never had to. None of these holier-than-thou, megalomaniac madmen have.

Mike Tyson said that everyone has a plan until they get punched in the mouth—maybe not the wisest words, but truer ones have never been spoken.

Donovan lay crumpled on the ground, and I celebrated it with a brutal kick to his side, sending him rolling over.

"Get up." There was a fire inside my soul, but I refused to let it conquer me. Instead, I used it to forge my focus and stay wholly in this moment. I was connected to my heartbreak, but I didn't let it direct me. "Stand up."

I heard him start growling about power, talking about how they had to pay—the council, the tribe, all of them. They'd robbed him of what was rightfully his, and even more, they'd kept him from the love of his life. I didn't even dignify his ramblings with an answer. Instead, I let him rant while I just stared, and none of what was keeping me upright as every inch of my body screamed out in pain was written on my face. Stoicism served well in a situation like this. Behind me I heard Grove, Johnny and Patrick struggle to get Verrakh up. I could feel them looking at me, but now wasn't the time to give them any kind of look. They had to finish the task at hand, just like me.

"You killed your friend." This time the statement hit, and I watched Donovan reluctantly let his head twitch in the direction of where we'd left Xander, once a humorous, dedicated companion, now just a broken husk. "You gave up on those who took you in, you turned your back on your family, and *for what?*"

I fished out the amulet, its wash of energy revitalizing me, and I forced myself to shut out the promise of power that came with it. Predictably, Donovan lunged, and I gifted him another right cross for all the effort. I closed my other hand around the amulet and smashed it across his head for good measure.

"Stay down," I ordered. And it was all he could do. He was beaten. I could see the concussion thwarting any sense of what was happening. Sadly, I suspected that he was too far gone to have listened to any kind of reason anyway. "Take your broken Judges. Take your archaic courts. Take your fucking fear out of my town, and take that goblin with you…and before you go…" I reached down and ripped the circular amulet containing Gale's essence from his neck, "leave this."

I was not a kind man, even if I tried to be an honorable one.

"This is my city, these are my people, and I'll rain holy hell on you if I ever see any of you again." I shoved him with my foot to keep him on all fours like the piece of shit he was. I let him sit in his defeat, taking no joy from the victory. There was a strength that I found in myself, and I couldn't help but wonder if it had anything to do with the stone, or if it was more connected to my understanding of myself.

I was the leader of a bunch of do-gooders who fought for the little guy, the glue between a group who dared to stand up to the darkness for everyone who couldn't. I left him in his ruin, the back I offered him was all he'd ever get from me. I joined my friends, who had successfully loaded our unconscious Stalker into Kaycee's borrowed, ancient pickup truck.

"She might be okay," Johnny said, somehow still looking ready to walk onto a stage. He was just an androgynous masterpiece of beauty and poise. How did he do that? "I think it was the paralytic stinger. I think she planned it that way too." My eyes widened which was no small feat, and as fast as she had been moving that evidenced some serious dexterity. The cops were close, but the concealing storm seemed to be coming down twice as hard as before.

"JANZEN!"

I'll say it again, anybody who already knows your name has nothing but bad news for you if they use it aloud outside of introductions.

I turned around and saw Donovan's dead body now limp on his knees, a scythe smile smeared across his paling, battered face. On his stomach was a series of crude sigils drawn in his own blood, and a gaping wound where it looked like something simply exploded out of him. The blood flowing out of him dripped skyward in a grotesque betrayal of physics, and about ten feet above his corpse it was coagulating into a blob. As the webbed strands of blood slithered skyward like some macabre Ouroboros, they created a great circle above his head, which hung limp between his shoulders.

At the center of this frame crafted out of Donovan's life essence was the Mistress of the Abyss, imagined in this blood-born form but fighting to emerge from this sacrificial ingression.

"Run," I whispered breathlessly. When the idiot elf dared to try to say something rather than take off, I turned on him and screamed, "RUN!"

***

Her scream ripped at the fabric of our reality, my sense of that sacred perspective fast fading as her roar tore me in half. Behind me I saw my people, my tribe, making way with Verrakh farther down the road, which left me center stage with a legitimate nemesis. The blood-framed portal was already closing; it was no small thing to open a passageway through the In-Between. Even if short lived, it was hard to speak on how impressive it was to do that out of your essence, but it also meant that Donovan had eviscerated what constituted a soul in our lexicon. The sarcophagus of blood started to wash away, and her smooth gray skin looked lovely until it reached out by way of an unnaturally thin and elongated arm, talon-like fingers sizzling morosely as she gripped the sanguine border of the spell that allowed her momentary entry into our world. Already it was failing, but not before she could open her mouth wide, her once elegant jawline stretching and popping into a hideous open maw.

There was a ghastly stream of power born from her banshee cry, an energy that seemed to play tricks with the atmosphere itself as it sailed at me. She was using physical force to try to keep her blood cage from closing shut, pressing a hand to each side and holding fast even as the frame of blood was being disintegrated by the In-Between's green-limned energy.

Acting without thinking, my arm came up with the pendant heavy in my hand. I was met with the strangest conflict of power I'd ever encountered, or ever could have conceived. It annulled everything for an instant, I felt like I had lived a lifetime in that moment, and at the same time never experienced it at all. It wasn't the quiet, it was the stillness. Whatever it was, it allowed me time, the space to find my breath, and in it… the last of my resolve.

I found the toughness of a soldier, the compassion of a monk, the stubbornness of a wildling, the pride of a queen and the swagger of a rockstar.

She screamed, so I screamed back. I screamed until my voice went hoarse and my lungs felt the fire of my fury, I screamed right into her fucking face. The pendant crackled, and I dug in and forged ahead. Each step felt like I was pushing against an immovable object, but if my feet could make any movement at all I kept going forward.

Always forward.

A funnel of energy ricocheted off and around me, and there was a moment where I felt an ethereal touch, a caress of hope that told me I could find a way to win. That hope stalled with my momentum, and then the first push that whipped through me killed it all together. My will was there, but my body was broken. I felt my left knee tear, a ligament at the least and the *crack* that followed it let me know that I may not ever walk the same way again. Still, I wouldn't relent, and even if I had to die, I would die fighting.

I knew my knee hit the ground, but I couldn't feel it, and through the channel of energy I could *feel* the smugness in this vile demigod. Wordless taunting whispered in my ears. There was the promise to wear my flesh, make me suffer for an eternity and more, but where she hit hardest was when she vowed to visit these things and worse on my people.

That was the only time that I wished I had something else in the tank, the only time I really dared think that this was unfair. Quivering, my arm bent back on itself until I couldn't take it anymore, I felt myself being dragged down by the anchor that wanted me to quit and just let it be over, and then…I moved.

I won back lost ground and was as surprised as the Mistress.

It was Maria. Her teeth were gritted, and she looked fierce as hell. I finally saw her for what she really was: a warrior. A person worthy of so much more than what she got. She braced my arms with hers, giving my arm the strength to hold the amulet up and push the fight back against the goddess.

When I tried to draw on some reserve of strength inside of me, there was nothing left. Every reservoir was depleted, no matter how much I needed it now.

As a woman much better than me once wrote—*Still I rose.*

Zachariah knelt beside me, taking my other arm and draping it across his shoulders for support, and then helped push me back up to my feet. I held onto the stone, I held on to my will and warded off the Mistress's demand to shut it all off.

Together we pressed forward, gaining more and more ground, but this was an ancient evil. An evil so old so we did not know what name to assign it; it wouldn't be taken down without demanding much much more of us. The portal wasn't ten feet away, but it may as well have been on Jupiter for all we were capable of touching it.

That was when the last piece of it all came together.

Bhalore, taking a position behind us, wrapped us in his strength and dug down deep, pushing us forward with bullish insistence across the last few feet. Bhalore with his faith, kept us and guided us to the finish.

There was a clap of some kind, another one of those indescribable pauses that seemed to suspend me *inside* everything… for what seemed like a lifetime.

And in that lifetime, I saw that it wasn't Maria who'd straightened my arm and lent me her fierce loyalty, it was Johnny B the rocker-bard, still by my side.

Nor was it Zachariah who kept me upright, steady and fixed on the path that I was walking. It was Grove, the silent soldier who kept his faith in me despite having seen more of me than most.

Bhalore, the only man who could make a moody and entitled teen stop taking himself so damn seriously….Alas, it wasn't my old friend; I'd see him again, and probably soon, but not today. It was Patrick, the Concrete Monk, giving freely of himself so that others would be safe. He was so selfless in this sacrifice that I honestly didn't think he'd even see it as one, he'd probably call it duty, or very simply just the right thing to do.

It all snapped back to the present, and the devastating eruption threw us all apart and me into darkness. My grip on the Wanderer's Heart was the last thing to go. The stone that carried a piece of

Maria's soul gave out first, breaking into a dozen shards in the blast and badly mangling my hand in the process.

EPILOGUE

"It's not that bad, actually, and I've been getting a full night's sleep, so that's dope."

It was nice to see everyone, and unlike everyone else in jail, my family wasn't at all uncomfortable visiting me here. In fact, they won me a lot of respect, which helped—I didn't really have a lot of street cred to my name.

"So, what's new?"

Grove surprised me by being the first one to light up with something to say. "I followed up on Nicholas Greene and believe it or not, he started going to therapy."

My eyebrows rose. "Huh. That's a way better use of his money than being a fucking creep. Maybe we should do that." I paused, the problem with my suggestion dawning on me. "Nobody would believe us though."

Kaycee snorted. "You have me, and that's half my job as it is."

We laughed, and the lightness I felt told me that Kaycee wasn't wrong about that. She took care of us and kept us well-fed, body and soul.

Grove was healing up nicely, although his bandages had covered almost all of his neck and half his right side. Kaycee had whipped up some kind of balm that saved him from some of the worst of the scarring. Patrick was next to him; he'd brought me some notepads and brain buster puzzles. I appreciated it. I was going to think about getting to those eventually during my stay, which was nice.

Johnny and Verrakh looked cozy, and quite happy. The paralytic agent had taken a few weeks to wear off, and during that time she'd worked her way into the group's good graces while lover-boy nursed her back to health.

She was also the new doorman at the Last Love, and I think Xander would have been fine with that.

Kaycee sat beside me, trying to be sneaky but failing miserably while she slid me cookies under the table. It wasn't like I could get into any more trouble, so I just took a handful and had my way with them.

I was pretty well-hated around here; I mean you can't go to jail in Ohio for destroying a statue of Jim Brown and expect to be well received. Grove's sister had a hell of time convincing them I wasn't whatever the social media radical of the week who was the current mainstream darling said I was. I think she did it by repeatedly telling them that I wasn't socially conscious enough to be destroying statues out of design, and that it was a stupid prank and not some kind of protest. She stopped short of calling me an idiot and an asshole, but only just.

Actually, I would rather be a terrorist than be the guy in Cleveland known for hating Jim Brown, but I digress.

She was a peach, and I think she might be into me.

Verrakh tried to bring me a gift, some kind of token harvested from the Judge's spiked tail that they'd had to dislodge from her shoulder. I'm sure it was nice, but I was glad that the screening process in security caught it. I think it was a thank you, a sentimental memento I suppose.

After the explosion, the cops were on scene pretty quickly. I guess I'd managed to get enough gibberish out that I directed them to get Verrakh out of there and leave me. It would take all of them to get her safely tucked away somewhere so that they could call Kaycee to take care of her. Undoubtedly, they beat feet to come back for me, but by then it was too late.

As for the police? I distracted them by trying to stand, but it wasn't really necessary. Those three men saw something they were going to wrestle with for the rest of their lives. It wasn't just the hulking death machine buried in a second-hand store a hundred feet back, or the sight of a ritualistically sacrificed gnome slumped over and onto himself beneath a macabre pool of blood.

It was hard to say which of those things really broke those men (all three subsequently resigned). No, those men had to deal with not just the shock of seeing and trying to absorb all of those sights, but also coming to terms with the fact that it shimmered a verdant green before eroding and vanishing right before their eyes. The In-Between wasn't just a barrier, it was a protector, too. Many of us suspected the energy itself was alive; a suspicion bolstered by the fact that it seemed to be cleaning up after itself.

Honestly, I think the only reason I didn't get charged with destroying a condemned building and blasting my way down an entire city street was that there was so much unwanted attention on all of this, that they wanted it behind them. I knew people from my community were furious, yet at the same time I knew nobody knew how to act.

I heard about Gale, about how after she came to and learned of Xander, the first thing she did was visit his hometown in Louisiana and rip his totem down from a stack that was meant to designate the pack's outcasts. When the elders threatened retribution and demanded that she respect the Balance, she uttered a single sentence that has rippled throughout our entire world, with implications that could affect all worlds.

"Fuck the Balance."

It was hard to pretend that that didn't tickle me but I did strive to keep up appearances. All of us still looked like we'd been put through a meat grinder, and apparently, I would walk mostly right again, and was even eyeballing a full recovery. Still, after getting a few pictures of Max and some more home-cooked food, I felt pretty good.

I was at peace with what had happened, what we as a family had taken on and defeated. I could survive another few months of this. More than getting out, what I looked forward to most was getting back to work.

I was so distracted that I didn't think anything of the chill that settled over the whole cell block. Instead, I gave each person a goodbye and sat back down, quietly eating my cookies and falling out of touch with the present. I'm a daydreamer especially when I'm relaxed, and with a bellyful of cookies, fresh off a morphine shot from med-bay, I was feeling totally zen.

My spine suddenly stiffened, there was a suffocating presence of *awful*, and my heart dropped. Instantly upright, something across the room caught my eye, and my sixth howled an inaudible warning, setting every hair on my body at attention.

It was Her.

THE
MONSTERS
AND MEN
TRILOGY
BOOK THREE
LAWRENCE DAVIS

It must have been possessed…which would explain why it was moving so awkwardly; struggling with stilted limbs that prevented it from erupting with the primal energy it usually displayed when on the attack. That's when the pieces started coming together. Unfortunately, there were six sneakers working me over in a classic beatdown, and another pair at the feet of the fallen prison guard who was trying to scurry away.

Then they stopped, and then I heard that muffled, distorted sound of people talking that was starting to become dangerously familiar to me in my bloodied state.

But I was too late.

I could see that Shawn was down, and that a Ghoul was clawing its way over his prone body for a quick easy meal. One of Helix' men tried to intervene and stop it, but the Ghoul was having none of it, and with bared teeth, bloodshot eyes, and a vice-like bone-twisting grip, turned on this meddler with a vengeance.

In an instant he was down in a tornado of flailing limbs as the ghoul rabidly attacked and tore into him. The harrowing screams, the ones of nightmares, filled the whole laundry room and probably reached far into every corner of the prison. Helix and his remaining partner-in-crime— knowing that this was quickly going from a beatdown to a murder charge—bolted over to try and stop the ghoul.

Misunderstanding my weak attempt to grab his ankle and stop him, Helix sent a quick departing kick to my midsection, and then stopped. They say you should never underestimate the age and experience of an old man in a profession where most men die young, and at 30ish he definitely qualified as an old man. This time was no exception, for in that moment's hesitation as he turned, he saw the macabre image of his cohort with his innards being torn out.

Helix cast a frightened look at me as a slow-burning realization began to spread like wildfire; he couldn't figure out why I tried to stop him in the first place, but he could see that I wasn't interested in retaliating. This was quickly spinning way out of control, and time waited for no man.

Although they did a pretty good job of getting the ghoul off their screeching friend, it was to no avail…he died in the struggle. The damn thing had been holding onto a still working organ that was torn out of him in the process of their rescue.

Sadly, I'm too concussed to point out the irony of that…at least out loud.

After robbing it of its snack, this inhumanly strong beast was in even more of a frenzy now, and I was still too head-rocked to get the words out and tell them to let go of the damn thing. We'd have been way better off letting it have the kill, because pulling it off turned it from just fixated to infuriated, which was absolutely worse.

Ghouls aren't complicated, and while that could make them easy to fight when you were prepared and equipped for it, that same simplicity made them terribly effective if they ever caught you off guard.

At this point I wouldn't say we were off guard, but we were definitely out matched and being trapped with this thing in a window-barred room didn't help either.

I never got the names of the two men Helix brought with him, but with one dead, suffice it to say that it was only a matter of time before the other one was toast. Ghouls relied on their strength and ferocity, and after he got his hand on the other one he would probably last maybe half a minute. Like I said, they aren't terribly complicated but they're effective. It would just wrestle you down, and scrap, bite and beat you until you went limp and made something of a more agreeable meal.

I grimace as I rather thoughtlessly was reminded of a Star Trek (or John Scalzi "Redshirts" if you wanna go real deep) reference that passed through my head, though the plight of the poor redshirts did buy me enough time to kind of get the last semblance of my scrambled wits together. I was locked in on the thought-loop of fuck, fuck, fuck as I stumbled upright.

As a side note…that's really what panic is ultimately. Something big, traumatic, ugly, or so violent that it knocks you out of your normal thought pattern. Then all the dread and anxiety of what's happening starts to act as a kind of mental molasses which insidiously evolves into something even more suffocating; a tar-like stranglehold over your ability to gather your head and make sense of what was happening. My military buddy used a solution called an OODA-loop; observe, orient, decide and then act.

Whenever I am at a loss, I run through a version of my own OODA-loop - either it'll get me back on track, or be the last series of thoughts going through my head when fate's hangman finally manages to get my ever elusive neck in its endgame noose.

But hey, you know what they say ... Death is the price of admission.

Sadly, we didn't have enough time to turn the tide on this one sided ass kicking….For that matter, we didn't have enough time to escape either. I was still reeling, Helix was so badly fear stricken that he'd become paralyzed, and with pinpoint focus, the ghoul turned from the most fresh kill to the pair of us.

It's about to come after us when a wrecking ball of blurring black crashes into it, sending it off its feet and sliding it back across the floor in a mess of uncoordinated limbs. It was soaked in the blood of the three people it had torn to ribbons, although Shawn was somehow alive and had managed to claw his way to the hallway entrance he'd been barricading five minutes ago. Shawn reminded me of a rat, and I hated how those types tended to get off a sinking ship—especially when they were the one that set the sinking into motion. Life wasn't fair, and there's nothing that I, fate, magic or anything in between could do about it.

When the dazed thing managed to find its feet and turn on us with a feral hiss it made quite the striking image.

Beau didn't even slow down long enough to let the thing finish that horrid sound before sending a nightstick into its face.

My body moved before my mind could catch up and I hurled my entire weight at the things retaliating arm to keep it from capturing my newfound ally in the throes of that death-grip it was so reliant upon. Beau was a big enough guy, a little over average height and heavy, yet once a warrior always a warrior, and Beau came from a fraternity of truly legendary warriors. I didn't know a lot about Army Rangers, but if what Grove had told me was true, there's no wonder the good-natured guard didn't hesitate in the face of brutality, even on such a horrendous scale.

"Don't let it get hold of you," I heard myself scream, and even though he didn't seem to understand exactly what was happening, he kept going. He thrashed it with a vicious shot right above the brow. Weapons training is important, and while I've belabored this point to death, there's two types of combatants ultimately: trained and untrained.

Beau was trained. The thing was untrained and lacked finesse, but what it lacked in discipline it made up in enough strength to actually whip me forward and then back, discarding me like a wet shirt stuck to his arm. Luckily I was up after an easy couple of tumbles on the tile.

Up in time to see Beau (quite skillfully if I might add) use his baton to actually intercept each attempted grab of the ghoul, and he's mangling those death-grip fingers with each smack. I didn't have time to choreograph the plotline of this bloodbath with my friend, but ever since his cousin introduced us he'd taken a shine to me. My hope was that given her background as a low-level witch who'd gotten support in our little makeshift network, that she'd advocated strongly enough for me to warrant him having my back, but this was above and beyond. This was a commentary on his character, and for a moment I remember something he'd said to me when first suspecting that something bad could be on the loose inside the jail.

These people are my responsibility.

Including me.

I rounded the table back to the original entrance that the now bleeding Shawn and company had blockaded earlier. On my way there I almost crashed into Helix who was paralyzed in the kind of fear that told me there would be little hope of him being of any real help in this. Still, I got a fistful of his bloodied shirt, tore him around and pulled his face into mine.

"Get the guards."

Normally I would get some bullshit about being a snitch, or him posturing about his status as some kind of Made Man in this hell hole, but Helix just had a seat in the front row of a real life massacre. Not some Hollywood depiction.

He had a front row seat watching the life leave his compatriots' eyes; he saw the minute the body went from being a working vessel of consciousness to just an inanimate bag of bones and flesh. To actually see what they wrote about in languages now dead… about what it was like to be feasted upon by an unearthly, wild, unruly monster was a totally different thing.

Helix would never be the same.

He'd seen people die, but nothing like this…even people gunned down in the street tend to die clean.

There was nothing clean here.

"GO!"

I screamed with such intensity that it jump started his budding panic and sent him into action.

http://wbp.bz/book3